THE MILE MARKER MURDERS

BOOK 1 IN THE TYLER BANNISTER FBI SERIES

C.W. SAARI

Virginia

The Mile Marker Murders
© 2011 C.W. Saari. All Rights Reserved.
www.cwsaari.com

First published in 2011 by BQB Publishing under ISBN 9781937084257

Republished in 2019 in the United States by BQB Publishing
(Boutique of Quality Books Publishing)
www.bqbpublishing.com

Printed in the United States of America

ISBN 978-1-945448-70-6 (p)
ISBN 978-1-937084-26-4 (e)

Library of Congress Control Number: 2011960924

Cover design by Rebecca Lown, www.rebeccalowndesign.com
Interior design by Robin Krauss, www.bookformatters.com

ACKNOWLEDGMENTS

I would like to thank the following wonderful people: Karen Todd, William S. Mann, Marilyn Olsen, Allen Boone, Cori Seifert, Charles Houchens, the Lexington 1st Writers Group (particularly Lynn Stidom, Carol Williams, Christine Deffendall, and Tommie and Stuart Osland), and especially my wife, Carol Saari, who was my chief critic and supporter. Collectively, their contributions made this work possible.

OTHER BOOKS BY CW SAARI

Prime Impact, Book 2 in the Tyler Bannister FBI series

CHAPTER 1

ATLANTA, GEORGIA

T he cell phone vibrated on top of the antique desk where FBI Special Agent Tyler Bannister had placed it when he got home that afternoon. He recognized the number as the one assigned to Gary Witt, the Atlanta FBI's Assistant Special Agent in Charge (ASAC). Bannister frowned as he set his wine glass down and picked up the phone. Witt rarely called agents directly, especially on a Sunday evening.

The street agents referred to Witt behind his back as "Dim Witt." He'd been in the Bureau thirteen years, but he'd never managed investigations in the field. After his first five years as an agent, he was promoted to FBI Headquarters as a manager. Seven years and three assignments later, the career board in DC decided to launch him to Atlanta where he could share responsibilities for Georgia investigations. Witt was slick, an excellent speaker, and always immaculately attired. He was a classic ass-kisser who believed perception was reality.

"I hope I'm not interrupting your dinner, Ty," Witt said.

"What's going on?" Bannister asked, hoping Witt would get to the point.

"Caleb Williamson is missing."

"What the hell do you mean, missing?"

"You haven't seen him, have you?"

Bannister thought a moment. "Not since he left to start his new job."

"Nobody else has, either. Apparently he never showed up for work.

I can't discuss details on this line, but two agents from Washington Field and an Agency rep are on a flight to Hartsfield-Jackson airport. They want to talk to you in the office first thing in the morning."

"How long has he been missing? Who reported it?"

"An Assistant Director called on a secure line from Washington an hour ago," Witt said. "He didn't tell me much, but he emphasized that they need to interview you. I'm sure you can appreciate the official concern, knowing Williamson's situation."

Bannister was stunned. Williamson was his best friend.

"Do you know the Bureau agents involved?"

"Not personally. The names provided were Doug Gordon and Steve Quattrone. Do you know them?"

"I don't think so," Bannister lied. He didn't want Witt pumping him for information. Doug Gordon was one of the best agents in Washington at investigating espionage. Although Bannister had never worked with him, he was aware of his reputation. Gordon was experienced, bright, and painstakingly thorough. One of his past major assignments was determining how much damage the United States had suffered from the treason of FBI supervisor Robert Hanssen. The name Steve Quattrone didn't register. Bannister didn't bother asking for the name of the Agency officer. His experience with CIA headquarters people was that they drove a one-way street. They listened to what you said, but never volunteered anything.

"Is there anything I need to know?" Witt asked.

"No," Bannister replied, hoping Witt would be tied up tomorrow during the interview. His wish was short-lived.

"Then I'll see you in my office in the morning."

"Does the Special Agent in Charge know about this?"

"Not yet."

"I'm not trying to tell you how to run things, Gary, but I'd give the boss a heads-up call. Atlanta may be able to provide some background. You want to cover your ass."

"I was just going to do that."

As Bannister hung up, his mind was already racing ahead. Caleb "Cal" Williamson was an experienced CIA officer. The Agency would never have assigned him as their Chief of Station in Vienna if he hadn't earned the reputation as a high achiever. As Chief of Station in Atlanta, he was responsible for clandestine activity in five states. Bannister had last seen Cal ten days earlier when they'd met for a jog on a Thursday morning. Because of his promotion to Washington, DC, Cal's last day in Atlanta was to have been that Friday.

During their run, Cal had told Bannister that he'd already moved all of his belongings to Virginia the weekend before. He was anxious to hit the ground running on his new assignment and didn't want the hassles associated with a move. Cal said he was driving up Saturday to his new place in Forest Hills and planned to get there in time for dinner in Old Town Alexandria. He figured Monday would be a long day jammed with briefings by everyone at Langley trying to impress him with current source information and state-of-the-art technology.

Bannister thought back to their jog. Cal had been upbeat. He was talking so much he had to slow down and catch his breath on a couple of hills he normally just flew up. He was looking forward to motivating his Washington staff.

It didn't make sense that Doug Gordon was on the case. Why put an FBI spy chaser on a missing person investigation? It sent the wrong message. It put Cal at the wrong end of the magnifying glass. Both the CIA and FBI had received criticism for their failure to detect the treasonous activities of the Agency's Aldrich Ames and the Bureau's supervisor, Robert Hanssen. Neither agency could afford to make mistakes if Williamson's disappearance was in any way connected to a foreign power.

Bannister couldn't do anything without more information. He resisted the urge to start making calls. He poured another glass of wine and settled back into his chair, listening to the boom of thunder in the distance. He often spent Sunday evenings reading a good book, but tonight he couldn't concentrate. Grabbing the remote, he switched on his plasma TV, scrolling up and down the channels a few times before realizing he wasn't watching the screen. The only thing he could think about was Cal.

CHAPTER 2

Bannister slept fitfully and awoke before his alarm went off at 5:30 a.m. He decided to go for a run to clear his head. In the back of his mind he feared that Cal was dead. He imagined the approach of the somber official, heard the words informing him of the worst. It had been a long time since he'd been shocked with the loss of someone close.

As he trotted down his driveway and past the gate, he remembered that night. The call had come at 10:00 p.m. from Lieutenant Duffy, an Atlanta police officer he'd worked with on several cases. The lieutenant had said he needed to talk to him and was waiting in a car at the entrance gate. Bannister was already standing at his front turnaround when the patrol car came to a stop. Lieutenant Duffy got out slowly, and when Bannister saw a second officer exit from the passenger side, he knew it was something bad.

"Ty, there's no easy way to tell you," Lieutenant Duffy had said. "Your wife is dead. Erin was killed in a car accident an hour ago."

Although it had been five years, he could still recall every minute of that night. He had followed the lieutenant to the morgue to identify Erin's body. He remembered his mind flashing through hundreds of images of their brief life together. When he saw her beneath the sheet, he knew it was over, and all he would have of his wife from then on would be memories. She had been killed instantly when a speeding Suburban went through a red light and T-boned her Miata.

Bannister had never experienced that kind of grief before. He knew that how a person grieved, and for how long, was personal. You made adjustments and tried to move on. Still, every now and then he would take out his favorite picture of Erin and look at it. In the photo she was leaning against a giant oak tree with a mischievous smile on her face. She looked so happy. For a few private minutes he'd let his mind drift, thinking about what might have been.

On this morning, Bannister tried to steel his mind to Cal's fate. Three of the five miles he covered went over the same route he had run with Cal. The air was thick but cool. The streetlights were on, and the only sounds were his breathing and the soles of his shoes hitting the asphalt. He thought about his conversation with Cal during that last run, and he tried to prepare himself with answers for the questions he'd be asked later that morning.

Both he and Cal enjoyed the solitude of running and agreed it was a time they often came up with solutions to problems. But all that was on his mind today were questions. Where was Cal? Was he alive? Had he been kidnapped? Who would take him? And why?

Bannister drove his usual route to the office down Century Parkway past the glass complex that was home to Atlanta's FBI. He keyed the Bureau radio to the proper channel to open the security gate for the cage where FBI vehicles were parked. The cars parked there overnight were plastered with a layer of wet leaves blown about by last evening's thunderstorm. Bannister walked to the back entrance of the mirror-like building. He stepped into the elevator and punched four, the floor for the main entrance. The reception area was impressive. Eight-foot carved wooden doors were flanked by floor-to-ceiling glass panels, each one four hundred pounds of inch-thick, blast-resistant glass emblazoned with the FBI seal. A white phone was mounted on the wall to the left, along with a simple sign stating the office opened to the public at 8:15 a.m. There was no one around.

Opposite the elevators was a door without markings. Bannister had to bend his knees and lean his 6'4" frame backwards to enter his code on the cipher pad, which was installed at a height sufficient for use by employees in wheelchairs. Two ceiling-mounted cameras recorded all his movements. Although assigned to the counterterrorism task force on the eighth floor, Bannister decided to check in on the fourth floor in case the guys from Washington had arrived.

As he walked past the intelligence squad area, Special Agent Mark Donovan looked up from his desk. Leaning forward, he said, "Hey, Ty. Something's going on. Five minutes ago I hear the door's buzzer. I look at the monitor and see three guys in suits in the hallway. I don't recognize them. I open the door to tell them the office won't be open for forty minutes, and they tell me they've got an appointment with Gary Witt. I call Witt and he comes straight out of his office and lets all three guys right in. Any idea what's going on?"

"I heard some agents from Headquarters are here to do some interviews on a Washington, DC, case." Not wanting to alienate Donovan if he happened to see him coming out of Witt's office later, Bannister added, "I was told they wanted to interview me."

"Well, don't forget the advice you once gave me," Donovan said.

"What's that?"

He grinned. "Admit nothing. Deny everything. Make counter allegations."

Bannister appreciated Donovan's attempt at humor, but he wasn't in the mood for laughs. As he passed Witt's closed office, he heard voices and assumed the DC guys were in there. Obviously Witt would be meeting with them alone before his interview. Not that anything different would be covered, but it gave Witt the chance to hear everything at least twice. Bannister went up to the counterterrorism task force space on the eighth floor. He had thirty minutes to kill.

—◌◌◌—

As Bannister was shown into Gary Witt's office, the three visitors stood up and introductions were made.

"Good to meet you, Ty. I'm Special Agent Doug Gordon. This is

Agent Steve Quattrone and Carl Holmquist who's the deputy in charge of the CIA's Office of Security. Thanks for coming in."

Witt remained seated. "Pull up a chair," he said to Bannister. "We'll be here awhile." Witt was short, about five foot seven, maybe a hundred fifty pounds. His complexion was white—chalk white—as if he hadn't been outside in at least a year. In contrast with his complexion, his hair was black and looked wet. It was combed straight back from his forehead, drawing attention to his beak-like nose. He looked like a hawk dressed in a blazer and slacks. The cuffs of his shirt extended out two inches from the sleeves of his navy blazer and displayed dark red square cuff links. The color matched his red patterned suspenders.

"Nice suspenders," Gordon remarked.

"Thanks," said Witt. "I consider braces to be one of my trademarks."

Bannister dragged a chair from the credenza and moved it next to Witt. He didn't want to look at Witt during the interview.

Bannister wondered what the visitors thought of Witt's office. It was tastefully decorated, but not due to any input from Witt. In a back corner, a standard walnut executive desk was placed diagonally so that anyone walking by could glance in and see how busy he was. He had the customary sofa, wing chairs, and coffee table with carefully arranged stacks of government magazines that nobody read. Destroying the ambience of the office decor was the one wall for which Witt did take credit. That was the "I love me" wall, with all his diplomas and photographs of himself posing with people he hoped others would recognize.

What stood out on Witt's wall were photos of him with President Clinton. There were six individually framed photographs of the President, Witt, and a third man. The uninitiated would be told by Witt that the other man was an uncle associated with the Democratic Party. What the uninitiated would not be told was that the photo session at the White House had taken less than thirty seconds, and the White House photographer had snapped eight photographs as he walked in a semi-circle. Witt had framed six of the pictures, each showing a slightly different angle of the Blue Room. At quick glance, the effect was that he'd had his photograph taken with the President on numerous occasions. But if you took a minute to stare at the pictures, you quickly realized they were all the same. You just as quickly concluded that the short guy in the photos had delusions of grandeur.

Special Agent Gordon took the lead. "Your official name is listed as Tyler S. Bannister. What do you prefer to be called?"

"Those who know me well call me Ty."

"Since I reviewed your personnel file before coming here, I'm assuming I know you well. I'll call you Ty."

Everyone laughed, except Bannister, who was feeling edgy.

Gordon quickly lost his grin, sensing Bannister's mood. Special Agent Gordon had a square face with dark eyebrows and penetrating dark eyes. He was also completely bald. One day in law school Gordon had decided to shave his head. He liked the look. He liked not having to worry about haircuts or combs or brushes or shampoo.

"We're here because we want your help," Gordon said. "Caleb Williamson is missing. He hasn't been seen in ten days. Other than his office staff, you were the last to see him. It's our understanding you know him very well."

"Besides being a professional colleague, I consider him a good friend," Bannister said slowly. "If he's been missing that long, I wish I'd been contacted sooner. Maybe there's something I could have been doing."

"The Bureau got the initial call last Tuesday." Gordon hunched his shoulders and opened his hands.

"That's right," said Holmquist, reaching up to adjust his tie. Holmquist was trim in a dark blue Brooks Brothers suit with banker's stripes. He had wavy, steel-gray hair, an engaging smile, and the polished look of a TV news anchor. "I got the authorization and made the call myself to your Assistant Director. I asked if he could furnish some FBI resources for a police cooperation matter, or a possible Hobbs Act violation—"

"Hobbs Act? We only use that statute when there's evidence of an extortion or kidnapping," Bannister said. "Is there any indication that Cal was kidnapped?"

"Ty, how long have you known Williamson?" Gordon asked.

"Three years," Bannister replied.

"When was the last time you saw or heard from him?"

"I saw him a week ago last Thursday when we met for a jog in Buckhead."

Bannister wasn't about to volunteer that he and Cal had a standing arrangement to meet at 6:00 a.m. each Thursday in the parking lot of the Presbyterian Church on Roswell Road. They would give each other until 6:05 a.m., and if one of them didn't show, the other took off. They had followed that arrangement for two years. If Bannister told them all that, Holmquist would certainly make a note in Cal's file that one of their case officers was violating the rule against following a set routine each week.

"We met at 6:00 a.m. in a church parking lot off Roswell Road and got in a good run," Bannister said.

"So, what did you cover?"

"You mean in miles or topics?"

"You can answer for both."

"We ran a five mile route through a residential area. In terms of what we talked about? Mostly current events. Cal mentioned a new restaurant he'd tried and recommended it to me. We talked a little about the Atlanta Braves and possible off-season trades."

Bannister certainly wasn't going to mention their discussions of Agency or Bureau politics. Nor was he going to volunteer information Cal had furnished about his colleagues. Bannister didn't intend to say anything that might reflect badly on Cal.

"That last Thursday, how did he seem to you?" Gordon asked. "What was his frame of mind? Did he seem preoccupied? Depressed?"

"No, he seemed normal. Maybe a little excited about his new assignment. Let me save you guys some time. Cal isn't depressed. He isn't suicidal. I'm not aware of any enemies he might have. He doesn't use drugs. He isn't in financial trouble. He isn't homosexual, and I don't think he has any sexual deviations. He isn't currently dating any particular woman, so I don't believe there's a jealous rival in the picture. Finally, he isn't a spy. I'll stake my reputation on that."

"I think you understand why we have to ask these questions."

Bannister unbuttoned the top button of his shirt and loosened his tie. His irritation was beginning to show.

Holmquist furrowed his brow and massaged his forehead with his hand. He looked like he wanted to say something but was holding back. Witt was fiddling with his pen and looking bored, which was typical of his demeanor.

No one said anything for a few seconds. Then Gordon broke the silence. "Before we go on, I know you're wondering why the Bureau is involved in this. You also want to know why counterespionage agents are handling the case."

"You're right."

"For us, Williamson is a special case. But he's just one of the thousands of people officially reported missing to the FBI across the country each day. Do you know how many people were reported missing last year in DC alone?" Gordon paused for effect.

"No idea," Bannister said.

"Five thousand. About three-fourths of those reported missing are located within forty-eight hours. In our capital last year, all but a hundred and thirty were found. But some just vanish and stay missing for a long time."

"Like Chandra Levy," Witt blurted out, earning glances from the others in the office.

"Williamson's been missing too long already," Gordon went on. "Missing persons either disappear voluntarily or involuntarily. Some may be escaping some type of stress they can't handle. They may want to start a new life—or end the one they're in. Then there are your accident or amnesia victims, abductions, nervous breakdowns, homicides. But when you're looking for someone in Williamson's position, you have to consider another possibility—defection."

Gordon paused, gazing at Bannister, obviously trying to evaluate his reaction. Bannister returned the stare.

Finally, Bannister said slowly and firmly, "Cal did not defect."

CHAPTER 3

The others exchanged glances.

Bannister sighed. "Look. Cal didn't display any of the classic signs. He's never been power hungry. He hasn't been passed over for a promotion. He doesn't have any debt or a high-maintenance girlfriend. And he just plain doesn't have any hot buttons someone could press."

Gordon leaned back and folded his hands. His tone became conciliatory. "I'm not implying he's a defector. It's just one possibility we have to consider. Do you remember the Waldo Dussenberry case?"

"Wasn't he a former CIA guy who sold secrets to the Libyans?"

"Right. No one could believe he was a spy. He was an archaeologist and Middle East expert at Langley who was indicted for espionage. Turns out he was leading a double life. He had two luxury apartments in Washington, DC—one for his seventy-year-old wife, and the other for his thirty-two-year-old mistress. Before his trial he disappeared. I found him. He was sitting in a chair in his apartment. He'd put a shotgun in his mouth and blown off the top of his head."

There was a momentary silence in the room.

"Last month, Williamson took a trip to DC to close on his house. He also had a briefing at Langley." Gordon looked carefully at Bannister. "Did you know about that?"

"Yes. He told me he was flying up on a Thursday night and staying at a hotel near his attorney's office. He said he needed to check in at

CIA Headquarters, but didn't say why."

"The officer he was replacing briefed him on the CIA's Russian recruitments and defectors. Those sources placed their lives in the Agency's hands. We all know what happened after the treachery of Aldrich Ames and Robert Hanssen. At least eleven top US agents were executed. Langley is holding its breath on Williamson's disappearance. We can tell you that one source, who was still being handled by Williamson, was extricated from his country last week. That source is now with the Agency's defector resettlement people."

"Have any of Cal's sources been recalled or dropped off the scope?" Bannister asked.

"No. To our knowledge, none of the sources he was briefed on have been compromised. This supports the position that Williamson is not a spy and that something else has happened to him. That's why we're asking you to help us fill in the blanks."

"Why don't you tell me what you already know?"

Holmquist spoke. "Cal Williamson has been an operations officer with the Agency for eighteen years. He has an outstanding record with no black marks. He was hand-picked by the DDO to revitalize Russian operations. He was the Agency's Chief of Station in Atlanta for three years. He was all set to start his new job as the group chief of what is still referred to as the Russian Desk.

"We've determined that Williamson was at the closing on his new home three weeks ago. He was represented at the closing by a law firm in Reston, Virginia. We also know earlier that same morning Williamson was at Langley for a two-hour meeting with the officer he was replacing. That officer gave him an extremely sensitive background brief. He was supposed to be at Langley last Monday for more briefings. He never showed. The Deputy Director of Operations said Williamson failed to check in for his 9:00 a.m. meeting. Calls were made around headquarters, and I was notified an hour later."

Witt was about to say something, but Holmquist continued. "There was no response when we called Williamson's cell phone and global pager. I called his new unpublished home phone. Again, no answer. We checked Williamson's 'J-file' for possible leads. I'd already reviewed his personnel file."

Holmquist noticed a quizzical look Witt gave Gordon.

"The Bureau would compare a J-file to a quasi-internal affairs record," Holmquist explained. "It's not an official file. It's a jacket where we put unsubstantiated complaints, evidence of indiscretions and identifications of questionable associates. Williamson's J-file had no entries. I then contacted the 24-hour command center and asked for a communications read-out.

"Williamson's secretary had e-mailed his itinerary on Thursday, his last day in Atlanta. Williamson indicated he would drive directly to Arlington via I-85 and I-95 with no planned stops. He called in at 06:00 Saturday, nine days ago, letting them know he was traveling to Arlington in his personally owned vehicle. That's the last anyone in official quarters had contact with him."

Gordon, motioning to Holmquist, said, "Go ahead and tell Gary what steps you've taken, and why you asked for the Bureau's help."

"Sure. I scanned our files and all database information on Williamson. He's fluent in French, and he's a level-two Russian speaker."

"Refresh my memory," Witt said. "What's a level-two?"

"It means conversational ability," Steve Quattrone said, primarily to let the others know he was also in the office. As if to emphasize his words, there was a loud thwack as Quattrone's wingtip shoe caught the bottom of the coffee table as he crossed his legs. "Sorry about that," he said sheepishly.

Ignoring the interruption, Holmquist continued. "He's correct about the Russian. I think Williamson's ability is probably higher than his last test score indicates. At least that's what we assume, based on comments he made to his Atlanta replacement. Apparently, he's improved his ability due to regular sessions with Agent Bannister. That's a point we need to clarify."

"I don't understand," Witt said, cracking his knuckles.

"I'll cover that," Gordon said, jotting a note on his pad.

"Anyway," Holmquist said, "I reviewed all our internal information. Williamson has been an exceptional case officer with a lot of success. He's only had one disciplinary action, when he overstepped his budgetary authority for a case in Vienna last year. He got an official reprimand. No big deal. Two months later the reprimand was negated when Williamson received a commendation for the operation's success. He was personally responsible for recruiting two of the Agency's best European sources. Those sources are still active."

"Does he have any personal issues?" Witt asked.

"Not that we're aware of. He's always been able to burn the candle at both ends with no problems. He's never shown signs of depression, he's not on any medication and doesn't have a drinking problem. In fact, despite the long days he puts in, he's extremely healthy. Last year he ran both the London and Bermuda marathons."

Holmquist continued, "We reviewed all his travel and nothing is out of the ordinary. We filed 'look out' notices with Homeland Security in case he tried to use his passport. Financially, everything appears in order. He has life insurance of three hundred thousand dollars. The beneficiary is his daughter. He bought his current townhouse and financed it privately, putting eight hundred thousand down. His loan for half a million checked out. No problem there."

"Whew," Witt said. "Eight hundred thousand, cash? Why is he working for the government?"

"With the Agency," Holmquist said, arching his eyebrows, "that's not unusual. During his overseas postings, Williamson invested in northern Virginia real estate. His market timing couldn't have been better."

"What about his ex-wife?" Witt asked.

"I'll get to her in a minute. I called in one of our 'Samurai Teams' from the Directorate of Science and Technology, the same ones we use when we have a defector who is 'temporarily out-of-pocket,' or for other sensitive matters. I met the team at an off-site and briefed them on what we knew. While two team members worked the databases, the others contacted state police agencies in Georgia, the Carolinas, and Virginia. Queries for 'John Doe' accidents and reported car-jackings were all checked out. Nothing to report. The tag on Williamson's Infiniti was run through all agencies to see if any citations were issued. The results were negative. Checks with parking security at airports, metro stops, and major shopping centers turned up nothing. Hospitals in the metropolitan DC area were also checked, with no hits.

"The finance team checked all his credit cards for activity. His Visa card was used once at a gas station outside Greensboro, North Carolina at 11:50 a.m. Saturday. It shows a purchase of seventeen gallons of premium gas. That's it."

Carefully crossing his legs, Quattrone asked, "What about his household goods?"

"He moved his belongings to Virginia a couple of weeks ago. When he left the Atlanta station ten days ago, he only took a small box of personal desk items. He didn't sign out a laptop. He did have a personal passport, in true name, and a clandestine passport package. Normally, that package would go by courier, but Williamson was authorized to carry it personally. In it was an official US Government passport with Williamson's photograph but with the name of Courtland Wilson. Everything else in the package supported the Wilson identity. This included credit cards, which had not been activated, a Virginia driver's license, and assorted wallet stuffers."

"We don't know a lot about his personal life in Atlanta. Maybe Bannister can help us out there. Williamson divorced his wife, Gina, three years ago while posted in Vienna."

"Does the ex-wife know he's missing?" Witt asked.

"Yes. She seemed shocked and upset. She kept saying 'CIA officers don't go missing. What aren't you telling me?' She eventually calmed down but wasn't able to give us anything of value. She let us put a recorder on her home phone and agreed to our instruction not to notify anyone about his disappearance."

Looking at Bannister, Gordon asked, "Assuming a worst-case scenario, who would benefit from Cal's death?"

"Probably his daughter, Dawn. Cal set up a trust with her as the beneficiary. She's also the beneficiary of his insurance policies, except for some money he's leaving to Tufts University."

"How's his relationship with his daughter?"

"Good. They stay in touch."

"Does the daughter have a significant other?"

"Not that I'm aware of."

"How would you characterize his relationship with his former wife?" Gordon asked.

"Fine. I know it's unusual to hear about divorced couples being friends, but in their case, that's the situation."

"He had a two-bedroom condominium here in Atlanta. Why did he upgrade to such a large place in Arlington?"

"He planned on retiring in the DC area and taking a job as a security consultant. He said he was looking for a permanent home. It had to be large enough to entertain and be in a convenient, desirable location. He wasn't into lawns or gardens. He hated traffic jams and promised his commute was going to be against the flow of traffic. As I remember, he said his townhouse was a mile from the Pentagon, four miles from the White House, and fifteen minutes from Langley."

"Gentlemen," said Holmquist, "let me go over some recent history. Both of our organizations suffered unbelievable damage from traitors. We had Aldrich Ames and Harold Nicholson. You had Special Agents Earl Pitts and Robert Hanssen. Numerous recommendations for change were not only made through congressional oversight, but also by both of our agencies. One change the CIA implemented after your Special Agent Hanssen was convicted was the 'Consent to Search' form. All our employees have signed an authorization permitting a search of their solely owned property if they are missing, and if there is a reasonable presumption their disappearance is not due to normal circumstances. Of course, our legal department is called immediately before any search is conducted, or if there is any evidence of a crime.

"About 4:00 p.m. Monday, I sent our Samurai Team to Williamson's Arlington townhouse. There was no response to the doorbell. The team bypassed his alarm system, which was turned on. They had to cut a key for the special Medeco lock on the front door. The team entered and took photos and video of all rooms prior to searching.

"The team confirmed that someone, presumably Williamson, was recently in the home. The refrigerator and pantry were stocked. A grocery receipt from a supermarket was on the counter indicating purchases made on Sunday. Two bath towels indicated recent usage. A check of the washing machine revealed laundered running gear, which was still damp. All of Williamson's official property was missing. We didn't locate his briefcase, passports, wallet, or keys. His car wasn't in the garage.

"At my request, a liaison officer contacted the Bureau, who sent out a Computer Assisted Recovery Team to do a search and mirror image of Williamson's hard drive. Next to the telephone in the kitchen was a Post-It pad. The top sheet had two notations. One line read, 'Flowers-Gina.' The second line said, 'Monday-Ty.' We made some assumptions. Gina Williamson's birthday was this weekend. She said she didn't receive any flowers." Looking at Bannister, Holmquist continued, "We're hoping you can shed some light on the 'Monday-Ty' message."

Before he could answer, Witt said, "I'm sure Bannister will help you in any way he can."

"I have no reason to doubt that," Gordon said.

He put his notebook on the coffee table and pulled out a beige folder. For a few seconds he stared at the recent photograph of Bannister who was listed as 6'4" and one hundred and ninety-five pounds. With his slightly tousled sandy-brown hair and green eyes, Bannister projected a rugged image, like a younger Robert Redford. Gordon looked up from the folder and glanced at Bannister. "I've looked through his file," he said.

Bannister's Atlanta file didn't have much in it except annual performance reviews, results of medical exams, firearms scores, and commendation letters. But it did reveal that Bannister was not a typical Bureau Agent.

Tyler Stetson Bannister had been named after his great-grandfather, the one of cowboy hat fame. Bannister was forty-seven and had been an FBI Agent eighteen years. He went to the Webb School, the most prestigious private academy on the west coast. Bannister had been born with a silver spoon, and attending that particular school was a condition of his trust fund. He went to college at Dartmouth, where he majored in International Relations and played on the lacrosse team. While at Dartmouth, he signed up with the US Marine Corps and was commissioned a Second Lieutenant upon graduation in 1982. He did well at the officers' course and was selected for the Reconnaissance Marines. Having a black belt in karate hadn't hurt.

Bannister was serving as a platoon commander when the brief war in Grenada broke out. He was with the initial invasion force of a thousand troops. For his actions on the second day in Grenada, he was awarded the Navy Cross for heroism. His citation indicated he personally saved a squad of Marines, was shot twice, and received the Purple Heart for his wounds. He was honorably discharged in 1987 and went to work for Mobil Oil in their international department, and he was still there when the FBI recruited him.

"You had four years of Russian at prep school and two more at Dartmouth," Gordon commented.

"That's right," Bannister said.

"Fluency in Russian has always been a vital need for the Bureau, and successfully recruiting a guy with your skills was a nice break, wouldn't you say?"

Bannister was silent.

"You were brought to Atlanta because the office needed a Russian-speaking agent experienced in counterintelligence."

"We had a sensitive espionage subject here," Witt interjected. "A source of the Agency fingered a subject who was living in Atlanta and working as a consultant for the CIA and Pentagon. The subject was cleared and that investigation fizzled. The real subject was never identified. In any event, Bannister stayed here. For the past three years, he's worked both intelligence and counterterrorist cases. He's on our task force and has been our liaison officer to the CIA."

Gordon said to Bannister, "I understand you were helping Williamson with his Russian."

"I was. Both of us thought it was a shame to know a language and not use it."

"We're exploring all connections," Gordon said. "Williamson's emergency contact form listed two people. One is the lawyer, who is the executor of a trust for his daughter. The other is you, Bannister. What we want to know is, why was Williamson interested in improving his Russian? And you were tutoring him in that language. How did that come about?"

"About two years ago during one of our runs, Cal mentioned he was still handling a sensitive source whose native language was Russian. When Cal returned from running the London and Bermuda marathons last year, he enjoyed telling me all about the races. Each time, however, he also winked and mentioned he had a good workout with his Russian."

"What did you think he meant by that?"

"I assumed he'd met with sources. Cal told me he hoped his next job would be the Russian desk, and being conversant would be advantageous."

"So, where did you do this tutoring?"

"Once a month we met for a ninety-minute lunch at a nice restaurant. The game rules were that other than ordering our food, the entire conversation would be in Russian. Absolutely no English."

"What did the FBI think about that?" Gordon asked.

"The Bureau didn't know." Bannister felt Witt staring at him but didn't bother to turn around. "There was no requirement to document it. As far as I was concerned, this was just a continuation of my liaison responsibilities."

There was silence for a few seconds while Gordon looked at something in his notebook. He resumed his questioning. "Williamson, at least we think it was Williamson, had some notes written on a Post-it pad near his phone. Do you know what the 'Monday-Ty' note meant?"

"No. When I last saw Cal, I suggested he give me a call after the dust settled and give me his spin of what it was like to be back in Washington. He said he'd call and give me his direct office number, official e-mail, and the like. He never phoned."

"Did you try to reach him?"

"No. I think we all know whenever you change assignments, things are pretty hectic for a while. I figured he'd get around to it sooner or later."

"One last thing. Did you know Williamson listed you as a person to be contacted in case of an emergency?"

"Yes. He trusted me and figured if anything ever happened to him, I'd be able to make some solid decisions in his best interests."

Gordon thanked Bannister and asked him to call if he thought of anything that'd be useful.

"Is that it?" Bannister asked.

Gordon nodded, and Bannister got up to leave. Gordon said, "Give me a minute," excused himself from the group, and followed Bannister outside the office. He closed the door, and as the two of them were standing in the hallway, he put his arm around Bannister's shoulder.

"Look, I tried to put myself in your situation. This has got to be tough. The just-not-knowing. As soon as I hear anything, anything at all, I'll give you a call," Gordon said.

Bannister sensed that he meant it, and that he wasn't an investigator with a hidden agenda. "I wish there was some lead I could give you to help find him. I feel pretty helpless right now, Doug. If I were back there, I'd focus on finding his car. I think that's the key."

CHAPTER 4

FIFTEEN MONTHS EARLIER—VIENNA, AUSTRIA

L illian Wells was living in one of the cultural capitals of the world. She had been told it would be a never-ending opportunity to experience new things. Now it just seemed never ending. When her husband, Felix Wells III, was assigned by the State Department to Vienna twenty-eight months ago, he had made her many promises. For her, the most important one was that before they left they would try and start a family. All of Felix's promises were the same—empty.

When Lillian turned thirty, Felix had literally waltzed into her life at a formal reception. He was handsome. He held his chin up high when he talked, and his voice was polished. His straight, bright teeth gave him a Hollywood smile. His clothes were expensive and carefully tailored. He impressed her with his first-hand descriptions of the world's historic sites. His enthusiasm for sampling what the world's great cities had to offer captivated her. Her interest in international causes intrigued him and he was impressed with her questions and the way she listened to everything he said. But Felix's love for Lillian blossomed after hearing a rumor she'd inherited a substantial sum of money. After a quick courtship, the two were married and Lillian became a diplomat's wife.

His infatuation with Lillian and his enthusiasm for their marriage began to fade after the first year. Other than physical intimacy, Felix shared less and less with Lillian. He'd seek her opinion for what he had chosen to wear, but he never offered his comments or compliments about how she was dressed. He didn't need to. Although Lillian didn't go to extra lengths with her makeup and hair, she chose her wardrobe for its simplicity and classic style. If pushed, she could accent her appearance with family heirloom jewelry.

Felix was only obsessive about his own appearance. He felt it beneath his lifestyle to help out around their quarters and left it to Lillian to do all the cleaning, cooking, and picking up. Lately she thought better than to ask Felix to handle even the smallest task.

To get his first overseas posting, Felix had to work hard to prove himself, and he resented it. He believed his superiors should have recognized his talents early and rewarded him without the necessity of a long trial period at headquarters. Finally, however, he had been assigned to Vienna.

As a Second Secretary in the Public Diplomacy Section, Felix stayed busy with appointments during the day and official functions at night. He never tired of the numerous invitations to cocktail parties and other social events, most of which, after the first few months in Vienna, he attended by himself. He consciously neglected to invite Lillian, who spent many evenings alone. It didn't have to be that way. She could have been an asset. Earlier in Vienna, Felix had discovered the men he was trying to curry favor with were ignoring him to talk with his wife. He resented that, too. Lillian was an excellent conversationalist and well read. She put people at ease and made them smile. Besides that, men always stole a second glance at her because of her natural beauty. Her perfect posture and the grace with which she glided across a room made her seem taller than she was. Her long, brunette hair cascaded to her shoulders in soft waves. She tried to wear her hair in a style that drew attention to her face and away from her breasts. To put it simply, she was well-endowed. She once asked Felix if he thought breast reduction surgery would make her more attractive.

"The only thing that would change would be that men wouldn't wonder if you had implants, and your friends wouldn't be as jealous. Why should you be concerned about what others think? And why would I ever want to waste that kind of money?" He had never asked her how she felt. He had quit asking her what she did during the day.

Lillian tried to stay busy. She spent hours organizing events for the Overseas Wives Club. When not scheduling club functions, Lillian attended Pilates classes and worked at improving her tennis game. It was on the tennis court that she would meet the man who would change her life forever.

On Friday mornings, Lillian drove to the tennis courts at the Prater, a public park in northeast Vienna. She liked the Prater. It reminded her of Central Park in New York City. Of course the Prater's amusement park was famous throughout Europe for its century old Ferris wheel, but the park had flowers and the woods where she could escape from the clanging sounds and glaring signs of the city.

The Prater's public tennis courts, near the banks of the Danube, welcomed her as if she were somehow a club member and not a just a visitor. Although she didn't advertise it, Lillian was an accomplished tennis player. She had been on her high school team and played well in league play for many years. She usually met one of the other wives at the park, but if her partner for the day failed to show, she would work on her backhand, taking advantage of the excellent practice walls at the end of the courts.

It was on a cool overcast Friday morning that she met Andre. Cecilia had called her earlier in the morning to cancel; she told Lillian she had some things she absolutely needed to do and thought it would probably rain anyway. It wasn't the first time Cecelia or one of the other wives had made a last minute cancellation. Lillian didn't mind. She drove to the courts alone.

She removed her baggy black sweatpants, but kept her jacket on because the air was misting. She had been hitting volleys against the practice wall for ten minutes when she heard a voice behind her.

"Did you read your horoscope today?" asked a man in perfect English. He was carrying a Prince tennis bag with several rackets in it.

"Pardon me?" Lillian said.

"Did you read your horoscope today?" he repeated. "What sign are you?"

"Libra," Lillian replied warily, wondering if the man was trying to pick her up.

"Well, you're in luck." He pretended to read something in his hand. "Your horoscope today says, 'You are about to embark on new opportunities, so don't procrastinate. Focus on what you want and refuse to let anything hold you back. The sun will shine on you today, and a stranger will help you with your backhand.'"

Andre studied things other intelligence officers overlooked. He stayed current on the latest women's fashions, knew about trends in cosmetics, read reviews of bestselling diet books, and studied astrology.

Lillian laughed. "How did you know the backhand was the weakest part of my game?"

"I was watching you. I admired your forehand and quick footwork. When you switched to your backhand, you concentrated too much on your grip and weren't aware of the angle of the racket face at impact."

"You talk as if you know a lot about tennis," Lillian said.

"Not as much as I know about women."

Lillian didn't know whether to blush or get angry. It had been a long time since a man who was not drunk had made a pass at her.

"I'm sorry for being so forward. Allow me to introduce myself. I'm Andre Neff."

"I'm Lillian Wells."

"It's so nice to meet someone with such a beautiful smile on a gloomy day."

"I'm sure the sun will come out," Lillian said.

"The weather forecast said cloudy all day."

"But my horoscope said the sun will shine on me today," Lillian reminded him.

"How right you are," Andre said, and Lillian could see his eyes sparkle.

"I really hate practicing by myself, so until your partner gets here, why don't we get in a few minutes of real practice?"

"My partner had to bail out on me today. I wouldn't mind if you did give me some tips," she said. "I haven't seen you here before."

"I've only been here a few times. I'm trying to get in more practice and maybe re-discover my old form."

They collected their gear and walked to a vacant court. Andre removed his warm-up. As Lillian starting unzipping her jacket, Andre deftly stepped to her side and helped her with it. His obvious manners did not go unappreciated. As Andre selected a racket, Lillian held her racket up as if examining the strings. She really was checking out his physique. He was about three inches taller than she was and solidly built. She noticed his well-muscled legs and tight butt. The muscles of his chest and arms were solid and defined. It was obvious he took care of himself.

Andre asked if she wanted to work on her backhand, or was she more interested in having a good physical workout? The answer for Lillian was easy. Some recent bouts of fatigue combined with weeks of frustration and boredom told her she needed a workout harder than her Pilates classes.

"Why don't we play hard singles for forty-five minutes and see how we both feel then, okay?" Lillian said.

As they got into their match, Lillian was hitting legitimate winners against him. Lillian was aware of a long dormant competitive feeling surfacing within her. She was not only having fun, but reveling in the intense muscle burn from the hard exertion.

At the end of forty-five minutes, they called it quits and walked over to the bench to towel off. Andre reached out and took Lillian's hand in his.

"Thank you for a wonderful time, even though I may hate you in a few hours when my body catches up," Andre said.

"I feel wonderful," Lillian said, and she meant it.

"If you're not in a hurry, it would be my pleasure to treat you to something to drink, perhaps a cup of coffee. Are you familiar with the Lusthaus? It's a restaurant about a five minute walk from here. The walk will give us a chance to cool down."

"I've been there. It has great coffee and sinful pastries."

Ten minutes later they were sitting under a Cinzano umbrella on the patio of the Lusthaus, each enjoying a bottled water and a steaming cup of Viennese coffee.

"Does your husband play tennis?" Andre asked.

Glancing down at her rings, Lillian said, "No, he's not into sports."

"Are the hours of his job too intense?"

"He's with the US Government, and he does work long hours." For a moment Lillian thought of the warnings the wives had received about discussing personal information with strangers, or answering questions about the embassy. Well, if Andre was a terrorist, then she was Superwoman. Switching subjects, Lillian asked, "What about you, Andre? What type of work do you do?"

"I'm a journalist. Mostly freelance. In addition to my current assignments, I'm helping a colleague who's trying to get a cookbook published."

One of Lillian's current projects with the wives club was organizing the publication of a cookbook for charity. "I'm working with our wives club on a cookbook right now," she said. "Perhaps we could compare notes someday."

"How about this time next week? I'd love to see your backhand improve to the level of your forehand."

Lillian stared at him for a few seconds, contemplating her situation. "Fine. Could we make it an hour later than today? It would work out better if it was closer to lunch." She wanted to avoid running into one of the other wives.

"I don't know your telephone number in case I need to leave you a message."

"I know," she said with a sly smile. "I guess you'll just have to trust I show up."

After Andre paid the bill, they walked the short distance back to their cars. The sun came out and bathed both of them with its warming rays. Lillian waved goodbye with a quick flutter of her hand. She turned around and said, "I'll be curious to hear what my horoscope is next Friday."

―――✺✺✺―――

The week couldn't go by fast enough for Lillian. Cecilia called her Thursday afternoon to see if she was playing tennis on Friday. Lillian told her she had arranged to take a lesson and she'd get back with her over the weekend.

Around noon on Thursday, Lillian's husband Felix called her from the embassy, advising her that he didn't have any commitments for that evening and asking if she minded fixing dinner at their apartment. Lillian wondered if Felix might be maneuvering for a night with her. They rarely made love any more. Whenever she brought up her desire to start a family, his interest in sex declined to almost nothing. Lillian wondered if Felix was seeing someone else. There were signs, but nothing definite enough to justify her confronting him.

Lillian prepared a pasta dish with shrimp and a Greek salad. After she and Felix had finished eating, she cleared the table. "Honey," she asked, "what would you think if someone told you I was having an affair?"

Felix laughed. "Who would want to have an affair with you?" He didn't emphasize the word "who" but stressed the word "you." Lillian felt sick. She couldn't believe Felix would make such a hurtful comment. She turned away from him and walked toward the living room. With her back to him, and hiding the pain which was obvious on her face, she nonchalantly stated, "Just curious."

―――✺✺✺―――

Friday morning finally arrived. The sun was shining through puffy clouds, and the wind ruffled leaves on the trees. Lillian spotted Andre walking toward the courts. They both carried tennis bags. Lillian had left her frumpy sweatsuit at home and wore a new designer outfit.

"I don't want you to be disappointed this morning, but I don't have your horoscope. Maybe after we're finished, I could read your palm instead," he flirted.

"Only if you win."

They went through a pre-game routine and decided to play an easier match and concentrate on quality ground strokes. For Lillian, it was invigorating. With her hair pulled back into a ponytail, she felt like a college girl on the court. She was surprised at the extra energy she had, even as the minutes flew by. All too soon their court time was up, and they retreated to the sideline to towel off.

"I failed to mention to you, Lillian, that I live five minutes from here in the opposite direction from the Lusthaus. If you wish, we could stop at my place. I could offer you a health drink or coffee. Besides, it would give me an opportunity to get your opinion on the cookbook layout I'm working on."

"That sounds like a plan. Let's do it."

After a short walk, Andre pointed to his three-story apartment building. The exterior was ornate and exceptionally clean, even for Vienna. "It was built in 1907, in the Jugendstil style," he said. "You probably know it better as art nouveau. It may seem rather bold and overly ornate on the outside, but wait until we're inside." As Andre held the door for Lillian, she entered a small lobby whose floor shone with bright blue-colored tiles. The light from a large brass chandelier with frosted glass-iris globes softened a wall mosaic depicting a view of a park fountain. On her left, Lillian saw an ornate curving staircase.

"We'll take the stairs," Andre said. "I live on the second floor."

Lillian was immediately impressed with Andre's apartment and its spaciousness and lighting.

"Did this come furnished like this?"

"No. I picked out everything in the interior. I thought modern, sleek furniture in a combination of black and chrome would offer a striking contrast without offending the period architecture."

On a glass coffee table in front of a black leather sofa, the cookbook project was laid out. There were photographs of prepared food items and a large white notebook with loose pages of recipes.

Andre prepared his coffee maker for a fresh pot. He put on a couple of CDs. The last one he chose featured twelve-string guitar selections by Andres Segovia.

Lillian took a seat and looked through the photos spread out on the top edge of the table. "Did your friend take these pictures?" she asked.

"Yes, he did all his own photography, and many of the recipes are his original creations. He enlisted my help with all the writing—you know, jacket cover, chapter introductions, and anything else requiring a creative flair."

"This project really looks promising," Lillian said.

"I wonder if it will be as promising as reading your palm. Please, let me see your hand." Andre reached over and tenderly placed his palm beneath hers. "This is your life line," he said, pointing to a line halfway between her thumb and index finger. Do you see how this line curves downward toward your wrist?"

"Yes."

"This contains details of your lifespan, which indicates you will live to be a very old woman," Andre said.

"Well, that's encouraging."

"The line that also begins between your thumb and index finger, which connects with your life line, and moves across the top of your palm, here, is your head line. Do you see it?" he asked, tracing the line slowly across her palm. "This line indicates your state of mind. What I see are very strong emotions in conflict with each other."

"Oh, really?" Lillian said with an arch of her brow.

"Do you see this line, here, which is parallel and above your head line? It spans the space between your little finger and index finger."

"Yes."

"This is your love line."

"And what does mine say?" Lillian asked as she slowly moved the tip of her tongue between her lips.

Andre folded her hand in his and their eyes met. Lillian's eyes were moist. "What's wrong? Have I done anything to upset you?" he asked.

"No," Lillian said as she wiped a tear from her eye. "For the past few months, I've just felt so isolated. I don't know what it is. I've been staying busy, but even with all the people around me, it's as if I don't see or hear them."

As Andre put his arm around Lillian, he could feel the tension in her shoulder. "If you wouldn't mind, let me help you relax."

Lillian said nothing and allowed Andre to turn her back slightly toward him. With his hands, he began a slow, gentle massage of her shoulders and neck. They said nothing, as they listened to the rhythmic chords of Segovia. After a few minutes of Andre kneading her muscles, Lillian slowly rotated her head in a circle, then Andre leaned forward and brushed her hair aside as he began kissing the back of her neck. She felt his warm breath and realized she couldn't even remember when she'd last felt this way. She knew it was wrong but felt powerless to resist. Her heart began racing as her breathing quickened.

Lillian knew the next move was hers: to continue or retreat. Andre's kisses took her choices away. She slowly turned to face him and looked into his eyes. Her unspoken question was met with his unspoken answer. He leaned in and kissed her. One kiss led to another, then another, each more passionate than the one before. He took her hand and led her into the bedroom. Was this really happening?

At the foot of his bed he stopped and said, "Aren't we entitled to continue and enjoy ourselves?"

Lillian didn't respond as a torrent of thoughts and emotions entered her head. Had Andre planned this from the beginning? He was so handsome. His actions toward her were those of a gentleman. Was she just another conquest for him? What if she was? She didn't care. *It's my life to live as I want.*

Lillian removed her blouse and let it fall to the floor. As she unfastened her bra, she exposed her breasts and placed Andre's hands over them. In their hunger for each other, they disrobed simultaneously, swept up in a wave of desire.

They fell onto the bed and showered one another with hot, moist kisses. As Andre reached for the nightstand where he kept his condoms, Lillian pulled his arm back towards her. He was too caught up in the heat of the moment as his body hovered over hers. Lillian entwined her legs around him and pulled him inside. There was no turning back.

Time seemed suspended. They both enjoyed exploring and being explored. It was obvious to Lillian that Andre was experienced as a lover. She knew she should feel exhausted, but all she felt was a pulsing sense of being alive and free.

Andre lay on the bed, slowly stroking her head and hair. Looking into her eyes he said, "You are a wonderful lover."

"I wish I could describe how you made me feel, but I don't have words," was all Lillian could say.

———

While Lillian used the shower, Andre went to the kitchen and pushed the on button for some freshly brewed coffee. When Lillian joined him in the kitchen, he handed her a cup of coffee, and she said, "Since I've been married, you're the only other man I've been with."

"Are you regretting it?"

"No. I should, but I'm not. You made me feel desired, that I was special. You made me feel like a woman."

Thoughts were flooding through Andre's head. He didn't regret the sex, but he could kick himself for violating one of his own rules. He hadn't used protection. It wasn't that he hadn't thought about it.

It was just that the passion Lillian had aroused in him was so intense he couldn't stop the desire rushing through his body. Only now did he recall a Russian proverb which translates: 'when a man's organ starts to rise, his brains fall into his ass.'

Lillian broke his train of thought. "Will I see you again?" she asked.

"I hope so," Andre said. "I would love to see you tomorrow, and the next day, and the day after that. But I do have to work. Regrettably, for the next two weeks I have business out of town." This was a lie. Andre knew Lillian would be thinking about him in the coming days. He knew her imagination would make him into something more than he was, and he wanted her excitement to grow. Operationally, he needed time to document moving her from a "developmental contact" into a "new source." His superiors would need to review his plan for their next rendezvous.

"Let me give you my phone number," Lillian said. "If you reach my voicemail, just say you're trying to re-schedule our tennis lesson, okay?"

—◦◦◦—

Andre hated the United States, but he loved his work. He was focused in his efforts against his American targets. His superiors rated his previous successes as exceptional. He was particularly skilled at recruiting women. If they didn't fall in love with him, they certainly became infatuated. He was skilled at balancing relationships. All his agents were still active, and none had yet been caught. He knew Lillian could be a valuable source for identifying vulnerabilities of US Embassy personnel. She could pinpoint who had drinking problems, and who were womanizers. She could tell him which couples were heading toward divorce, and who might be in financial trouble. She would have access to official lists and addresses. Information she had access to could help confirm the identity of CIA and defense intelligence employees. To get this information from her would take time, however, and the clock was working against him. His assignment in Vienna was ending in two months. He would then return to Moscow for thirty days of briefings, paperwork, and additional training before his next posting to Washington, DC, as a correspondent with TASS, the official Russian news agency.

CHAPTER 5

When Lillian got the call from Andre two weeks later, she could barely keep the excitement out of her voice. It was she who proposed they have dinner that Friday. She told him her husband had to travel to Amsterdam again for a conference and would not be back in Vienna until midweek. This wasn't the first time Felix was leaving on a Friday for a conference that started on a Monday. Why would he want a free weekend in Amsterdam? But this time she didn't care. She knew Felix never gave a moment's thought to what she might be doing.

Andre had agreed to pick Lillian up at the entrance to the Hotel Sacher near the Vienna Opera House. He'd made dinner reservations at the Korson, a restaurant known for flawless service and memorable meals. Andre pulled his car into the circular drive in front of the hotel, and a white-gloved doorman held the door open for Lillian when she came out.

Andre had dressed for the occasion. His dark blue suit with banker's stripes draped over him rakishly. His white Oxford shirt was accented with a burnished gold tie. Lillian was wearing a black evening gown with lace décolletage. A string of opera-length pearls drew attention to her not-so-subtle breasts. Tonight, she didn't care if anyone stared. She felt provocative. She didn't wear her rings but carried a luxurious black-knit shawl and a gold-chained purse. On the drive to the restaurant, she had awkwardly offered to treat him to dinner, but Andre insisted she was to be his guest for the entire evening.

The Korson was a romantic restaurant done in quiet taupe tones. A small fountain in the entrance displayed a bronze statue of a maiden set amid an impressive floral arrangement. Venetian glass lamps, strategically placed around the dark furniture, sent warm inviting light across each table. Comfortable armchairs with high backs were upholstered with discreet stripes of maroon and gold. Heavy sterling flatware and quality china were accented with fresh red roses in crystal vases.

Andre gave the maître d' his reservation, and the couple was directed to a quiet booth. A waiter and sommelier appeared simultaneously to explain daily specials and assist with the selection of an appropriate wine. Andre ordered a glass of champagne for each of them. As they flirtatiously stole glances at each other and sipped their aperitifs, they pretended to concentrate on the many entrees listed in the green leather-bound menus. Lillian, perhaps to show her intended submission to Andre, suggested he order for both of them.

Looking at the other couples in the restaurant, Lillian assumed many were there celebrating an occasion. Well, she too was celebrating something special, and the night was just beginning. When the waiter returned, Andre ordered eggs with shaved black truffles. For their main course, he ordered seared scallops with chicken dumplings in a chicken jus and a bottle of Pouilly Fusse. They would complete the dinner with the restaurant's signature chocolate truffle mousse with raspberry sauce.

They savored their food, smiling and laughing, and occasionally touching hands. They talked about their families, where they grew up and where they went to school. She found out Andre was fluent in French as well as English and Russian. Lillian tried to focus on the conversation, but her mind kept whispering that they had so little time left. She didn't want to say anything that would lessen the pure enjoyment she was feeling, but she heard herself blurting out that she and Felix were to return to Washington in six weeks, as her husband had orders to return to his section at the State Department. She waited for Andre's reaction. With a slight smile, Andre revealed he had landed a job with a Russian news agency and also would be assigned to DC—he would report there in three months.

"Oh, Andre, that's wonderful," Lillian said a little too loudly, realizing she'd be able to see him again. "Have you been to the United States before?"

"No. This will be my first time. I really don't know what to expect, but it's a fantastic opportunity for me."

He told her he still had reporting assignments in Zurich and Moscow and felt an obligation to finish writing the cookbook assignment for his friend. From his breast pocket he pulled out a business card and gave it to Lillian. On the card he had written an e-mail address he could check from any cyber café. Lillian reached into her purse and took out one of her diplomatic calling cards with only her name engraved on the front. On the back she wrote down a new e-mail address she had not shared with anyone else. It was reserved solely for him. As she handed him the card, her hand lingered lightly on his.

"When I'm with you, all my senses are heightened," she said. "I feel like I could tell you anything."

"I'm glad you feel that way."

"This week I got a telephone call from my best friend in the States who naturally asked me if there was anything new in my life."

"Did you tell her about us?" Andre asked.

"No. I can tell her just about anything, and I have in the past. But I couldn't even think about mentioning anything about us. Right now what we have is so private. And special."

Before Andre could say anything, their waiter returned to the table.

"I do hope the food has met your expectations," he said.

"It's exceeded them," Andre said with a smile, and Lillian chimed in, "Everything has been absolutely delicious."

As the waiter spun away, Andre asked, "So, what's important to you in a friendship?"

"I guess finding someone who has interests similar to mine but who accepts me the way I am. Why do you ask?"

"You've cast such a spell over me. You've been in my thoughts every day. I've found it very hard to concentrate. You've just made me step back and think about what's important."

"And have you come to any conclusions?"

"I've only known you for such a short time," Andre said, "but I feel as if I've known you for so much longer . . . like I've known you forever. I feel an inner peace when I'm with you."

"I feel the same way. Somehow we've managed to compress time."

"Men take so much longer to develop friendships and most guys are lucky to have one or two good friends they can talk to. Even then, they don't talk to their friends like women do. You mentioned your best friend is in the United States," he said. "How long have you known her?"

"We were roommates in college. I guess that makes it fourteen years. Do you have a best friend?" Lillian asked.

"I used to, but not anymore. My older brother was my best friend. He was killed in a helicopter crash." For once, Andre was truthful.

"I'm so sorry," Lillian said, not knowing what else to say.

"That's all right. It's been a long time. You're lucky to have a best friend. Lots of people who are married believe their husband or wife is their best friend. But many of them are wrong. To work, your spouse has to be unselfish, be willing to listen to you and not judge, to genuinely care about you as a person. If you're lucky enough to have that kind of relationship, then life can be wonderful. If you don't, you'll look to someone else with whom you can share your experiences."

"You mean like us and what we experienced," Lillian said smiling.

"Exactly. We shared something special, something that was missing from our lives. No one can take that away from us."

—◦◦◦—

As Andre drove them back to his apartment, Lillian could feel her body warming with expectation. Once inside, there was no small talk and no pretensions. Both knew what they wanted to do. Their desire had been simmering for the past two hours. They held each other and kissed deeply. Their hands explored each other, fingertips stroking each other with care and excitement. Their bodies melted into each other as they made love with no thoughts of tomorrow.

CHAPTER 6

After the meeting with the Washington agents, Bannister returned to the task force. Agents Ramirez and Campbell were standing near their desks. Mercedes Ramirez and Ford Campbell were rookie agents who had been assigned to the task force six months earlier. Derek Barnes, a gruff and salty senior agent on the team, assigned nicknames to all new agents. He obviously didn't care whether they objected or not. Ramirez and Campbell were dubbed the "Pit Crew" because they both had car names, and both were assigned a lot of dirty work the senior agents didn't want to do.

Stu Peterson came out of his office. "Ty, grab your notebook and follow me down to Witt's office."

"What's up?" Bannister asked as they walked toward the elevator.

"A new case. Witt just took a phone call and asked me to assign an agent to work an extortion. "

Extortions usually went to the bank robbery squad. There had to be a different angle to this one to have it referred to the task force.

Witt was perched at his desk, talking on the phone. As Bannister and Stu walked in, Witt waved for them to sit down in two armchairs in front of his desk. He finished his call and looked at Bannister with his hawk-like stare. "I just took a call from Adam Kush, director of security for Global Waters Company. You know him, don't you?"

"Yes. We did some work for him during the '96 Olympics." Bannister had been to Kush's office a few times since. He didn't see the need to tell Witt that Kush's personal assistant, Robin Mikkonen, was a Special Agent applicant recruited by Bannister. Mikkonen was in her final background stages, awaiting orders to the FBI Academy.

"He said he received a FedEx package this afternoon with a demand note and a vial with an unknown substance in it," Witt said.

"Where's the letter and vial now?"

"He still has them. He locked them in his safe and called us."

"According to Kush, the letter mentioned a 'biological agent,'" Stu said to Bannister. "Go over to their offices and take Ramirez with you. She's our microbiologist," he added for Witt's education. "Make sure you take at least one other Hazmat trained agent."

"I'll take Ford Campbell," said Bannister. "Did the letter identify the biological agent?"

"I don't think so. Kush didn't read the letter over the phone."

"FBI Headquarters has to be immediately notified of any extortion involving the threat to use a biological agent. I'll see what the letter says. If there's a threat, the United States Attorney has to authorize an investigation. And the letter should be sent to the laboratory ASAP."

"If the US Attorney gives you the green light, have Ramirez run the vial over to the Centers for Disease Control," Stu said. "Make sure the CDC is told the vial is part of a criminal investigation and has to be handled properly to preserve prints and other evidence. And interview Robin Mikkonen. Kush said she was the one who opened the package."

"If I'm not in the office, reach me on my cell," Witt said. "I want to be called as soon as you've determined what's going on."

"Has the boss been notified? I'm assuming he's still at Quantico."

"No one's called him yet. I better do that," Witt said. "Is there anyone else you think needs to be advised?"

"I'd let our media coordinator know, but tell her this is being tightly held. If CNN gets wind of this, all hell will break loose. I'll call the security director at the Centers for Disease Control. He can press some buttons with their toxicology division."

"I'll handle the media," Witt said.

Peterson looked at Bannister. "I'll let Kush know you're coming out."

Bannister went back up to the squad area to find Ramirez and Campbell.

"Mercedes," Bannister said to Ramirez. "I guess you got an assignment to go with me to Global Waters."

"No problem. Stu called from the ASAC's office and told me and Ford to hang around until you got back."

People liked Mercedes. She was single, petite, and tough, with a positive work ethic. She stood five four and was lucky if she weighed a hundred and ten pounds. She wore her dark hair short and curved in at the neck. She didn't smile much but was thoughtful, bringing in homemade cookies whenever she knew someone had a birthday or Bureau anniversary. She was a no-nonsense person, but could still laugh at her own jokes. She'd worked three years in a Biosafety Level Three laboratory at the Centers for Disease Control prior to becoming an agent. She knew protocols for dealing with unknown substances and had excellent contacts.

Ford Campbell was standing near Mercedes's desk. Bannister brought them up to speed.

"We'll take three cars. You two might have to run an unknown substance to the CDC."

The Pit Crew agreed to follow Bannister to Global Waters. It was rush hour in Atlanta, which started well before 4:00 p.m. and didn't let up until after 7:00 p.m. The interstate was its normal four-lane parking lot in each direction. Bannister decided to take an alternate route to Global Waters' offices on Marietta Street. With luck, they'd be at the guard gate in twenty minutes.

Heading west into the sun, Bannister kept Ramirez in his rear-view mirror as his thoughts drifted to Robin Mikkonen. He'd first met her a year ago when he'd set up an appointment with Adam Kush to discuss a new threat awareness program the Bureau was promoting.

It was Robin, Kush's assistant, who had come down to retrieve

Bannister from the lobby that day. She was absolutely striking, a statuesque blonde with long, silky hair, and what agents referred to as bedroom blue eyes. She introduced herself and shook his hand firmly. Robin had her own office, which led directly into Kush's.

While waiting for Kush to get off a conference call, the two had made small talk. Robin was intriguing and easy to be with. Bannister found out that she'd majored in Business and International Studies at Georgia Tech, including a year abroad studying politics in Paris at the Institut de'Etudes Politiques. She was fluent in French and her family's native language of Finnish. When she said she had always been fascinated by the work of the FBI, Bannister invited her out for coffee the following week. Eventually, he had encouraged her to apply for the Special Agent position. When Robin's formal FBI application was submitted, Bannister discovered she had a martial arts black belt in TaeKwonDo and had attended Georgia Tech on a scholarship. She'd been notified three weeks ago of her selection to New Agents Training, pending completion of a background investigation.

Bannister was still thinking about her when he pulled up to the guardhouse of Global Waters, with Ramirez and Campbell behind. He identified himself to the guard who said he had their names, told them where to park, and lifted the gate.

Ramirez got out of her car, carrying a silver metal case in one hand, a square black evidence suitcase in the other, and a large Bureau-issued purse with two-inch shoulder straps.

"You look like you're going away for a week, Mercedes," said Bannister. "You want me to carry one of your bags?"

"No, I've got it. You told me to bring the whole kit, remember? I can handle this if you'll get the doors for me."

Campbell trailed behind, carrying his notebook and photo bag.

They walked through a revolving door on the side of the complex toward a round reception console, which also served as a security monitoring station. The lobby was three stories high. One wall had seven-foot sculptured bottles with a cascading water fountain. Their shoes echoed on the black marble floor as they approached the guard and a receptionist seated behind the circular counter. The guard had his back to them, staring at monitors displaying eight changing camera views. The receptionist called Kush's office and announced an escort would be right down. Bannister hoped it would be Robin.

His wish materialized a few minutes later when Robin Mikkonen walked confidently into the lobby. She was wearing a beige Prada suit with a white silk blouse. Her two-toned heels automatically drew attention to her long, tanned legs.

"Hi, Robin. I was hoping you were still working here."

"Hello, Mr. Bannister. I'm glad they sent you to handle this."

"I'm going to feel uncomfortable unless you call me by my first name," Bannister said. He introduced Special Agents Ramirez and Campbell.

Robin proceeded to escort them to Adam Kush's suite on the executive floor, leading them through a high open archway into the office where Kush was waiting. Kush was a barrel-chested man of medium height. He was bald on top with reddish-brown hair and short, graying sideburns. He favored hound's-tooth-patterned sport coats, and always looked like the only thing he was missing was a bird-hunting shotgun.

After introductions, Kush said, "Robin, why don't you fill them in while I go to my safe and get the package. And by the way, Agent Bannister, I'm not too happy with you for hiring away the best assistant I've had in twenty years."

Mercedes and Ford looked at each other with furrowed brows. Bannister told them Robin was a Special Agent applicant. With a wave of her hand, Robin directed them into Kush's conference room, where they took seats at his round table.

"A FedEx letter was delivered to our offices this afternoon addressed to Mr. Kush," Robin said. "Our company instituted fairly elaborate security measures before the 1996 Olympics and has continued to update them. We have a separate mail facility next to the employees parking garage. Maybe you saw that small concrete building?"

"Yes, we parked right next to it," Bannister said.

"We have an x-ray machine in there, which detects any abnormalities in items being examined." Robin made eye contact with Mercedes and Ford, then continued. "All FedEx, UPS, and snail mail is scanned. Once each piece is scanned, a distinctive red mark is placed on the lower right corner. It's then sorted and routed to the appropriate corporate division. One of my job functions is to screen Mr. Kush's mail and eliminate junk mail."

"So, you opened the FedEx package?" Bannister asked.

"I have authority to read any mail addressed to him except for handwritten letters."

Adam Kush came out from the back of his office wearing blue latex gloves and carrying a large plastic envelope with two printed sheets inside and a FedEx envelope. He laid the package down on his conference table. They could see the envelope held a two-inch glass vial containing a clear liquid. The vial was sealed with what looked like a glass threaded stopper.

"I have no clue what that is," Kush said, pointing to the vial.

Wearing the cloth gloves Ramirez had given him, Bannister slid the FedEx envelope out of the plastic sleeve and examined the outside. "Robin, do you recognize the sender's address?"

"I think the name's a fake. Joe Kammel. But the address is for the Ralston and Evans law firm at One Peachtree Center in Atlanta."

"We don't have any business account with that firm," Kush added.

The letter was typed in large print on two plain white pages. Bannister read the first sheet aloud:

Various Global Waters products have been treated with a biological agent. The vial attached is proof of our capabilities. Unless our demand is met, altered products will be placed by our operatives in open display cases in two cities on

November 19. One city is in the United States; the other is an international capital. We demand five million in US one hundred dollar bills. If you agree to our terms, place a classified advertisement in the November 8 Atlanta Journal-Constitution. Ad should appear in personals section and state: Your offer has been accepted. Include a contact number. This contact number must be a 404 exchange number, which we will call between 1:00 p.m.–2:00 p.m. on Thursday, November 12.

He then read the second page:

Put the money inside a canvas bag. Place the canvas bag inside a large, black trash bag tied with a red pull-tie. The bag will be delivered by one of your employees driving a white Global Waters panel truck. The truck will be directed to a specific site where your driver will receive instructions. The truck must be ready to leave Global headquarters at 1:00 p.m. EST, Thursday, November 12. Driver should have a cell phone to communicate with you. Do not follow the truck. Your driver will not be hurt if you follow directions. Do not notify the police or other authorities. Do not place any tracking device or dye pack inside the bag. We have countermeasures equipment. If a tracking device is located, we will execute our plan. If payment as instructed is not received, we will execute our plan. Failure to follow our instructions will result in messages being sent to both The New York Times and The Washington Post with the following statement: Certain Global Waters products have been treated with a biological agent and placed on food shelves in specific United States and foreign cities. Your failure will require us to demonstrate the full extent of our capabilities during the New Year's Day celebrations.

"You read this letter?" Bannister asked Robin.

"Yes. It's serious, isn't it?"

"Sure looks that way. You took the right steps. Anyone else know about this?"

Robin looked at Adam Kush, who said, "I advised the company president and our general counsel. I told them I was contacting the FBI.

Our president called an emergency meeting for 7:30 a.m. tomorrow. I have to call him as soon as we know what's in the vial. I think he'll follow whatever the Bureau recommends."

"Did you handle the letter?" Bannister asked.

"I used gloves. Robin's prints should be on it. You have her prints on file, right?"

Bannister nodded.

Mercedes and Bannister asked Robin a few more questions. Agent Campbell then took photographs of the FedEx envelope and its contents. He carefully set the vial on a black card along with a six-inch ruler and took several photos of it. Campbell then placed the FedEx envelope and the printed pages in separate plastic evidence envelopes. Bannister had him accompany Kush to a copy machine where Campbell made photocopies of the now-sealed items. Mercedes enclosed the vial in a tamper-proof biological hazard container.

"Mercedes, I'm going to interview Mr. Kush," said Bannister. "While I'm doing that, I want you and Ford to take the vial to the CDC. Let our office know your route and give them time checks. I'd like you to stay there until the substance is identified and call me immediately, regardless of the hour. Ford, once the CDC has the vial, go back to the office with the film and get six sets of prints developed. In the meantime, we'll work off the photocopies."

As Mercedes and Ford collected their gear, Robin called the lobby and walked with them to the elevators. Bannister returned to Kush's office. Kush motioned him to one of the two black leather recliners facing a large picture window with a view of the downtown Atlanta skyline. Kush took off his jacket and walked over to the door, reaching behind it to retrieve a wooden hanger. He hung up his coat and walked back to the other chair. Bannister watched his heavy body slowly settle between the arms of the chair.

"So Adam, what's your take on this?" Bannister asked.

"I'm worried. I think there's something in that vial."

"I agree. I'll feel better once it's identified."

"I was working here in security twenty-something years ago when Tylenol capsules laced with cyanide killed seven people in Chicago. The killer was never caught. After that episode, I looked to see if we had a product tampering plan at Global." Kush raised his eyebrows and let out a deep sigh. "We didn't. I set one up, and every couple of years I dust it off and bring it up to date. I never thought we'd have to use it."

"Can you keep a lid on things until we know what we're dealing with?"

"I hope so. We don't want this leaking out. I don't know who's behind it. We could be facing a crackpot, disgruntled employee, terrorists, or maybe even a competitor. I know we can't ignore it. Our written policy, the one I developed, is to involve the FBI. That's why I called you guys."

"That was a good decision, even if the letter said not to notify the authorities. How's Global's financial health?"

"Excellent. We bottle and sell just one product, and that's water. That's all we're about. We currently market twelve different brands, and last year we sold twenty million cases in the United States and seventeen other countries. Our profits have increased annually for the past seven years."

"I didn't realize you were that successful."

"A lot of people don't. I think it's because we don't spend the big bucks on television advertising like the soft drink giants. Speaking of soft drinks, want one?"

"No thanks."

Kush walked over to his walnut credenza. He opened up a small refrigerator and popped the lid on a diet Coke. "Because of our success, Nestle Waters and two other companies are maneuvering for a hostile takeover bid. We have a significant cash surplus, and our board of directors has been pressing us to expand into sports drinks. One thing we can't afford right now is any kind of scandal."

"Do you have any thoughts about who might be behind this?"

"No, but somebody did their homework." Pointing his finger at Bannister for emphasis, Kush said, "It could be someone on the inside."

"Why do you think that?"

"My address on the FedEx envelope said 'Drawer 1734.' That's for internal routing. Outside people could get the P.O. box number from the Internet, but not the number 1734. What's your read?"

"I don't have enough information yet, but I tend to agree with you. Someone has gone to a great deal of effort and planning. If there's a poison or biological agent in that vial, then we're dealing with extremely dangerous people. I say 'people' because if we're to believe the threat, the worst-case scenario calls for simultaneous placement of your doctored products in the United States, and abroad. There's a possibility the subjects may have law enforcement or military experience. You noticed they used the terms 'tracking device,' 'dye pack,' and 'countermeasures capability.'"

Kush nodded.

"No one besides your company president and corporate attorney know about this, right?"

"Right. Our president and general counsel both said their number-one concern is public safety. Naturally, they want to avoid bad publicity. You remember what happened to Coca Cola in Belgium in 1999?"

Bannister shook his head.

"In June of 1999, over a hundred Belgian students at several schools got sick. They had all consumed at least one Coke product, and the public was quick to point a finger at Coca Cola. This happened at the same time there was a dioxin scare in Europe, and a sort of psychological hysteria swept Belgium and France. Coca Cola finally located some transport pallets, which had been sprayed with a fungicide that might have washed onto some of the cans and caused some of the illness. But they never did figure out how all the students got sick." Kush pointed out his window to a beige fourteen-story complex about five blocks away. "That's Coke's international headquarters. In any event, no one died or got seriously ill, but Coke ended up spending over $300 million recalling products—and Coke's image was tarnished for a while."

"What you're saying is that Global's executives are concerned with damage control, right?"

"Correct. In the morning I'll brief them on what we know and recommend an action plan. A lot will depend on what the Bureau finds out tonight and what you want us to do."

"At least whoever sent the letter has given us some time. Have you recently fired anybody who might want to get back at you?"

"I'm sure we have. I asked Personnel to pull all terminations and resignations from the corporate office for the past two years. I'll have that information in the morning. You've got to let me know when you find out what's in that vial."

"I'll call you right away," Bannister reassured him.

"Right now, I think we'll follow the extortionist's instructions and count on the FBI to do two things: catch whoever's responsible, and recover any tampered products. We'd also like to make sure our pay-off money doesn't get lost if it gets that far."

"The letter said not to contact the authorities. Most of the bad guys say that, but just in case they've got someone on the inside, let's keep this thing on a need-to-know."

"Absolutely," Kush said.

"I'd like to tell my boss you're prepared to place the ad tomorrow."

"Go ahead. I'll have it ready along with a phone number the extortionist can call."

"What about the money?" Bannister asked.

"I know the FBI doesn't front ransom money. We have emergency arrangements and can have the five million here within twelve hours."

"I'd like to go with your person to the newspaper."

"No problem," Kush said.

"I'll give you a call when I get the CDC results and check with you in the morning. I think that's it for right now." Bannister stood up. They shook hands, and Bannister gave Kush one of his cards with his cell phone number.

On his way out of the office, Bannister walked by Robin's desk. She was still there, sitting with her chin cupped in her hand, her elbow on her desk.

"Thanks for your time and for answering my questions," he said.

"Sure. Anything else you'd like to ask me?" She looked up at him with a saucy expression.

Bannister paused for a moment. "Just one. After this case is resolved, will you go to dinner with me?"

"The answer is yes. I'd love that."

"I'll bet you have a few questions for me, too. About the Academy."

"Lots of questions. So many, in fact, that it might take longer than one dinner."

CHAPTER 7

Tonight, as he did every Monday, Terry Hines was enjoying the Irish pub scene. He wasn't actually in Ireland, but in the Old Crom Pub on Peachtree Street in Atlanta, which was as close as he could get to the real thing. At least this year. He was quietly celebrating his plan, and so far everything was clicking. Global Waters had received his FedEx earlier that day.

The owners of Old Crom had spent two million dollars creating a bar with five different sections, including an old cottage and a museum room offering a history of Irish pub culture. This was Hines's favorite place to have a beer. It was early, and he took an empty seat at the end of the bar.

"Start you off with the regular?" the bartender asked.

"You got it, Jason," Hines said.

It took Jason a careful minute of pouring to build him a pint of Guinness with a solid inch of head.

Hines wanted to be financially independent by the time he turned forty. That was why he had changed his major from electrical engineering to business. Six years out of graduate school he had no debt. With eight years to reach his goal, he'd only saved twenty-two thousand dollars. At that pace, he knew he'd never make it. As he waited for his beer, Hines thought back to that day a year ago when he had brewed his scheme.

It had been his first trip abroad. As an international marketing manager, he was in Vienna representing Global Waters at a three-day joint ventures business symposium. He'd attended the essential break-out sessions as well as meet-and-greets. His corporate requirements were covered in the first twenty-four hours, and he was bored. Fortunately, during one of the initial breaks, he'd run into Andre Neff. Andre, a reporter for a Russian trade journal, had just completed an analysis of the Russian market for mineral water. He was intrigued with Hines's questions and his interest in Russian investment opportunities. During their last break, the two talked shop some more and had a few laughs. It was Andre's idea they get together that night for drinks.

Andre lived in Vienna and suggested they meet at the bar at the Hotel Bristol, a landmark where the elite had been meeting for drinks since 1892. After Andre and Hines had a few cocktails, their conversation turned serious. Hines confided in Andre that he had access to his company's technology and strategies. It was then that Andre asked him if he could line up venture capitalists willing to invest an initial three million dollars for a plant to produce bottled water for distribution in St. Petersburg. Andre's research had convinced him the return on investment would be at least ten million dollars a year. He said the only Russian company currently developing the mineral water market was Narzan, but they were only in a few smaller cities and could not satisfy the thirst of millions of Russians who desired clean water and were willing to pay for it.

Andre said the untapped market was enormous, and that he had connections inside the foreign ministry who could facilitate all the paperwork. For a price, of course. All he needed for a partnership was someone with industry knowledge and financial backing. Hines remembered telling Andre that when the Bristol Hotel was built, the Rockefellers and Carnegies were using family inheritances in the United States to take risks and seize opportunities. Hines didn't have an inheritance to give him a head start, but he assured Andre that, like the Rockefellers, he wasn't afraid of risk and would seize an opportunity to build his own fortune. Maybe it was the alcohol talking, but Andre said the two of them had that opportunity in Russia and with proper timing, they could, in the words of the Wall Street gurus, be the gorilla on the block.

After a couple of drinks later and a few back slaps, the two exchanged information and agreed to stay in touch. It was during the walk back to his hotel room that Hines decided to make a daring move to fulfill his dream.

As soon as he got back to the US, he obtained a false identity in the name of Sean O'Brien. He used that identity to register the name of a new company with the Georgia Secretary of State's office: *US Euro Trans-Consultants*. The name meant nothing. The company was fictitious. The president and only officer listed was Sean O'Brien. It took Hines several months to open charge accounts and establish credit for Sean O'Brien. Hines had the credit card bills sent to a mail drop box; he paid the bills immediately with money orders. What he was waiting for was a foolproof opportunity to make a one-time financial killing. It was while sitting in the Old Crom Pub that he had come up with the key to his future.

It took him two weekends of scouting dozens of mini-marts around Atlanta before he found what he was looking for. The small commercial office space at the end of an L-shaped strip mall had a "For Lease" sign in the window. Next to the vacant office, across the alley, was Mike's Mini-Mart. The Mini-Mart's hours were perfect—7:00 a.m. to 11:00 p.m. Its large steel trash dumpster may have seemed like a paint-splattered, foul-smelling eyesore to some prospective tenants. To Hines, it was the one feature that had sold him on the lease.

Hines still had the wig, mustache, and glasses he'd worn when he got his O'Brien driver's license. Donning his disguise and wearing a blue-denim shirt over torn, faded blue jeans, Hines had felt confident posing as a foreign graduate student from Emory University. He felt a rush reliving the lease transaction.

"Good morning, Mr. O'Brien," Candace Miller, the leasing agent, had chirped when she first met Mr. O'Brien to show him the vacant office.

"Good morning, Miss Miller," Hines said, and waited as she opened the door to the empty space.

"As you can see, it's a basic office. The walls and ceiling have all been repainted in an off-white tone. This carpeting was installed by the last tenant and is in excellent condition. The office's wiring has been updated to handle multiple pieces of office equipment and is cable-ready with six phone jacks. What do you think? Anything missing?"

"It looks perfect. I like the window treatments."

"The wooden blinds were custom-made. They let in the morning sun, but when shut will give you total privacy."

"I'm ready to sign the papers."

Hines had followed Miller to her office and backed his white rental car into a space at the far end of the lot to keep anyone from seeing its license plate. As he walked through the front door, Miller directed him to her small glass-walled office in the back of Best Atlanta's one-story, gray-brick building.

"I'm assuming you have everything I need to sign."

"I think so. You told me you and your partner were setting up a business arranging international home exchanges and vacation property swaps for Atlanta area residents."

"That's right."

"Do you want him to be a co-signer on the lease?" Miller asked.

"No, I think it's easier to deal with just one person."

"I like the name of your business—US Euro Trans-Consultants. It has a modern ring to it," Miller remarked as she laid out the lease papers on her desk.

Hines paid two months of the lease in addition to a thousand dollar security deposit. He gave her $3,600 in cash, explaining that he was still in the process of setting up commercial bank accounts, business cards, a business phone, and the like. He was careful to keep his fingers off the original documents. After giving him a receipt for his payment and copies of the documents, Miller said everything was in order and he could take possession by the end of the week.

—◈◈◈—

Jason the bartender checked back with Hines. "So what's the big grin for?" he asked, interrupting Hines's train of thought.

Hines had been smiling to himself as he went over his plan. "Oh, I was just thinking about a girl that was here last week and how close I came to hooking up with her."

"Well, I'd save the smiling practice until someone's sitting next to you. You want another pint?"

"Yeah, I feel I could use one more tonight," Hines said. He was enjoying rehashing all the details he had so carefully worked out.

—◈◈◈—

Once he had the office keys, Hines had set about renting equipment. To give the impression of a business office, he rented two office desks, chairs, and a floor lamp. Later, black landscaping plastic was tacked across the entire length of the wooden blinds to block anyone from seeing inside.

The first weekend he had used his SUV to bring down from North Carolina a ground penetrating radar unit he had rented for a week. After midnight, he wheeled the unit up and down the empty alley by the office. It surveyed everything below the alley's asphalt surface to a depth of sixteen feet and plotted all the information into a digital control unit. Once the images were downloaded to his laptop, Hines saw there would be no problem with sewer lines, gas lines, or electrical conduits.

From a Georgia company he'd bought a portable auger, PVC casing pipes, hydraulic pipe supports and plates, and burlap bags. Everything was pre-paid with money orders and shipped to the storefront. He tracked the delivery date and took a vacation day from his regular job to ensure he was at his new office when the carrier arrived with his supplies.

The second weekend, Hines rented a concrete cutting saw. Along the back wall of the office were numerous boxes containing the equipment delivered earlier from Georgia. He covered the desks and chairs with plastic and spent four hours cutting out a four-by-four foot section of the office floor. He rested frequently, not being big on muscles. Although he was six foot, he only weighed one forty-five. Dust was everywhere. It took six cuts to remove four seventy-pound sections. With difficulty, he carried out the slabs, one at a time, and loaded them into a panel truck he'd leased. After sweeping up inside, he placed a sheet of plywood over the hole in the floor. Pleased with his work, Hines headed back to his apartment, stopping alongside a steep ravine where he slid each of the concrete blocks down the embankment.

Over the next three months, working mostly at night during the week and early on Saturday and Sunday mornings, Hines dug a tunnel from his rented office space, underneath the alley, and out to a point directly below the steel dumpster by Mike's Mini-Mart. The dumpster, which stayed in the same location, was emptied by a blue trash truck like clockwork every Wednesday afternoon. Hines had filled and dumped each of the three-dozen burlap bags at least ten times with soil and rocks from the tunnel.

During this same period, using the alias Sean O'Brien, Hines completed a correspondence course in welding. He had reviewed the DVDs on cutting-torch basics and techniques numerous times. He had no doubt that when it was time, he would be able to handle a real oxy-acetylene torch.

From the Internet, Hines ordered castor beans from two different seed retailers. He'd followed the instructions from an "underground" manual to make the specific toxin he wanted. He used extreme care when grinding the beans to obtain the oil. When the process and curing were finished, he had a vial of poison.

From a college contact, he was put in touch with a man who sold him a stolen cell phone with a cloned subscriber number. The stolen numbers entered into the phones were only good for the current billing cycle. For another hundred dollars, his seller said he could bring the phone back and have it re-programmed with another stolen number the next month. The phone Hines had bought the previous week could be used for another eighteen days before the subscriber even got the bill. Hines knew he'd only need it for a few calls.

His second purchase was for five yards of Flectron material. This discovery, via the Internet, was his answer to the problem of how to thwart law enforcement's tracking devices. He had researched methods the government and military used to prevent interception of signals from computers and other sensitive electronic equipment. Flectron was a copper-plated nylon rip-stop fabric used to make protective clothing for people working with electromagnetic power line transmissions and microwave radiation. Flectron was designed to keep electrical waves or radio frequency beams from entering into anything covered with the material. Hines reasoned that it would also keep any transmitting device, such as a cell phone, pager, or tracking device, from letting its signal escape from inside a covered item.

Once the roll of Flectron material arrived, Hines only needed three hours to hand-sew a six-foot by three-foot duffel bag. He attached a four-foot Velcro strip along one side to seal the opening.

While he nursed his beer, Hines reached into his wallet and pulled out a card on which he had written his five remaining "to do" items. The first item was "buy oxy." He was picking up the portable cutting torch this weekend. The second item was "car rental." Next Tuesday evening he'd rent a car from the airport for three days. The third item was "plate." He would drive the rental to the long-term parking lot at Atlanta's airport that same night where he would steal an out-of-state license plate. The fourth and fifth items were "cruise-pack" and "offshore." Friday he was leaving on a one week's cruise to Costa Rica, Cozumel, and Grand Cayman. Grand Cayman was where he'd open his new "offshore" account. When he returned to Atlanta, he'd contact

Andre Neff and get specifics about investment opportunities in Russia. In the meantime, he'd have an entire cruise to bask in the sun and think about the lifestyles of the rich and famous.

Hines reflected for a final minute, trying to think if there was anything he'd overlooked. There wasn't. He knew that. The excitement grew each time he went over his plan. He put the card back in his wallet when he heard Old Crom's house band, The Charms, singing their first set from the room around the corner. He waited until they finished their rendition of the ballad *Lakes of Coolfin* and drained his glass.

As Hines got up to leave, Jason said, "See you same time, next week?"

"Nah, I'm going to be out of town, but you can go to the bank on my being here the week after." Hines enjoyed the subtlety of his parting comment.

CHAPTER 8

When Bannister left Global Waters, traffic was still sluggish. By the time he got back to the office, Stu and the rest of the task force had left. He called the Assistant United States Attorney on duty and read the letter to her. She authorized prosecution and gave him an okay for a trap and trace on the telephone number Global would put in its ad. After calling the Bureau's operations center, he went to the breakroom where the vending machine still had one beef-and-cheese burrito. He heated it in the microwave and brewed a pot of coffee.

Just as Bannister finished writing up the interviews of Robin Mikkonen and Adam Kush, Ford Campbell stuck his head in the door.

"I guess we're the only ones left. The film's at the photo lab. The tech was still there doing a bank robbery photo spread. She said no problem doing our prints tonight. She's on approved overtime."

"Any hitches at the CDC?"

"No. One of the scientists doing the testing used to work with Mercedes."

"Hopefully they got along. Did they give you any idea how long it would take?"

"Within twenty-four hours. They're making this a priority and want to be exact in case this ends up in court," Campbell said.

"In that event, there's no use in your hanging around the office."

Bannister's cell phone rang and he recognized Ramirez's number. "It's Mercedes now," he said.

"It's ricin!" Mercedes was almost shouting. "They ran a time-resolved fluorescence immunoassay test and—"

"Whoa! Take a breath."

"Sorry. One of the standard tests they conducted is for ricin. It came back positive. The CDC is going to run a polymerase chain reaction or PCR test tomorrow. They're the only lab that does a PCR test since it involves looking for the DNA of the ricin protein."

Bannister turned to Campbell and said, "Ricin."

Ramirez went on, "She told me that a five-hundred microgram dose, about the amount that could fit on the head of a pin, could kill the average person."

"Good work. Take a statement from whoever is doing the testing. I don't know when Witt's going to order us to circle the wagons, but I'll call you if there's any change."

Bannister called Stu and gave him the update. While Stu notified task force members, Bannister called Witt.

"The CDC confirmed the vial contains ricin. We have a definite biological threat."

"This is serious," Witt said. "Save me from having to look it up. What is it, exactly, and how toxic is it?"

"Ricin is extracted from the oil of the castor bean plant. It's extremely toxic. If it's inhaled or injected, it's bad news. There's no known antidote."

"How quick does it work?" Witt asked.

"You've got to get medical attention immediately or it's usually fatal. Death normally takes three to five days. The problem is, by the time a victim's symptoms are diagnosed—severe dehydration, decreased blood pressure, and a build-up of fluid in the lungs—it's too late."

"Should I call an emergency meeting tonight?"

"It's your decision, but I don't think we'd get anything more done tonight. I'd let the boss know and confirm the worst. He might not want to stay in Quantico."

"Okay, we'll meet tomorrow at eight. Can you prepare an operational plan?"

"It'll be ready. I'll notify headquarters. I'd like both the technical and surveillance supervisors to attend."

Campbell returned from downstairs with the photos, and Bannister called Adam Kush with the bad news. Kush agreed to restrict knowledge of the FBI's plans to essential company personnel and advised him that Global would hold an emergency meeting in the morning. Bannister suggested the others call it a day. He knew for the rest of the week they'd be running on high test.

Everyone left but Bannister, who set to work on preparing an operational plan.

—⟡⟡⟡—

GLOBAL WATERS—TUESDAY, 8:00 A.M.

There were two people at Global besides Kush and Mikkonen who knew about the letter. One was Leo Abramowitz, their chief lawyer. The other was Global's International Relations manager, Terry Hines, who had sent the letter.

Everyone Adam Kush had requested to be at his emergency meeting was assembled when he walked in with Robin Mikkonen. There was no usual meeting banter. Seated at the table were Global's General Counsel, Operations Director, Chief Product Development Engineer, and International Relations manager.

Kush addressed the gathering. "A situation developed late yesterday requiring us to activate an emergency plan. Robin, hand out these copies of our contingency plan and the letter we received. Gentlemen, take a few minutes to read the letter. The vial with the unknown substance was sent to the CDC last night for testing."

"Do you think someone would actually carry out this threat?" asked Global's Operations Director.

"It's possible. I called the company president right away, and he instructed me to bring in the FBI," Kush said.

"The letter said not to contact the authorities. Aren't we putting the company at an unnecessary risk, getting the FBI involved?" asked Terry Hines.

"We're not the ones putting the company at risk," Kush said. "Whoever sent that letter is the one creating the risk. The CDC has determined the substance in the vial that accompanied the letter is ricin—a deadly poison."

Leo Abramowitz said, "One or more crimes have already been committed, and the FBI has the resources to investigate them."

"Are we going to pay the money?" the Operations Director asked.

"Our position is that we will cooperate with law enforcement and not interfere in their investigation. It's my understanding they will coordinate closely with our security department. Isn't that right, Adam?" Abramowitz asked.

"Correct. Our general liability insurance policy covers payment of a ransom up to five million dollars. However, it's silent about making extortion payments," Kush said.

"The company president can authorize providing the FBI with the five million. I'm sure he'll turn over the money if this thing isn't solved by the payoff date. But he's going to ask me about what to say to the Board of Directors if anything happens to the money," Abramowitz said. "And by the way, our product recall insurance coverage is twenty million dollars."

Global's Chief Product Engineer scrunched his face. "That may not be enough. Our emergency plans have pretty well defined what steps we take if we have a batch of contaminated water. I don't have any heartburn over that. But I don't know of any company that's faced a biological threat. Hell, we don't even know if they'll carry it out. And if they do, we don't know in what country or city."

"Well, our planning calls for us to prepare for a worst-case scenario," Kush said. "If any of our bottles get poisoned, even if no one drinks the stuff, the costs of a recall will be astronomical. I don't know if you remember the Tylenol case. Johnson & Johnson recalled thirty-one million bottles. But I think the biggest loss to any company took place when Intel had to recall its defective Pentium computer chip. It cost them over five hundred million. I could point out other cases, but you guys get the point."

"I know our plans call for a massive and immediate notification to all our people. Don't we have a duty to give them a heads up?" the Operations Director asked.

"Not exactly," Kush said, swiveling around in his chair. "We're not going to let any advance information out until we know a recall is required."

"We'll have statements ready for immediate worldwide publication and network coverage," said Abramowitz. "We'll do everything possible to minimize damage to our goodwill, and limit liability."

"In the meantime, I want all of you to familiarize yourself with our contingency plan and prepare any questions you might have. We'll meet again Friday, and then every day next week until this matter is resolved," Kush said.

"Who's handling the advertisement with the newspaper?" Hines asked.

"Robin's going there with the FBI. That's it for now. I want all of you to keep your cell phones with you at all times," Kush said, pushing away from the table.

As he headed to the door, Hines stopped him.

"Adam, two months ago I put in for a week's vacation to take a cruise. It's supposed to start the day before the scheduled pay off. Do you want me to cancel?"

"I don't know. Let me get back with you Friday. If we need you here, the company will reimburse you for any cancellation fees. If I remember correctly, the Business Development Coordinator is really sharp and the two of you are almost interchangeable, right?"

"I wouldn't put it that way, but yes, we've always tried to make sure if anything happened to cause one of us to drop out of the picture, the other could handle the job."

"You have a tentative okay, but check with me later. I appreciate your team spirit," Kush said as he left to call the company president.

———⟐⟐⟐———

FBI—TUESDAY, 8:00 A.M.

Stu Peterson had assembled the team members as well as the technical and surveillance supervisors. Witt walked in and said, "Good morning, men. We might as well begin." Mercedes Ramirez winked at Bannister in response to Witt's greeting.

"We have a new extortion case. It's also a biological threat involving the toxic agent ricin. The victim is Global Waters, and whoever's behind it is demanding five million dollars cash. I've assigned the case to Ty Bannister, and he'll outline his plan."

"Before we do anything, I'd like all of you to take a couple of minutes to read over the letter. Then give me your initial thoughts," Bannister said.

Derek Barnes was the first to speak. In his slow, gravelly voice he asked, "Why Global Waters? Why not someone really big, like Coke?"

The technical supervisor said, "I agree. Normally it's always about the money. Why five million, why not ten? And the language about 'countermeasures' makes me think we're not dealing with the normal knucklehead."

Stu Peterson added, "I know we have confirmation the substance with the letter is ricin, but I have reservations that whoever's behind this would actually poison Global's water if the payment isn't made. I also question whether the subject or subjects have a collaborator in Europe."

It was quiet for a minute before Ford Campbell added, "Whoever's behind this has to realize a major corporation that's threatened isn't just going to make a ransom payment without contacting authorities, especially the FBI. They must think they're smarter than us and can get away with it."

One of the task force agents with a background in explosives said, "I'd focus on the payoff if we're going to catch the subjects. They've got to know that a van driving around town with five million is going to be followed in some way. I don't think the van is the last leg of the transfer. I'd be looking at a second transfer to a plane or boat or maybe even the subway. Just food for thought."

"Good point," Bannister said. "Anyone else?"

The surveillance supervisor spoke next. "A couple things bother me. Why a canvas bag inside a trash bag? Why not a suitcase? Or backpack—you know, something easier to carry. And we can't make the assumption the driver is going to toss the bag out somewhere. The subjects may force the driver out and hijack the van."

"That's happened before," Bannister said.

"I don't want to sound presumptuous, but I think we're dealing with a college-educated person," said Mercedes Ramirez. "If you look at the wording of the letter as well as the grammar and punctuation, it could be something one of us wrote. And I'm sure you've already thought of it, but I'd ask the lab to run the letter through psycholinguistics and see if they can't work up something about the sender's profile."

"If there are no other questions right now, how about letting us know how you want this handled?" Witt looked at Bannister.

"Each of you has a copy of the plan in front of you. I particularly need the surveillance assignments and recommended technical installations as soon as possible. Right now, I intend to use one of our agents as the driver, with a second agent concealed in the back of the van. I want the van equipped with interior CCTV, external camera coverage, a global positioning system, and an infrared strobe on the roof, just in case the money exchange drags on into the evening."

All eyes shifted to the technical supervisor.

"No problem," he said.

"I'll get together with you later to go over marking the money and installation of a sensor in the canvas bag," Bannister said.

"Do you anticipate any problems having a plane up at all times?" Bannister asked the surveillance supervisor. "And we'll need enough ground units to make sure we don't lose sight of the van."

"Weather's always an unknown, but we'll have a contingency plan in place," he responded.

"You'll also be responsible for the arrest team. Treat any subject as armed and dangerous."

"You bet," he said.

"You've got a couple of days to get everything organized. We'll meet Friday morning to go over details. The lab may have something for us to work on by then. E-mail me any questions or thoughts you have. I'm going to Global now to pick up their advertisement for the newspaper."

"Okay, let's make sure we cover everything," Witt said as he adjourned the meeting.

CHAPTER 9

ONE YEAR EARLIER—WASHINGTON, DC

D r. Connie Bradford had been Lillian Wells' gynecologist before Lillian moved to Vienna. Even though she and Felix were buying a house in a new neighborhood, it gave Lillian comfort to be able to return to the same doctors and dentist she'd had before going to Europe. What she found a little unsettling this afternoon was that Dr. Bradford asked her to come into her private office to discuss the results of the exam and lab work. Normally, the doctor talked with Lillian in the examining room. She didn't have time to wonder what it meant. Dr. Bradford came in almost as soon as Lillian sat down.

"Lillian, you remember when I asked you if there were any changes in your general health since I last saw you? You mentioned you'd lost a few pounds and have been more fatigued the last two months."

Lillian frowned and tilted her head. "I thought it was due to the stress and pressure of moving from Vienna back to Washington. It did occur to me I might be slightly anemic or something."

"I'm sure the relocation had some effect on you. But just to rule out chronic fatigue syndrome or a thyroid imbalance, I had you sign a separate consent form for additional tests. Do you remember that?"

"Yes." Lillian grew alarmed. "What are you trying to tell me, Dr. Bradford? Do I have cancer?"

"No, you don't have cancer, but you tested positive for HIV."

"What? No! No, that's not right." The blood drained from Lillian's face, and she slowly shook her head back and forth, not believing what she had heard. "There must have been a mix-up in the lab. I can't have HIV."

"Lillian, listen to me. I had a second blood test conducted, which confirmed the first. I'm sorry to have to tell you this."

Dr. Bradford came from around her desk and sat in the chair next to Lillian. She reached over and took Lillian's hand. "We need to talk about what you should do from today forward. And there are some other questions I'm required to ask you."

"How could this have happened?" Lillian asked softly, stunned and still in denial.

"During the past year, have you had sexual relations with anyone, male or female, other than your husband?"

Lillian bent forward and placed her hands on her forehead. Without lifting her eyes to meet the doctor's, Lillian said, "Yes, with one man. We had sex twice; the first time was without protection. Are you saying Andre—I'm sorry, that's his name—infected me?"

"You've told me you have never used illegal drugs, never received any injections other than inoculations for overseas travel, and have not had any body piercings or tattoos, right?"

"That's correct."

"Then if you've only been intimate with your husband and this Andre, there's a very strong probability it had to be one of them. After a person is exposed to HIV, it takes from two weeks to six months for antibodies to develop." Dr. Bradford was silent for a minute. "They'll have to be notified and should be tested. You understand that, don't you?"

"It could be my husband. I've suspected him of having an affair, although I don't have any proof. And I've also thought he might have been with prostitutes during one of his trips to Amsterdam."

"I'm going to recommend a counselor for you to talk with. She's extremely competent and understanding. She'll help you in ways I can't. Having HIV and AIDS aren't the same thing. HIV is a virus that attacks your immune system. Eventually, it can cause a range of illnesses that we commonly call Acquired Immune Deficiency Syndrome, or AIDS. I'm going to start you immediately on an antiviral drug program. The names of the drugs won't mean anything to you right now, but I'm prescribing AZT, 3TC, and Efavirenz. There are over twenty drugs being used to treat AIDS, but those three have been shown to work the best. I want to see you back in my office next week. If you want to bring your husband to my office and have me discuss this with him, let me know."

"I don't know what to think right now. I don't want my husband to know about the other man until he's tested. If his test comes back negative, then I'll tell him about Andre. You won't tell Felix, will you?"

"No, our relationship is privileged. But he needs to be told."

As Lillian walked out of the doctor's office toward Felix's leased Lexus, she started shaking and thought she might break down and cry. Thoughts were cascading through her head so fast she couldn't think. She didn't even know if it was safe for her to drive. There was no one for her to call. She couldn't believe this was happening. There must have been a mistake somewhere. She needed to focus.

The sun was shining directly through the window of the car, and its warmth on her face felt good. She needed to make sense of everything. She always had lists, and plans, and ideas and things to do. A person always in control. Until an hour ago. She'd never imagined this happening to someone she knew, much less herself. Of course, she'd occasionally thought about how someone might handle a diagnosis of cancer, but when she tried to imagine herself in that situation the answer was always, "Don't be negative. Cross that bridge when you come to it."

Well, I'm there now, and it's because of you, Felix. You sonofabitch!

How long did she have? Could people with AIDS really live a normal life?

I don't even know who I can talk to. Who would even understand me if I did tell them? Mom and Dad are gone. Mary Claire would understand or at least she'd try. She knows me better than anyone but would feel so betrayed because I never mentioned anything about Andre. All I know is I just don't deserve this, and one of the men in my life is responsible. But which one? If it was Felix, then I put Andre at risk. It has to be Felix. It just has to be. He never wanted me to have children, and now he's made sure I never will.

And with that, the tears came. After she cried herself out, she felt a little stupid. By the time she finished, she knew she would confront Felix, get the truth, and make sure he was tested. She trusted Dr. Bradford, and she would call the counselor in the morning for an appointment. She'd be able to talk with someone who understood. Knowing she had a plan helped. But how would she tell Andre?

Felix called Lillian at six o'clock and suggested they have dinner at a nearby Chinese restaurant. She didn't feel like eating, but she had no intention of cooking for Felix that night. The hour they spent at the restaurant went the way their meals out always did. Felix talked about himself, his day at the office, and all the opportunities he saw in his immediate future. Lillian merely listened, picking at her fried rice. Felix never asked about her doctor's appointment. Once they returned to the apartment and changed clothes, Lillian said she wanted to talk.

"Sure," Felix shrugged as he sat down in the love seat, kicked off his loafers, and put his feet up on the ottoman. "So what do you want to talk about?"

"I went to the doctor today," Lillian said, still standing. "She diagnosed me with a problem."

Felix waited, looking slightly impatient.

"I have a sexually transmitted disease," Lillian said.

She let the words sink in for a moment, but Felix showed no response.

"The only way I could have gotten it is from you." She said this in a matter-of-fact tone without raising her voice. She was surprised how she had controlled her emotions.

Felix clenched his jaw and furrowed his brow, but still said nothing.

"So, who have you been seeing? Who have you been having sex with?"

"I haven't been having an affair, if that's what you're asking."

"That's not what I'm asking. Who have you been fucking? That's what I'm asking. You got infected from someone and I want to know who!"

"Okay," Felix said. "Okay," he said again.

Lillian waited for him to speak. Felix put his feet on the floor and leaned forward, hanging his head like a young boy caught cheating by his teacher. "I've been with some women in Amsterdam. I don't even know their names."

"You slept with prostitutes? You paid for sex? Answer me!"

"I paid a prostitute in the red light district. The other two were women I picked up in the hotel bar. One-night stands. They didn't mean anything to me."

"Goddamn you, Felix. Obviously our marriage vows didn't mean anything to you either," Lillian said quickly, even as the thought of Andre entered her mind. She took a deep breath.

Felix asked, "So, what do you want me to do?"

"I want you to get a blood test tomorrow. And I want you to make sure your doctor tests you for all sexually transmitted diseases."

"I don't know if I can get an appointment that soon."

"Oh, you can get an appointment. Use some of your high-level connections if you have to. Or go to a public health clinic. I don't care where you go. Just get it handled tomorrow and get the results."

"So, what is it that you have?" Felix asked.

"We'll discuss it after we discuss your lab results. And I don't have anything else to say to you tonight. We'll talk tomorrow."

Lillian left the living room, walked into the den, and turned on her computer. While she waited, she breathed in and out deeply four or five times. It took another minute for her heart to quit pounding so hard. She logged onto the Internet and from memory entered an e-mail address and typed in her password. There was one message. It read: "Greetings from center court. Everything is going well here in Moscow. I'll be leaving for Washington this week. I have a lot to do when I arrive.

I am anxious for a personal tour. Can you fit me in? If you have a new number, please send it to me or e-mail it later. Andre."

After reading the message for the third time, Lillian put her finger on the delete key and pressed. If only her problem could be eliminated so quickly.

———ⁿⁿⁿ———

The following morning, Felix went to his doctor for a blood test. The results were positive for HIV. He returned to the apartment a devastated man and shared the results with Lillian.

"It's HIV," Felix said.

Lillian had nothing to say.

CHAPTER 10

Bannister called Adam Kush as soon as the FBI briefing was over.

"How'd your meeting go?"

"Fine, no problems on this end. The president authorized the withdrawal and use of the five million. I was planning on having the money delivered here next Wednesday afternoon. I'll have to hire some armed guards to babysit the dough. I was thinking, though, you don't suppose this is all a setup to try and steal the money once it's delivered to Global, do you?"

"No, but it's smart to think of all the angles. There are too many unknowns for someone to try and rip off the money from your headquarters. Does Robin have the ad ready for the newspaper?"

"Everything's all set. When you get back from the newspaper, how about briefing me on the Bureau's plan for next week?"

"Sure thing."

Driving over to Global Waters, Bannister thought of Robin. He wondered how a woman could totally captivate his thoughts. Even with the constant underlying worry he had been feeling ever since Cal had gone missing, he kept thinking about her. And he was less concerned about the seriousness of the ricin threat than he was pleased for the opportunity it gave him to see her again.

What made one person attracted to another? The first two years after Erin died, he hadn't dated. It wasn't because of grief. And it wasn't that he didn't meet plenty of attractive women. But once he'd start talking to a woman, he inevitably found himself comparing her to Erin. It wasn't fair to the woman, and maybe not even to him. He had his share of dates and always tried to act like the perfect computer match, but somehow when he smiled it seemed forced. He never led any of them on, and he would attempt to explain that it wasn't anything to do with them. He didn't know if they completely bought his explanation, but at least he tried.

Robin was different. She was the first woman since Erin who was able to hold his attention. Being around Robin gave him an inner calm and a feeling of excitement at the same time.

He called her cell phone. When she answered, her mellow voice and inflection made the words she spoke sound like she was genuinely interested in talking with him. She agreed to meet him at Global's front entrance.

Two minutes later, Bannister swung the car into the turnaround next to the fountain. Robin breezed out of the building. He barely had time to stop and walk around to open the passenger door for her."

"Ah, you're a gentleman," she smiled. As she stepped into the car, her hair brushed past his face, and he caught the subtle scent of her perfume, an air of fresh citrus.

"It's my pleasure. At the Academy, your male classmates will have mixed reactions. Like when you're leaving the gun vault and heading to the firing ranges, some guys might open the door for you just because you're a woman. Others will step right in front of you and make you catch the door yourself because they don't want to treat you differently than any other trainee."

"Well, I'll just have to make a mental note of that—and be sure to thank those who hold the door."

It was a ten-minute ride to the newspaper. Downtown Atlanta was like most big cities; finding a parking space was always a problem. Luckily, a van was pulling out of a spot on Forsyth Street as Bannister turned the corner.

The Atlanta Journal-Constitution's circulation department was two doors down. Robin handled the placement of the ad, and Bannister was impressed when she asked to speak to the classifieds' supervisor. Neither of them wanted to risk the ad not getting into the Sunday edition. She arranged for the proof of the ad to be faxed to her at Global to make sure there weren't any typos. They exited the newspaper's office, and Bannister called Stu to let him know the ad was placed and that he was returning to Global Waters to brief Adam Kush on their game plan.

"Have you ever worked this type of case before?" Robin asked when they were back in the car.

"Not exactly. I've never seen one which involved a biological poison. And the amount of money involved is large. I once had to stake out a drop site in a cornfield in Ohio in the middle of winter. My partner and I lay on the frozen ground among dead corn stalks for six hours, waiting for a subject to retrieve a garbage bag with two hundred fifty thousand dollars."

"Did he show up?"

"Yeah. An hour or two after daylight we noticed a car drive past the field twice. When we spotted the car the third time, a guy stopped and ran about thirty yards into the field to grab the bag. We were to the side about twenty yards away. We both jumped up and pointed our M-16 rifles at him. We scared the hell out of him. Did I mention we were wearing all white Arctic winter gear, gloves, and boots? We would have scared anybody."

"Did the guy have a record?"

"No. He was only nineteen. He just stood still like he was in shock. He wet his pants. The guys who had to take him to booking were pissed off about that, no pun intended."

Robin smiled. "I have a feeling our subjects are older."

"I agree, but I wouldn't be surprised if they're not. We're seeing criminals today who are smarter, younger, and more dangerous. And they're all interested in making money the new-fashioned way—stealing it."

When they got back to Global Waters, the receptionist said Adam Kush had left a message for them to go directly to the executive dining room to meet him.

Kush came in as they entered.

"If you don't mind," Kush said. "Let's eat and brief at the same time. Help yourself to the buffet."

Bannister welcomed the chance to satisfy his appetite, so he selected a few beef medallions, some sautéed potatoes, and four spears of grilled asparagus. He grabbed a piece of cheesecake surrounded by plump strawberries. He had to admit this was a pleasant break from the junk food of yesterday. But it seemed wrong to enjoy good food when he didn't know where Cal was, or what he was eating. If he was eating.

"So, are you ready for next week?" Kush asked.

"We are. Let me outline what I've set up. Two of our tech guys will make installations in the money as well as in the canvas bag containing it."

"What kind of installations?" Kush asked, taking a sip of water.

"Global positioning system, GPS trackers. These are state-of-the-art, and we don't have to worry about a power supply or antenna. They're about the size of quarters. We'll put one inside a currency bundle and the other in the liner of the canvas bag. We'll also have a motion sensor in the bag, and that will let us know if the bag is moving and to send a signal to activate the GPS tokens."

"And you'll be able to track the bag anywhere?" Kush asked.

"We have about a five-mile range and our plane will handle that. The driver of the van will be one of our agents. The cell phone, with the number you put in the advertisement, will also have a GPS tracker in it, in addition to a microphone and camera. The van will have an infrared light, which will look like a spotlight from the air. We're also installing a kill switch in the van. Like you mentioned earlier, if someone's going to skip the money drop and just try and carjack the van, the engine will stop."

Robin got up to get some coffee from a side bar and brought the pot over to fill their cups. "Have you thought about what happens if this thing drags on into the night?" she asked.

"We're good to go for at least thirty-six hours," Bannister said. "We have ground surveillance units, including foot teams, aerial coverage, and an arrest team. We have a modified plan if there's heavy rain or fog. Adam, when you requested the money, did they provide the serial numbers?"

"Yes. They're not all sequential, but we have all the numbers," Kush said.

"One of our evidence recovery team members will also come here next week with our tech guys to take photos."

"Has the Bureau made any notifications on the international level concerning the ricin?" Robin asked. She plucked a strawberry from Bannister's plate and put it in her mouth. Her eyes were watching him.

For a moment he struggled to regain his focus. "The FBI, CIA, and other intelligence agencies are mining all their databases for any ricin connection," he said. "So far, there's nothing. To be honest, I don't think there are any operatives overseas. But we have to consider that contingency just as you have with your product recall plan."

"I agree with you, but God help us if someone poisons our water," Kush said.

Robin answered her cell phone. "Adam, the van is ready in the basement." She stood and pushed her chair in. Kush and Bannister stood, too.

"Thanks," said Kush. "Your agents can take it today and put your gizmos in it."

"I'll send Ford Campbell over to retrieve it since he's going to be driving it next week. I'd also like him to be totally briefed by your operations and dispatch-people."

"No problem. I've arranged for him to be given a uniform and ID badge. Unless you say otherwise, I'd suggest he go through the half-day orientation program we have for our new drivers. Just in case he's asked questions about Global deliveries or routes, I want him to be able to furnish an educated answer."

"Right." Bannister picked up his notebook and started walking out of the office. He thought of something else he wanted to say, and turned to speak, not realizing Robin was right behind him. She almost tripped into him. He had just enough time to catch her by the arms.

"I caught you just in time," he murmured.

"You caught me," she said with a smile that made him melt. "Just in time."

"It might be a while before I see you again."

"Duty first," she said, her eyes sparkling. "But I haven't forgotten about that dinner you promised me. If I have to report to the Academy before our date, I'm going to make you come up to Washington to take me out."

CHAPTER
11

T he FBI's inspection team from Washington was due to arrive in Atlanta in two weeks for their triennial turn-the-office-upside-down inspection. The message from the team of three inspectors and their twenty-six assistants was, "We're just coming to Atlanta to help you out." The best thing an agent could do during those two weeks would be to stay as far away from the office as possible. Hopefully, the Global Waters extortion case would be resolved by the time the inspection team arrived.

On Friday morning, the operational team reviewed next week's plan. Everything was in order. Global's van, with its hidden modifications, sat in the Bureau's garage, ready to be ferried over to Global next Thursday morning. Ford Campbell and a SWAT agent, who was to be riding in the back of the van, had been briefed by Global. Campbell had also been fitted with a uniform. The tech guys showed him how to operate the special cell phone and the kill switch on the van.

As the clock hit five, a stream of FBI support personnel headed for the elevators and the start of their weekend. Bannister called Adam Kush and went over details for the umpteenth time. They were now in a waiting game. Bannister went to the breakroom for a soda and had just popped the tab and sat back down at his desk when an FBI lab supervisor called with some preliminary findings. The supervisor in the fingerprint section confirmed what he'd already guessed. She said latent fingerprints were detected on the envelope and letter; the prints on the envelope were identifiable with Robin and three FedEx employees. The only prints on the letter belonged to Robin. No help. Bannister had no sooner hung up when the phone rang again.

"This is Marty Bracken in Quantico. I'm with Behavioral Sciences."

"How you doin'?" Bannister had never met Bracken but recognized his name. "I appreciate the fast response. Were you guys able to come up with anything?"

"We've got a few ideas that might help. I guess this thing's going down next week."

"Right."

"This is only preliminary, you understand. But we ran the wording of the note against the known extortion letter file and also plugged it into a new computer program that uses artificial intelligence. For six years we've been analyzing the behavior of offenders identified with weapons of mass destruction threats. The artificial intelligence is new. Since it's still in its early stages, you should treat the information as educated hunches. You'll get this in an official communication later, but I thought you'd want to take a few notes now. You ready to copy?"

"Fire away."

"As you probably anticipated, there were no matches from the known extortion file. However, the AI program spit out a summary of your subject's possible traits. There is a high probability the writer of the letter is a college graduate; he's male, Caucasian, and has probably lived close to downtown Atlanta for three or more years. He's most likely between the ages of twenty-nine to forty. The subject has visions of grandeur, feels a sense of entitlement, does not respond well to criticism, does not work well with others, and does not believe in showing kindness or consideration toward others."

"How the hell can your computer figure all that out from a two-page letter?" Bannister asked.

"Look, I don't know. This artificial intelligence thing's experimental. That's why I said treat the information for lead purposes. Maybe none of the information is ident with your subject. Maybe it's right on. Two other things: Your subject may have had one or more unstable relationships in the past year or two and is interested in travel and adventure."

"I'll be really curious to see how much of that information pans out."

"So will we. If you end up catching this guy, we'd like you to fill out one of our forms so the computer can crunch your findings."

"Thanks. You've given us ten times more than we had before your call."

"No problem. Good luck."

Bannister was still thinking about the subject's profile when Robin called.

"Hello, Ty, hope I'm not interrupting you."

"No, I was just thinking about our case."

"Well, I was thinking about you. What I mean is, I'm running in a ten kilometer race tomorrow morning in Buckhead. I know it's kind of late notice, but would you be interested in running it and maybe getting a cold drink afterward?"

For a few seconds his mind shifted to Cal Williamson. The last time Bannister had done a six-mile run was with Cal during one of their early morning workouts three weeks ago.

"Are you there?" Robin asked.

"Sorry. Yeah, that sounds like a possibility. What time, and where is the start?"

"Race time is eight, and it begins and finishes at Phipps Plaza."

"I have a proposition for you. If I agree to do the run with you, you'll have to join me for breakfast—at my place. It's right near there. I'll do the cooking. What do you say?"

"Okay, as long as you're not trying to get out of taking me to dinner." Bannister listened to her laugh. "How about we meet at the race registration table about fifteen minutes before the start?"

"Great. I'll see you in the morning."

This would be his first time seeing Robin while off duty. It felt a little weird, but he looked forward to it.

———✺———

The next morning he met Robin as planned. There were about eight hundred runners milling about who didn't seem fazed by the forty degree temperature. She spotted him first.

"This is great!" Robin said as she walked up to Bannister and gave him a hug. She was wearing black tights, a running jacket, and a pink baseball cap. Her long, blonde hair was pulled back in a ponytail. "It's kind of nice knowing you don't always wear a suit," she said with a wink.

The run started exactly on time. When ninety percent of the participants were type-A personalities, race officials didn't want to be even one minute late.

"Adam said you were a serious runner," Robin said. They were no longer running in place, but moving out quickly with the mass of participants.

"When people hear you run a lot, they always label you as serious. I just enjoy running."

"You don't have to run with me, you know. We can meet at the finish."

"And miss out on your wonderful conversation? Definitely not." He wanted to stay with her. "I'll try and run your pace, unless you're a secret track star."

"No, I'm going to try and run an eight-minute mile pace. That will show me I can handle the runs at Quantico. Maybe you could check my form."

"I already have," he said.

———✺———

The race itself was going smoothly as the churning mass of huffing bodies wound its way down Peachtree Road through the commercial section of Buckhead. Things were uneventful until after the halfway turnaround. Bannister felt a burning, shooting pain in his right thigh. He slowed his pace and pressed hard on the outside of his leg. The pain disappeared. He didn't say anything to Robin and hoped she hadn't noticed. This same pain occurred a couple of times before, during runs with Cal. Cal had asked him what was wrong. He remembered telling him about his wounds from the invasion of Grenada and his orthopedist informing him there were some bone fragments in his leg. The orthopedist said the damage might make him a candidate later in life for osteoporosis or arthritis. Cal said to get it checked out by a neurologist. Bannister always feared getting disabled but decided to ignore his friend's advice.

Fifty minutes later, Bannister and Robin were back at the finish line where they each grabbed a bottle of water and some orange slices.

"I'm parked right over there," Robin said, pointing to her Jeep, wiping the perspiration off her forehead.

"I'm across the street," Bannister said. "I'll drive over here, and you can follow me to my house. I'm only five minutes from here."

He gave Robin his address in case they split up. They took Roswell Road past the Rib Shack to Habersham and turned onto Valley Road. A minute later they pulled into his drive and waited for the gates to swing open. Robin followed him under a high canopy formed by six mature elms on each side of the drive, and parked in front of the house. Bannister parked in his three-car garage.

Robin came around the corner carrying a black duffel bag. "Gosh, Ty, this is where you live?" Her eyes swept from left to right, noting the stone archways, tall leaded-glass windows, and the stone tower anchoring the right side of the building.

"Yeah, this is where I live. For as long as I can remember, I thought it'd be neat to live in a huge stone house. I still feel that way. Come on, let's go in through the garage."

"Nice car," Robin said, pointing toward a silver Mercedes.

"Yes. I don't think you'll see many of these. It's a 1957 Mercedes 300

SL Gullwing. It belonged to my grandfather. When I was a kid, I loved the way the doors swung up into the air. My grandfather took me for a ride around his ranch whenever I went to visit. He knew I loved that car the same way he did, so he left it to me when he died." Bannister took Robin's bag.

"It's beautiful."

"If you want, we can go for a drive through the neighborhood after we eat."

Once inside, Bannister poured each of them a glass of orange juice and put the crème Brule French toast casserole in the oven. "How about we clean up while breakfast is baking? You can use the guest bathroom behind the den. There are plenty of towels, and feel free to use any of the stuff that's on the counter. I put it there to be used, so don't be bashful."

Twenty minutes later he was back in the kitchen, having changed into Levis and his favorite sweatshirt. The green color had faded years ago, and the white Dartmouth letters were barely visible. Robin came out in jeans and a black cashmere sweater. Her hair was still damp and her face was bare of makeup, except for some shimmering gloss on her lips.

"Whatever you're cooking smells great. And by the way, has anyone compared your guest bath with one in a five-star hotel? I can't believe you had all those perfumes and colognes on the vanity."

"I didn't do that. That's Amelia. My housekeeper. I told her if I had guests, I wanted them to be treated like I'd like to be, so she had someone at Nordstrom's pick out all that stuff. Besides, if someone forgets something, it's nice to know they don't have to worry about doing without."

The oven timer went off, and Bannister removed the French toast, which he set on the table with slices of cantaloupe and fresh strawberries.

"I thought you might like the strawberries," he said with a knowing smile as he poured them coffee.

"One of my favorite foods."

The obvious flirtation thrilled him, but he was again struck with the idea that here he was, enjoying the luxury of his beautiful home, delicious food, and the company of a fascinating woman, when Cal was . . . he didn't know where Cal was. He had hoped the race and his date with Robin would distract him from this feeling that he should be doing something more to find his friend. But these enjoyments only seemed to taunt him.

While they were eating, he asked Robin to tell him about her family. She said her parents and younger sister lived in Palo Alto, and she was going to California to spend Christmas with them.

He found himself already missing her.

"Have some more," he said.

"This is so good. And your place is so beautiful, right down to the fresh flowers."

"You'd have to credit Amelia for that. But she knows what I like."

"On the job you seem so hard and professional. It's nice to know you have some rounded edges."

Bannister unlocked the Gullwing and the doors swung up. He helped Robin into the passenger seat and showed her where the seatbelt latch was. He started the engine, which responded immediately with its throaty thrum.

It was an unusual car, with its door sill armrest and the rear-view mirror mounted on the dashboard instead of stuck in the windshield. "It takes a little getting used to," he said. "The car is meant for a racetrack or straight and level roads. It's a little unpredictable under high-speed cornering."

They drove out onto Valley Road and went up and down the wide, gracefully curving streets of Buckhead. He was amused and gratified by her obvious enjoyment of the car.

"Do you know how to drive a stick?" he asked.

"Yep. My Jeep's a manual," Robin said.

With that, he pulled over into a side road off Tuxedo Drive. He opened the doors and got out.

"What are you doing?" asked Robin.

"Giving you a chance to drive."

"I can't drive this car. What if I hit something?"

"Nonsense. It's just a car. Come on, you'll like it."

Robin climbed into the driver's side, and after an adjustment to the seat and mirror, they took off. He could see the excitement in her face. She was a little tentative at first, but once she got the feel of the Gullwing and how it responded, she pulled it through a series of smooth turns and accelerations. He let her drive it back to the house and into the garage.

"I notice the speedometer goes up to one-sixty," she said. "Does it really go that fast?"

He just smiled.

They went inside the house and Robin collected her things.

"Thanks for sharing your morning with me, Ty," she said. "I had a great time and a super breakfast. And I never dreamed I'd get to drive a car like that. What more could I ask?"

"What more could I ask? A strenuous workout, a healthy breakfast, a fast ride—and all in the company of a beautiful woman."

"You're sweet," Robin said. She leaned in and gave him a hug, his second of the morning.

"I guess I'll see you at work," she said.

"You will." Bannister watched her get into her Jeep. Robin waved out the window as she headed down the driveway. He carried Sunday's copy of *The Atlanta Journal-Constitution* into the house and found the classifieds. The extortionist's ad was printed correctly with no typos.

CHAPTER
12

Monday morning at eight-thirty, Special Agent in Charge Leon Brennan called Bannister, Stu Peterson, and Gary Witt into his office to discuss the Global Waters case. SAC Brennan had returned from the FBI Academy at Quantico. Brennan was an executive respected for his intellect as well as his common sense. Before he joined the FBI, he and his four brothers had run the family farm in Iowa. The Brennan family raised flowers and seeds, which they sold worldwide. Unlike a lot of farms struggling in the Midwest, theirs was successful. Leon was the youngest and went to college, then applied with the FBI to fight white collar crime. In his early Bureau years, he'd solved several major cases and rose fast through the investigative ranks. At forty-five, he was one of the youngest bosses in the Bureau and was considered by many to be on a short list for promotion to Assistant Director.

With his steel-gray suit, white shirt with dark-striped tie, and gold-rimmed glasses, Brennan looked like a successful tax attorney. Unlike a tax attorney, however, Brennan smiled a lot, not because he was so happy, but because he knew it put people at ease. He was smiling when the three of them walked into his office.

Following Witt into Brennan's corner suite, Bannister thought about a quote from a salty agent who'd helped break him in a long time ago. It was one of Murphy's laws, the one that said: "If there is a possibility of several things going wrong, the one that will cause the most damage will be the first one to go wrong."

"Have a seat, gentlemen," said Brennan. "While in Virginia, I was kept informed of developments on this case. Let's hope the poisoning part never happens." Looking at Bannister, he added, "I appreciate your calling me this weekend with the latest lab input."

"No problem."

Brennan remained seated at his desk with his back to the glass wall overlooking the I-85 traffic heading to downtown Atlanta. Taking out his black-and-gold Mont Blanc pen, he looked down at a notebook to refresh his memory. "Gary, are you comfortable with not cutting the locals in on this?" he asked Witt.

"I don't see any problems, Leon," Witt replied. "It's our jurisdiction and we can't risk a leak."

"And you're going to coordinate everything from the command center, right?" Brennan asked.

"Not exactly." Witt cleared his throat before continuing. "I'm going to be the on-scene commander, and Bannister will be back here for coordination. He knows all the players and who to call if we need additional equipment or personnel."

Brennan's smile disappeared. He looked at Bannister and Peterson, then back at Witt. When Witt looked down at the operational plan he had brought to the meeting, Brennan glanced at Bannister and nodded his head as if to signal he trusted his judgment.

"Okay," Brennan sighed. He said to Witt, "Just make sure there are no screw-ups on this thing. We don't need bad press. And I don't want headquarters breathing down my neck."

"We're totally ready. They won't get away," Witt said.

"Good. Make sure you leave me a current copy of the operational plan, and let me know if there are changes. I'll be in the office Thursday afternoon."

As the three men stood up and filed out of the office, Witt turned and said to Bannister, "I hope I didn't catch you off guard just now when I told the boss I'd be the on-scene commander instead of you."

Bannister didn't answer. He was irritated with Witt but not surprised.

The ASAC had a reputation for changing direction mid-stream. "We'll pencil in the switch on the ops plan," was all he said.

For the next three days, FBI agents working the case had rehearsed their assignments and reviewed contingency plans. Now it was Wednesday afternoon and everything was ready. The money would be delivered by armored truck to Global within the hour. Bannister looked up at the large ceiling-mounted TV in the squad area. It was always tuned to CNN with the volume set low. The meteorologist was announcing tomorrow's forecast for sunny skies and a high around fifty—optimum surveillance conditions.

Bannister was at his desk, wrapping up loose ends. Stu stood in the doorway of his office with his hand resting high on the doorjamb. Instead of phoning agents to come to his office, Stu had a habit of looking out over the tops of the work stations and shouting out for whatever he wanted. When Bannister glanced his way, Stu waved him over.

"Grab a seat," Stu said as he sat down in his high-backed leather chair.

When Bannister was settled, Stu began, "You know, Ty, the boss is well aware that you had to make decisions in the Corps and in the Bureau. The kind of decisions where lives are at stake."

"Then why didn't he pull the plug on Witt's grandstanding?" Bannister asked through clenched teeth.

"Brennan still needs to back his ASACs. He let Witt do his bantam strut because he knows your plan for tomorrow is sound and you'll make things work. But I don't like the idea of Witt being at Global Headquarters calling the shots without one of us nearby to rein him in." Stu crossed his arms and leaned forward with both elbows on his desk. "I'm hoping he'll have the smarts to coordinate with you before making any harebrained decisions. I'll make sure our people in the command center know you're the one to contact first."

"Thanks. This isn't an ego trip for either of us. If Witt would take a hands-off approach, we could make him famous."

"I tried to convince him to stay here in the office. I told him any major decision would be routed to him for approval, but he didn't buy it. Then I tried a different tack."

"Which was . . ."

"I told him if he stayed here he'd be bullet-proof if anything got screwed up. You'd be the fall guy."

"Thanks," Bannister said wryly.

"Not really, but that's what I told him. I said if things went right, there'd still be room for him in the picture."

"How did he respond?"

"He didn't. He pulled rank and gave me an order. He's going to run things from Global. You're to be the coordinator. He mentioned something about the inspection team coming in and maybe second-guessing his leadership."

"What he should have learned about leadership is that you empower your qualified people and turn them loose to accomplish the mission. If they need support, provide it." Bannister glanced up at the picture of Stu and the other US hostages on the day they were released after 444 days of captivity in Iran.

"You and I know that," said Stu. "Witt's never been in the military or in harm's way. I don't even know if he's supervised a serious case before. Put your disappointment aside and look at it this way. We've covered all the bases, minimized the risk to outside personnel, and we should be able to take these guys down at the right time," he said.

"I just wish he'd follow the three D's of leadership like most Washington guys."

"What are those?" Stu asked.

"Decide, delegate, and disappear!"

Stu laughed. "So we'll assemble here at seven-thirty in the morning. The tech guys will do their stuff with the money around nine, and then we'll wait for the call."

———⟨∂∂∂⟩———

On Thursday at 11:30 a.m., as Witt left to drive over to Global, Bannister called Adam Kush from the FBI's operational center. Everything was ready at their end. The global positioning trackers and motion sensor had been concealed in the money and the bag. The five million in hundred dollar bills weighed seventy pounds, and the banded packages fit in a large canvas mason's bag. The van was inside Global's garage. Agent Campbell was behind the wheel and a SWAT agent was concealed in the back. The surveillance teams were stationed at pre-positioned locations. The Bureau pilots were inside the FBI's hangar chowing down on chili dogs and sodas one of the agents had brought back from The Varsity.

"So are you ready for this?" Bannister asked Kush.

"Ready as we'll ever be. We're using the conference room as our operations center. I've got to admit, the adrenaline is kicking in, and we haven't even gotten the call yet. I just had to pop a couple of Tums."

"I know the feeling. Waiting around is the hardest part."

"What's strange is Witt coming over here. I haven't seen him for a year, and to be honest with you, we're not exactly excited about his being on the scene. I'm sure there's a story behind that."

"Keep my cell phone number handy."

"Don't worry; your number's programmed into my phone. Since your agents are here with the money and have rechecked everything, I'm cutting the armed guards loose."

"Remember, the cell phones you and agent Campbell have are identical, and all conversations are being relayed here to the command post. We'll be listening to the audio live and recording it."

—◈◈◈—

At 1:15 p.m. the extortionist called the number in the advertisement. Adam Kush didn't wait for the second ring, and picked it up immediately.

"This is the Ambassador," said a female voice, using the prearranged introduction.

"This is the Deputy," Kush responded in the exact words the extortionist had requested.

"Have your driver leave in two minutes and take 14th Street to Peachtree Street and turn left. Have him call this cell phone number as soon as he makes the turn onto Peachtree." The caller read out the cell phone number and hung up.

"Agent Campbell, did you copy?" Witt, who was pacing inside Global's security office, asked nervously.

"Ten-four," Campbell said. "I've got the number and I'm heading out now."

Four cars surveilled the white Global van as it wound its way through light traffic to Peachtree Street in midtown. Two cars were ahead of the van on parallel streets, and two trailed behind at a discreet distance. The Bureau plane, which had been circling above the Georgia World Congress Center, banked northward as it monitored the van's progress.

"Bannister, this is Witt," the ASAC said as he called the command post on a secure FBI radio.

"I copied the caller's transmission," Bannister said.

"One of the subjects is a woman."

"Might be," said Bannister.

"What do you mean 'might' be? I heard her voice," Witt said.

"The caller could be using a portable telephone voice changer. I know that's what I'd use. They're pre-programmed with up to twenty-four different voices, male or female, as well as different accents."

When Campbell made the turn seven minutes later onto Peachtree Street, he dialed the extortionist's number.

"Pull into the front circular drive of the Woodruff Arts Center and stop," the female voice ordered and hung up.

Campbell knew the Arts Center was less than a mile ahead. The surveillance teams reported no unusual vehicles following the van.

While Campbell pulled into the front drive of the Arts Center and kept the van running, his eyes rapidly scanned back and forth across the marble entranceway. No cars were moving and there wasn't anyone on foot. Five minutes later the phone rang.

"Go back the same way you came. When you get to Northside Drive, turn south to Bankhead Highway and turn right. After you make the turn onto Bankhead, call." Click.

—◦◦◦—

On a large map board, Kush was tracing the van's route. Witt continued pacing back and forth, his right hand unconsciously jingling change in his pants pocket. "They may lead this van all over the city," he said.

"You're right," Kush replied. "Bannister told us to be prepared for this thing being mobile for up to twenty-four hours. I've got additional people on call."

—◦◦◦—

When Campbell reached Bankhead Highway, he dialed the number again.

The voice said, "Continue down Bankhead for two miles. When you get to Garry Avenue, turn right. There's a small shopping center there. At the entrance is Mike's Mini-Mart. Pull into Mike's and call."

—◦◦◦—

Witt called Bannister on the radio. "Any luck on the trace?"

"We're working on pinpointing the caller's location. With all the cell towers in that area, it's going to take some time. Right now, we've identified the subscriber as a woman in Marietta, Georgia. My guess is either it's a stolen cell phone or a cloned number, but we're checking it out."

"Okay, let me know what you come up with as soon as you get it," Witt said.

"Why don't you sit down," Kush suggested as he noticed Witt

stumble over one of the rubber floor mats near the computers. "We might be here for a while," he added as he swallowed another Tums.

———◊◊◊———

Campbell called the number again once he pulled into a parking space in front of the Mini-Mart.

"Take the bag and put it in the dumpster on the left side of the Mini-Mart," the female voice ordered. "Then leave immediately."

Campbell turned off the engine. "I'm assuming you guys have an eyeball on me," he said. "I'm about to step out of the van. I don't see anyone outside the store. There's a red Taurus parked on the far right near the big ice machine. No one's in the car. I'm exiting the van now, and I'm going to put the bag in the dumpster."

Campbell got out, slid the side panel door of the van open, and took out the black trash bag with the canvas money pouch inside, being careful to hold it with both hands. His every move was being watched by six agents, four in cars and two in the plane. He walked fifteen feet to a large brown Dempsey dumpster. He put the bag on the ground for a few seconds to open the lid. He then dropped the bag to the bottom of the trash bin, closed the lid, and notified the command post he was returning to the van so they could send the electronic signal activating the motion sensor in the bag.

Once back inside the van, Campbell said, "Delivery made. No one coming out of the store. I'm returning to base."

The surveillance teams stayed at their observation sites as the arrest team, in two cars, moved into position.

The two GPS devices were silently beeping their signals every ten seconds.

"I guess we're in a waiting game now," Campbell muttered to himself.

———◊◊◊———

Ten minutes went by, and then two things happened. The signal from the motion sensor went off briefly, then its signal and those from both of the GPS locators went silent.

As soon as Bannister heard the signals go silent, he called Witt on the radio. "They're taking the money. We gotta move in now!"

"Stand by," Witt told Bannister. "I'm calling the plane and ground units for a situation report."

In a few seconds, both responded. No one had approached the dumpster.

"All units, sit tight," Witt ordered.

Back at the command center, Bannister was irate. Stu Peterson walked over to the command center console in time to hear Bannister yelling, "I don't know how they've done it, but the bastards got the money, and Witt's sitting on an empty nest!"

"What makes you so sure?" Stu asked.

"I had two GPS locators placed in the money bag and one motion sensor as a backup. Somehow, three different technical devices went out at the same time. That's not coincidence. And it's not faulty equipment. I checked those units myself a half-dozen times. What it means is that someone's a step ahead of us."

The next phase of the agonizing waiting game began.

After one hour, Witt was overcome with impatience and called for a surveillance unit to break cover and go to the store, buy something, and then take some trash out to the dumpster. One of the agents was ordered to look inside and verify the bag was still there. At the same time, a report from the phone company came in. The location of the cell phone used by the extortionist was in the exact sector as the mini-mart. Bannister relayed this information to Witt.

"We're holding tight at the mini-mart. All units, be aware the caller's cell phone has been traced to this vicinity," Witt said.

"Watchdog to Base," one of the units called in a minute later.

"Go ahead."

"We've confirmed the bag is still in the trash bin."

Bannister asked if agent Hollister had lifted the bag to make sure the money was in it.

"We've had a half dozen agents watching that dumpster, and no one's gone near it. The bag's still there," Witt said.

The next five hours dragged by with no activity except for the normal traffic into and out of the mini-mart. The sun disappeared on the horizon. Finally, Witt made the decision to abort.

"Base to Watchdog," Witt called. "Retrieve the package. I want all surveillance units to keep an eyeball on Watchdog until the package is back at Global."

Agent Hollister returned to the trash bin and reached down to retrieve the black plastic garbage bag with the red tie. He knew immediately something was up when he went to lift the bag. It couldn't have weighed more than two pounds.

The other agent had already popped the trunk when Hollister got back to the car. He and his partner opened the bag and saw shredded newspapers. They immediately radioed Witt.

"Base from Watchdog. The money's gone. Repeat. The money's gone. There's nothing in the bag but newspaper. What do you want us to do?"

"Secure the trash bin until I get there," Witt blared into the phone.

CHAPTER 13

As soon as Bannister heard the transmission, he said to Peterson, "Stu, the team here can continue coverage and work the leads. I'm going to Mike's Mini-Mart."

"Go ahead. We've got things under control here. It looks like you were right. Someone's got a six-hour head start on us."

The direct route to Mike's Mini-Mart was Spring Street to North Avenue and over to Northside. Bannister hoped to get there before Witt. He knew that whenever the ASAC had the chance, he liked to use lights and sirens. It was unlikely the display would get him there any faster, but it certainly heated up the scene once he arrived. Bannister found that fast, alert driving and going through traffic lights after checking for oncoming traffic worked best with unmarked cars, which was all the FBI drove.

He pulled into the lot from the north as Witt, with blue lights flashing from his visor, and the alternating wig-wag lights blinking from behind his grill, entered Mike's lot from the south. Witt swerved to narrowly miss hitting a steel pylon holding up a giant billboard.

Agent Derrick Hollister was standing beside his Bureau car, talking on a cell phone. Bannister parked the Buick near the road, got out, and gave Hollister the "time-out" signal. Hollister concluded his call immediately.

"Have your partner go inside, identify himself, and tell the manager we have a crime scene here and we're going to be around awhile. Make sure your partner tells him to stay off the phone."

"I don't believe in magic, but your guess is as good as anyone's about what happened to the money," Hollister said.

"I'm not guessing. Give me a hand with this dumpster." Bannister walked a few paces toward the rusting bin that emitted an odor like burning cheese.

"Watch where you step," he warned. As they shoved the dumpster toward the rear of the alley, a long strip of pink insulation rolled out from underneath it. Exposed directly below the dumpster was a square hole.

"Someone have a light?" Bannister yelled.

Hollister produced a flashlight and offered it to Bannister, who shined the beam down into the shaft of a tunnel gaping from beneath the asphalt alley. Witt rushed over and his mouth dropped open.

"I'll be damned. He's dug a tunnel." Witt stood there gawking down the hole.

Bannister wanted to say, "No shit, Sherlock," but instead called the plane. "Eyeball One."

"Go ahead," one of the pilots responded.

"Download all your video coverage for the past six hours to the command post computer."

"It's already done."

"Pull the arrest teams and have them start canvassing the businesses across this alley. Hollister and his partner can start interviewing the employees in the mini-mart. We'll need a forensics team to search this tunnel and wherever it ends up. My guess is that it empties into the office space there." Bannister pointed directly to a building about twelve feet from the dumpster.

"I need an agent to go down and see where this thing goes. I'd do it myself, but it looks a little narrow for my shoulders. We'll need a warrant to get into that office. I'll get the duty US Attorney on the line as soon as I have enough detail."

Witt was still leaning over the hole. At least he wasn't barking out orders. Bannister gave him credit for that.

"Gary, would you mind turning off the blue lights in your car?"

"Yeah, sure."

"Call Adam Kush and confirm his money's gone, at least temporarily. And then give the boss a call and fill him in. He's probably home by now."

Mercedes Ramirez pulled up and walked over to where Witt and Bannister were standing. She looked down into the hole, shaking her head. "I went back to the office to follow up on the ricin report and Stu told me what happened. I thought maybe you could use me here. Yes?"

"Thanks, have you got your disposable hazmat suit?"

"I have a couple of them, but I don't think they'll fit anyone else. They're in the trunk with the evidence kit. I also have a portable searchlight. You want me to check out this tunnel?"

"Mercedes, I don't know what's down there. I don't think it's dangerous, but if someone is willing to send ricin in the mail, they're capable of anything."

"Don't worry. I'll take it real slow."

"If you see anything suspicious, stop and get out."

"Let's see where this thing ends up." Ramirez put her portable searchlight on the ground and climbed into her white Teflon suit with built-in boots and gloves. She would have just used the hard hat, but Bannister made her put on the hood.

A six-foot wooden ladder constructed of two-by-fours had been secured into one side of the tunnel's opening. Ramirez carefully descended the five rungs into the shaft. When her feet reached the bottom, Bannister lowered the searchlight to her.

"I'll have to do a duck walk down here," Mercedes shouted. "It looks like this thing goes horizontally for about twenty feet or so. The tunnel's circular. It's got either fiberglass or plastic sections bolted together, and there's an aluminum track on the floor. There's some kind of small cart at the end."

A few moments later, they heard Mercedes's voice again. "I measured eighteen feet to where there's another shaft going up, and another wooden ladder attached to the wall. It looks like the opening is covered with plywood. Do you want me to continue?"

"No, come on back," Bannister called down to her. "We'll wait for a warrant."

As Ramirez climbed up out of the tunnel, Bannister was already on the phone for a warrant, having been patched through to the same Assistant US Attorney who had authorized prosecution.

Hollister, his partner, and one of the arrest teams had returned, having identified the four businesses across from Mike's. The assistant manager and clerk inside Mike's were of no help. Of immediate interest was the office closest to the tunnel—US Euro Trans-Consultants. The full range of FBI records checking began on that business and all the others in the vicinity.

Witt said he'd remain on the scene while the search warrant was drafted. Bannister called the Technical Supervisor, Ernie Gonzales, with the bad news.

"Yeah, I heard. One of two things happened. Either our tracking devices were located and destroyed, or someone managed to block their signals," Gonzales said.

"They went out too fast after the drop. They wouldn't have been able to search the money and bag that fast."

"That's what I thought. I've got a theory on how this could have gone down. I don't know if Witt's told you yet, but the boss called a meeting at the office for nine-thirty tonight. We'll talk about it in a couple of hours."

Bannister noticed Witt scraping his left shoe, trying to remove a wad of gum someone had spit onto the pavement.

Ramirez walked over in her jump suit and silver hard hat. Even though the temperature was dropping, she'd worked up a sweat inside her suit and her bangs were plastered to her forehead. Looking in Witt's direction, she whispered to Bannister, "Real gumshoe, eh?"

Bannister laughed. "I'm going downtown to the US Attorney's office," he said. "How about identifying the door lock on the front of this business?" He pointed to US Euro Trans-Consultants. "Make sure one of Gonzales's tech guys comes out with the forensics team so we can key the door rather than breaking it."

"Gotcha."

"One other thing. See if any of these businesses have cameras focused on the outside."

—◦◦◦—

An hour later, with search warrant in hand, Bannister pulled back into the last vacant space at Mike's Mini-Mart. Surprisingly, no local police or media had stopped by to investigate all the activity. A van with the crime scene recovery group was getting their equipment ready. Ramirez was in charge of logging all evidence, and the search team was reporting to her. Ernie Gonzales's guy advised there were no alarms. He said he could pick the lock easily and cut a key for it after they were inside.

Everyone wore latex gloves. Once the lock was picked, Bannister opened the door and flipped a switch on the wall. Two overhead lights illuminated an eerie scene. Everything inside was coated with a layer of gray dust. Two large windows and wooden blinds had been completely covered on the inside with black plastic stapled to the wall. In the room were two office desks with matching chairs. That was it. No other furniture. The floor was covered with light brown industrial carpeting, which appeared to have been vacuumed. Everything else was coated in dust. The door in the rear led to a spartan bathroom with nothing in it except a toilet, sink, and mirror. One of the techs took photographs.

The chair behind the second desk was sitting on a square sheet of plywood. Bannister rolled the chair aside and lifted the plywood board. Staring at him was the end of the tunnel. Eight feet down was a red pull cart that looked like a gardener's wheelbarrow.

"Well, the money's not here," Witt said.

"You're right, Gary. I think the last time it was here was two o'clock, or five minutes after Campbell put it in the dumpster." Bannister let that sink in. "The search team will probably need a couple of hours to process everything. If you've got things under control, I'm heading back to the office. I want to see what the analysts have been able to find."

"I'll be back for the briefing," Witt said.

"By the way, make sure the alley's blocked off before we secure. I don't want some citizen to drop out of sight."

At the office, the command center was buzzing under the able direction of Stu Peterson.

"Ty, Germaine's come up with something you need to hear," Stu said, beckoning Bannister into his office.

Germaine White was an intelligence analyst assigned to the task force. She was a single black female who favored bright-flowing dresses and pastel-colored shoes. When she walked through the office, her glasses swayed from a gold-colored cord. She was the only employee who worked inside the special security room everyone called the "vault."

Germaine lived with her mother, had never married, and was rumored never to have had a date. Most of the office considered her intense, high-strung, and opinionated. But one undisputed thing about her was that she knew her job and was a damn fine analyst. For some reason, she considered Bannister her best friend in the office. It might be because he flirted with her. More likely it was because he appreciated her work and always sent her a short note thanking her for her effort on a case.

Holding a sheaf of papers, Germaine said, "As soon as Hollister phoned in the names of the businesses next to Mike's Mini-Mart, I started researching all of them. The name Sean O'Brien may be of interest to you."

Bannister knew how Germaine liked to draw out the steps she had taken, as well as explain the link analysis she used to reach her conclusions. He listened patiently.

"The tunnel was dug from an office space leased by US Euro Trans-Consultants. The company was listed last year with the Secretary of State's office and their filing named only one officer, Sean O'Brien, as president. The stated purpose of the business was to arrange international home exchanges and vacation property swaps. O'Brien has a Capitol First credit card and a Georgia driver's license. Prior to a year ago, neither he nor his business existed, at least according to a hundred databases queried with his name and date of birth. Nothing. Nada. Zilch!" Germaine shifted the papers.

"Thanks, Germaine. That's good work. See if you can get a photo from DMV."

Bannister walked over to the ops center, pulled out a chair at one of the computers where the surveillance video had been forwarded, and started reviewing it. He was interested in the thirty-minute window between 1:45 and 2:15 p.m. At 2:06 p.m., footage from Eyeball One showed a figure emerging from the office space leased by US Euro Trans-Consultants. It appeared to be a white male wearing a baseball cap with a brown duffel bag slung over his shoulder. The photographic angle from the plane was too vertical to reveal the subject's face. The man turned around, apparently locked the office door, opened the trunk of a white sedan parked nearby, and placed the duffel bag inside. He then got into the car and drove slowly out of the strip mall onto Garry Avenue. The camera, which was focused on the area around the dumpster, lost coverage of him as soon as he turned onto Bankhead Highway.

That's our subject, Bannister thought. The timing was perfect and the duffel bag had to be stuffed with Global's five million.

—◦◦◦—

SAC Brennan's meeting started ten minutes late. The key players were in the conference room, including Germaine White, whom Bannister had invited. She'd been successful in getting a driver's license photo of Sean O'Brien and had printed twenty copies.

Brennan walked in and sat down. "It's been awhile since I've called a meeting this late in the day. I appreciate all of you being here, but I'm sure you realize the importance of this case." Brennan motioned for Witt to open the meeting.

Witt methodically went over the events leading up to that evening. He explained how everything had been done by the book, but because of the tunnel and the failure of their technical installations, the unsubs—unknown subjects in FBI language—had gotten away.

"Ty Bannister is the case agent, and he'll explain where we're going next," Witt said as he took his seat at the end of the table opposite Brennan. It seemed like he deliberately avoided making eye contact with the boss.

"First off," Bannister said, "I want to thank all of you and your teams for your efforts. You did what you were supposed to do. Today isn't ending the way we expected, but I think tomorrow will be different. The forensic team is still at the mini-mart processing the crime scene. Germaine, would you hand out these sets of photos?" Bannister handed her a stack of prints.

"Germaine crunched all the systems and came up with a guy who may be one of our subjects. The first picture you're looking at is a driver's license photo of Sean O'Brien, listed as the president of the company leasing the space from where the tunnel was dug."

"This DL photo looks like a disguise," Ernie Gonzales said.

"That'd be my guess. If you look, his hair is really bushy, and his mustache looks like the one worn by Gene Shalit, the movie critic. Not to mention the thick glasses," Bannister added.

"The second picture was cropped from the air surveillance video and shows a guy, maybe this O'Brien, getting into a sedan outside the office about eight minutes after we lost contact with our technical devices planted in the money bag."

"I told you I had an idea about that," said Gonzales. "The extortion letter mentioned something about countermeasures. It's possible our unsubs used some type of shielding to block the signals, but we won't know for sure until we catch these guys or locate the money."

"Gary debriefed all of our people who were near the dumpster," Bannister said, "and no one was seen approaching it after the money was placed inside. The forensic team discovered that the steel bottom of the dumpster had been cut out and replaced with a piece of plywood covered with trash. When the money bag was put inside the dumpster, the bad guys were directly below. Somehow they deactivated or blocked our sensors from sending a signal out. They then dropped the money bag down the hole, substituted their own trash bag with paper filler in its place, and slid the plywood sheet back over the entrance. When Hollister looked in the dumpster about an hour later, he radioed to say the money was still there. What he actually saw was the substituted trash bag."

"So what are our priorities, Ty?" Brennan asked.

"Tomorrow I want a full court press on this O'Brien, which I'm guessing is an alias. I've placed a lookout notice on him with Homeland Security, so they'll notify us if O'Brien attempts to fly anywhere. I plan on interviewing Best Atlanta's leasing agent. I want any original papers O'Brien signed preserved for testing. Let's get a good description of the white sedan and run rental records from the major car rental agencies. I want up-to-date info sent to Quantico, and let's see if their computer is able to add some details to the subject's profile."

Gonzales asked, "What's Global doing?"

"Gnashing their teeth, for sure. I'll be talking with their security director as soon as we're done. We don't want them losing confidence in our ability to catch whoever's responsible. Meanwhile, we still need to keep a lid on this."

"Let's do what we're good at," Brennan said. "We'll reconvene tomorrow afternoon at four. You're all dismissed."

Before returning to his desk, Bannister walked by the vault and gave Germaine a short list of items he wanted her to check out first thing in the morning. He locked his desk and drove back to Mike's Mini-Mart, which was scheduled to close in ten minutes.

When he arrived, the forensics team was loading their equipment back into the van. The dumpster had been loaded onto a flatbed truck, which was taking it back to a secure area at the office. Gonzales was staying at the office until it arrived. Ramirez gave Bannister an update. The alley had been taped off in both directions, and the team had set up sawhorse signs with flashing yellow lights.

Bannister called Adam Kush. He didn't mention O'Brien, but let him know they were following up on leads from the search of the leased office.

He was on Northside Drive heading home when his cell phone went off. He assumed it was Kush calling him back.

"Bannister, this is Doug Gordon."

Bannister's heart quickened a few beats. Special Agent Gordon was spearheading the investigation into Cal Williamson's disappearance.

"Do you have any news?"

"We found your friend's car tonight at Dulles Airport. I had it taken to the Lab at Quantico. They'll start processing it as soon as it gets there."

"I thought you guys had already searched the airport." Bannister hoped the frustration and anger he felt wasn't creeping into his voice.

"We did," Gordon said. "His Infiniti wasn't there the night we searched. One of our teams went back to all the airports today and found it in long-term parking. It had a Minnesota license plate on it. Somebody switched tags."

"How do you know they didn't miss the car during the initial sweep?"

"It's rained here for three days. We haven't had any additional precipitation since it stopped yesterday afternoon. Williamson's car didn't have any water spots on it. I think it was driven to the airport within the past twenty-four hours."

"Any sign of Cal or what might have happened?"

"No. A preliminary exam of the car didn't reveal anything. There was no evidence of foul play. You said you and Williamson were the same size, didn't you?"

"That's right. Why?"

"I don't think he drove the car to the airport. The front seat and rear-view mirror were adjusted for a person about six feet tall. Since your friend is six-four, that means someone else may have been behind the wheel."

"That probably means something happened to him."

"It might. But some of the company guys speculated if a person was going to defect, they might deliberately adjust the seat to throw us off."

Bannister felt a flash of annoyance, but said nothing. He knew there was no way in hell Cal had voluntarily disappeared. The guy had too much going for him.

"I'll keep you posted on any developments. In the meantime, you've got my number. If you think of anything or just want to talk, give me a call."

"Thanks, Doug."

CHAPTER 14

ONE YEAR EARLIER—WASHINGTON, DC

Within forty-eight hours of discovering she was HIV positive, Lillian was a changed woman. She'd decided she had two choices: She could be depressed and wallow in self-pity, marking time until AIDS grabbed hold of her body. Or she could take charge of her situation. She decided to fight and direct her energies to give herself the best chance of being a long-term survivor.

On Tuesday, Lillian met with the counselor Dr. Bradford had recommended and discovered the woman to be warm, compassionate, and knowledgeable. Her attitude was so positive, Lillian scheduled semi-monthly meetings with her for the next three months.

When she called Dr. Bradford to give her feedback on the meeting, Lillian asked for a prescription to help her sleep better. She wanted to ensure her energy level was high for the next few weeks. Dr. Bradford, however, suggested waiting at least two weeks to make sure there weren't adverse side effects from the daily intake of AZT and the cocktail of other HIV drugs. Lillian guessed the real reason was the doctor wanted to minimize the possibility one of her patients might over-dose on Valium.

She then drove directly from one counselor's office to another—that of Homer Vinson, attorney-at-law. Vinson specialized in family law, or more accurately, the law dealing with the dissolution of families. He was a divorce specialist who had represented one of Lillian's friends, successfully tracking down thousands in assets the cheating spouse had tried to conceal. Lillian knew Vinson was highly respected in the legal community. Walking into the atrium of his building, Lillian felt proud of the way she was taking charge. Once seated inside his office, she asked Vinson to represent her in divorcing Felix.

He was a large man whose three-hundred-pound girth looked formidable in a dark-blue, three-piece suit and white shirt with blue awning stripes. His huge neck made his bowtie look like a butterfly had landed at his shirt collar. Vinson's ham-like arms were spread wide on his desk as he leaned forward. His sallow jowls framed a head of curly white hair which floated downward covering his ears. He looked like a lawyer and his voice was mellow and reassuring.

Lillian patiently listened to his expected spiel about marital counseling and a trial separation. When he was finished, she was blunt. "Mr. Vinson, my marriage to Felix is broken," she said. "Forever. It's over, and it's been over for quite some time. I'd hoped his posting to Vienna would change everything. It certainly did, but not in the way I'd hoped. When my husband told me he didn't want children, and nothing I said could convince him otherwise, it was as if a part of me died." Lillian paused and took in a deep breath.

"Is that when you decided on divorce?"

"When I returned to Washington, I found out I was HIV positive, and that Felix was responsible." Lillian looked at Vinson when she mentioned HIV. His eyebrows lifted, but he continued to listen carefully.

"I just couldn't believe I married and stayed married to that lying, cheating, supercilious piece of shit for a husband!" She took a breath, embarrassed by her emotional outburst. "I'm sorry."

"That's quite all right. Do you have any evidence Felix was responsible for infecting you?"

"Yes. I made him get a blood test, and I have a copy of the results. He admitted his infidelity to me."

"Will he contest the divorce?"

"I see no reason for him to do that. I don't want a court fight. Isn't it extremely expensive to go to court?"

"It can be. As you're probably aware, my fees for appearing in court are four-hundred an hour, plus an additional two thousand a day. What property do the two of you have that might be an issue?"

"We don't have a house. Each of us has our own property, which we've managed to keep separate. My parents died before we were married. I inherited their home in Basking Ridge, New Jersey, and about a million in stocks. My broker has handled everything for me over the past ten years. I think my investments have grown to four million. Funny thing is, that might not be important if I get AIDS, right?"

"Let's not worry about what might not happen." He slowly drummed his chubby fingers up and down on the blotter as if his hands were slow moving spiders. "Let me make sure the assets you have are protected and that Felix pays what the law demands. Don't sign anything unless I tell you."

"I plan on asking him to move out this weekend. Right now he's sleeping in the spare bedroom. We barely talk."

"Okay," Vinson said as he got up from behind his desk. "Don't worry, Lillian. I'll handle everything. Once he moves out, I'd prefer any contact he has with you to be through me first. Do you have any problem with that?"

"No, sir, I don't."

Vinson offered Lillian his right hand, and then he gave her a grandfatherly pat on her shoulder. "We'll get through this legal matter just fine. And my office will help you with any medical referrals or problems with doctor's bills or tests. I look forward to seeing you again Thursday morning."

Felix didn't return to the apartment that night until after eight. Lillian didn't bother asking him where he'd been, but could tell from his wet hair and the splattered dark drops on his suit coat that it was raining again.

"Did you have dinner?" Lillian asked in a surprisingly civil tone.

"Yeah, I stopped at Blackie's House of Beef with a couple of people from work," Felix said as he put his briefcase down beside the coffee table and went to his bedroom to change clothes. He returned a few minutes later.

"Before you grab the remote, I have something to say," Lillian said. "I saw a lawyer today, and I'm filing for divorce."

"I figured that would be coming. I haven't talked to a lawyer yet. I thought about it. I guess I'll have to put that on my list of 'to dos.'" Felix sunk back into the sofa and his voice returned to its normal sarcastic tone. "Do you intend to rake me over the coals?"

Standing with her hands on her hips and looking down at Felix, Lillian said, "I don't have any specific intentions except to end this marriage as soon as possible. And one other thing."

"Yes?"

"I want you out of here."

"Do you have a timetable on that, too?"

"Don't be an asshole like you normally are, Felix. The sooner the better."

"All right. Quit the name calling. I'll be out this weekend. Is that fast enough for you?" Felix turned on the television, raised the volume, and looked away from her stare.

"That would be fine," Lillian said as she turned and went into the bedroom and closed the door.

She hadn't worried about Felix getting physical with her. It would have been totally out of character for him. She sat down at the small desk and opened her laptop. She'd decided on a short message. Although she hadn't yet figured out how to tell Andre, she knew she'd have to. Her e-mail to him simply said: "Please call me soon. I need to talk to you. Lillian."

Lillian logged off and called Mary Claire Vine, her best friend. She hadn't talked with her since leaving Vienna.

"Hello, this is Mary Claire," the voice answered.

"It's me, Lillian. How are things in Chicago?"

"Freezing! Where are you calling from? Are you in DC?"

"Yes. I'm back. So much has happened this month. I don't know where to begin," Lillian said.

"What's wrong? You sound like you're in some kind of trouble."

"I just needed to talk to you. I asked Felix for a divorce."

"I'm so sorry. No I'm not. That didn't come out right. I'm sorry for how you must be feeling, but I'm not sorry you're leaving Felix. He's never treated you the way you deserve. I don't think he's ever thought of anyone except himself. You feel like talking?"

"I do, but maybe tonight's not the best. I just wanted you to know. I saw a lawyer today and told him my marriage was over. I worked hard at it, Mary Claire, but I couldn't get it to work. At some point the love just left."

"Lillian, don't blame yourself. Listen. I've got oodles of vacation time and my boss has been encouraging me to get away. I was thinking I'd pay you a surprise visit after you got settled. What would you think if I came down to see you for a couple of days?"

"I don't want you to do that. Why would you want to waste your time with some depressed person?"

"I know you. You're strong. Remember when I came to New Jersey when your parents died?"

"I'll never forget that. I needed someone to cry with and you were there for me."

"Yes, and you needed someone to tell you it was all right to laugh again," Mary Claire said.

"You've always known what to say."

"Well, I'm not going to come to DC to spend time with a blubbering idiot. But I want to see you again. There's so much to catch up on."

Lillian could sense the excitement in Mary Claire's voice. "I really can't wait to see you."

"We'll put our heads together and come up with a good game

plan for you. Hey! Consider it a done deal. I don't want to hear any arguments. I'll book a flight for this Sunday and you can plan on my being around until Wednesday night. What do you think?"

"You're the best friend anyone could have."

"You'd do the same thing for me. I'll make reservations tonight and e-mail them to you tomorrow. Let me know if there's any problem. Do you mind picking me up at the airport?"

"Absolutely not. This is great. I'll call you tomorrow."

Lillian and Mary Claire talked a while longer and both realized how much they missed seeing each other. Lillian drew a hot bath and added some luxury bath oil she'd brought back with her from Vienna. Her body slowly sank into the tub and the heat of the water, like gentle hands, drew out the tension that had been building all day. She thought of Andre and different ways to explain to him what happened. She knew he had to be told but couldn't decide on the words to use.

Thirty minutes later, with a cup of hot tea on her nightstand and her body wrapped inside a nightgown and flannel robe, Lillian propped herself up in bed. She opened Lorna Landvik's novel, *Angry Housewives Eating Bon Bons*, and had read a few pages when her cell phone rang. She grabbed it automatically and glanced at the unfamiliar number on the screen.

"Hello, this is Lillian."

"How good it is to hear your voice again. I hope I'm not calling too late."

"Andre! Oh, thank you for calling. You must have gotten my e-mail." Lillian didn't care if her excitement sounded in her voice.

"I did. I'm here in Washington. How are things with you? Are you all right?"

"Things have turned upside down. It's complicated, but I'm leaving my husband."

"I guess the normal thing to say is, 'I'm sorry to hear that.' But I think I know you better," Andre said. "You've been so unhappy. Maybe fate is telling you this problem will soon be over."

"You're so positive. I've missed you, and I need to talk to you. When can I see you?" Lillian asked, trying not to sound overly anxious.

"I thought about that before I called. I know this is short notice, but could you meet me for coffee tomorrow? I need to talk to you, too."

"I'll make time. When?"

"Do you know the Starbucks across from the Springfield Mall?" Andre asked.

"I'm sorry, I didn't hear where. It sounded like a car squealing."

"I'm calling from a pay phone. I said Starbucks across from the Springfield Mall. How about meeting me tomorrow morning at 10:00 a.m.?"

"I'll be there. I can't wait to see you." Lillian could feel her heart start to race.

"I know you've had a lot on your mind. I'm just curious, though, have you told anyone about us?"

"No, not yet," she said.

"That's good. I'll explain tomorrow. So until then, as they say in America, sleep tight," said Andre.

Lillian chose a pair of black slacks, black boots, and a cream-colored blouse topped with her new waist-length, chocolate-brown leather jacket. She twisted her hair up in a bun to draw attention to her dangling gold earrings and gold band necklace. She felt chic and polished.

At a few minutes before ten, Lillian was delighted to see Andre walking toward the Starbucks entrance.

"Good morning. You look fabulous," he said as he embraced her for a second, giving her slight kisses on both cheeks in the European fashion.

"And you look wonderful, too." Taking in his blue blazer with a white turtleneck, Lillian said, "You look like a movie star."

"I guess I should take that as a compliment," Andre said.

He held the door open for Lillian, and the two went into Starbucks where they ordered lattes. Andre told her he had completed his assignments in Zurich, including the editing of his friend's cookbook, and then had gone to Moscow. He said he'd been busy on a story about the Moscow Circus, which he hoped would get picked up by one of the major travel magazines. Lillian told him about her last week in Vienna and a side trip to Florence and Milan she had taken before returning to the States, but she couldn't conceal her distracted state.

"Did you want to talk about your husband?" Andre asked as he looked into her eyes.

"I kept putting off facing reality and what it meant," she said. "Felix never wanted children and I did. Then he admitted he'd been cheating on me. When he didn't show any emotion telling me about it, I knew our marriage wasn't worth saving."

"Right now you're hurting, but it's not the end of the world. You have so much going for you. You're intelligent, unselfish, and beautiful."

"Do you really think so?" Lillian asked.

"Yes, and I have firsthand experience that you're in very good shape," Andre said with a rakish smile.

"I know you're trying to cheer me up, and I appreciate that," Lillian smiled as she reached for Andre's hand. "Last night you said you had something you wanted to talk to me about, right?"

"I did say that, but what I'd rather do is show you something that's been in my family for many, many years. It's extremely rare and valuable, but I know I can trust you. It was never supposed to leave my country, but I brought it here. It's about ten minutes away. Come with me. I'll drive and then bring you back to your car."

On Friday morning, Homer Vinson called Felix Wells at the State Department.

"Mr. Wells, this is Homer Vinson. Your wife retained me as her lawyer. Do you happen to know where she is?"

"No, why?"

"She was supposed to be at my office yesterday morning, but she never came in. When I called her cell phone, I got her voicemail. I also left a message for her on the answering machine at your apartment."

"I know. I listened to your call and saved the message for Lillian."

"Well, this morning I tried to reach her again without success. I left another message on your apartment phone, then called your work number, which she had given me."

"You've got to know we haven't exactly been having lengthy conversations," Felix said, irritated. "For your information, I haven't seen Lillian since Wednesday night when she told me she wanted a divorce."

"What about yesterday?" Vinson asked.

"I just said I haven't seen her since Wednesday. Are you interrogating me?"

"No. Don't get upset. Your wife hired me to represent her, and that's what I intend to do. I would like to talk to her as soon as possible. So she never came home yesterday?"

"I don't know. Her alarm usually goes off about five minutes before I leave for work. Yesterday morning I went to work at seven-thirty. I didn't hear her alarm, so I figured she was sleeping in. Her door was closed."

"What about last night when you got home?" Vinson asked.

"I got to the apartment about seven and yelled out I was home. I knocked on her bedroom door. When she didn't answer, I looked in the room and saw she wasn't there. I assumed she must have left to go out with a friend or something."

"Did she come home?"

"I don't know. I went to bed about eleven and she still wasn't back."

"So what did you do today?"

"I went to work as normal. As a matter of fact, I have an appointment with my lawyer this afternoon to discuss the divorce. Are you saying you think she's disappeared?"

"Right now I have some concerns. When you hear from her, have her call me immediately. If I'm not in the office, my answering service will call me. I've placed a priority on her call."

CHAPTER 15

ONE YEAR EARLIER—ARLINGTON, VIRGINIA

T he last time Felix Wells III had been to a police station was twelve years earlier when he needed two sets of fingerprints for his State Department application. This time it was to make a report. Felix had met with a lawyer to discuss his divorce and used that opportunity to mention Lillian's apparent disappearance. His lawyer strongly urged him to file a missing person report with the Arlington Police Department and to cooperate with authorities. If the police attempted to question him formally, he would invoke his right to remain silent and call his attorney.

———⦿⦿⦿———

Detective Weber had been with the Arlington Police for eighteen years. Normally he was on call for any homicides, but since they only had six in the past two years, all of which he had closed, he was helping out this week with missing persons duty. The majority of complaints involved teenage runaways. Most returned home or surfaced somewhere within forty-eight hours. Some were found in jail where they'd been locked up for miscellaneous crimes. Other missing persons cases involved drug users who overdosed, hospital patients who wandered off, and elderly residents with Alzheimer's who went on errands and simply forgot where they lived. Occasionally, the missing person turned up as a suicide or murder victim.

Detective Weber was buzzed by reception and met Felix Wells at the entrance to the detective bureau's bullpen where four other officers were working at their desks. The open area looked like a newspaper office. Black binders and stacks of papers were on every desk. Screen savers on a dozen computer monitors silently changed scenes as the two men shook hands. The detective was wearing a light gray suit. His iridescent silver blue tie drew attention away from his gray, leathery face and a nose that looked like it'd been broken more than once. He had tired eyes with prominent crow's feet.

As the detective bent down to pick up a Post-It note from the floor, Felix stepped over a wet spot on the dirty gray carpeting blemished by one too many coffee spills. The office was stuffy, and the air smelled stale because the police department had cut back on heating and air conditioning for the start of the weekend.

"You're not going to smoke during the interview, are you?" Felix asked.

Detective Weber glared at him.

The interview room looked like a handball court. The detective flipped on the lights and pulled the chair out from behind a black, steel desk and sat down. He pointed to an empty chair.

"Have a seat, Mr. Wells. Do you mind if I call you Felix?" Weber knew the importance of establishing rapport with complainants.

"No, go right ahead."

One of the fluorescent lights buzzed and blinked. After getting identifiers and background information from Felix, Detective Weber began the interview.

"What makes you think your wife is missing?"

"I haven't seen or heard from her in over two days."

"Is that unusual?" Weber flipped over a yellow page of his notebook.

"Normally, I would say it is. But this week's been a little different."

"In what way?" Weber asked.

"Well, Tuesday night when I came home from work the first words out of Lillian's mouth were 'I want a divorce.'"

"I see. Are there kids involved?"

"No. We don't have any children."

"Okay. What happened next?"

"Nothing. I told her I didn't have a lawyer but would probably call one the next day. We talked about our situation, and both of us agreed we didn't want a court fight."

"Did she—it's Lillian, right?—act mad or upset?"

"No, as a matter of fact she was kind of calm," Felix added.

"So, you weren't shocked by her asking for a divorce."

"No, but I didn't think she would spring it on me so soon."

"What happened after that?" Weber asked.

"Nothing. She went into her room, and I watched TV until I went to bed. I got up and went to work the next day."

"So when exactly was the last time you saw or talked with your wife?"

"Tuesday night."

"Today's Friday. You didn't see or talk to her Wednesday or Thursday?"

"No. I came home about 7:00 p.m. Wednesday and checked to see if she was there. She wasn't. The same thing on Thursday. She didn't leave me a note. I checked the messages on the answering machine and there were two for her. One was from her lawyer, asking her to call him. The second was from Lillian's friend in Chicago, asking her to call or e-mail her about the plan."

"What plan was that?" Weber asked.

"I don't know. It could have been anything."

"Does your wife have a cell phone?"

"Yeah. Why?"

"Have you tried to call her since you last spoke with her?"

"Yeah, I tried her number after her lawyer called me at work this morning and said he'd tried unsuccessfully to reach her. He left messages on both her cell phone and our apartment phone. She missed an appointment with him yesterday."

"Let's call her now," Weber suggested.

"Here, use my cell phone." Felix handed it to the detective. "Just hit speed-dial two."

It didn't ring but went directly to voicemail. "This is Detective Alvin Weber of the Arlington Police Department," he said into the phone. "Please call me as soon as you get this message." He left the police department's main number and his extension, then handed the phone back to Felix.

"Maybe when she hears a police officer needs to speak with her she'll call back. Does your wife work?"

"No."

"How about you? What line of work are you in?"

"I'm a foreign service officer with the State Department."

"Do you or your wife have any enemies?"

"No. Everyone likes Lillian. As for me, I can't think of anyone. Of course, we always receive briefings that any of us could be a target of terrorists."

"I think things are a little bit different here in the States." The detective wanted to get back on track.

"Does your wife have her own car?"

"Yes. It's a leased Lexus. In my name," Felix said.

"I'll need a description of it, including the vehicle identification number and license plate. We'll put that into the National Crime Information Center's computer. Does your wife have any family or friends in the area where she might be staying?"

"I don't think so. Her parents are gone, and she was an only child. Her best friend lives in Chicago. I don't think Lillian is close enough to anyone around here to impose on them, even if it were only for a couple of days."

"Does your wife have any kind of medical condition, or is she taking any medication?"

"Why's that important?" Felix asked.

"There's always the possibility she may have had some kind of reaction requiring hospitalization."

"My wife's a healthy woman and never . . . well, at least until recently . . ."

"What do you mean?" Weber said, picking up his pen. "Has your wife had a recent problem?"

"You may as well know. She was diagnosed last week as being HIV positive. And so was I."

"I'm sorry to hear that," Weber said. "How did Lillian handle the news?"

"How do you think she handled it? How do you think I handled it? It was a shock to both of us! I don't think the reality of what it really means has hit yet."

"Are either of you drug users?"

"What the hell does that mean?" Felix's voice got louder and his face flushed red with anger. Weber noticed two of the other detectives glance toward the interview room. He gave them a thumbs up.

"I'm not trying to upset you, but that's one of the most common ways people contract HIV—infected needles. And, of course, there's the other common way," Weber rocked back in his chair. "Unprotected sex with another person."

"I don't think we need to get into that here," Felix said.

"Look, I'm trying to work with you, Mr. Wells. Is Lillian currently involved with someone else?"

"No. At least I don't see how she could be. We've only been back to the States for a couple of weeks. We've been living in Vienna, Austria, where I was assigned for the past two and a half years."

Weber made a note on his pad. *Husband infected wife?* "Finding out you've contracted HIV is a life-changing event," he said. "You'd agree with me on that, wouldn't you?"

"Yeah, sure."

"Well, do you think your wife is the kind of woman who might think about suicide?"

Felix was silent for a moment. "I don't know."

"Have you checked to see if any of her clothes or cosmetics are missing?"

"No."

"You haven't?"

"No. Look, I figured that's what you guys would do. That's why I'm here." Felix got out of his chair and stared at the detective.

Detective Weber raised both his hands in the air in mock surrender. "Let's not get all wrapped around the axle on this. Please, sit back down. Being missing isn't a crime. Even if Lillian is voluntarily missing, the important thing is to concentrate on locating her as soon as possible. We also want to make sure nothing has happened to her. In whose name is the contract for her cell phone?"

"It's in my name."

"Good. Then we won't have any delay in dumping all her incoming and outgoing calls. Do you have a home computer?"

"We do, but it's in transit with our shipment of household goods. We each have our own laptops and e-mail accounts."

"Would you happen to know Lillian's password for her e-mail?"

"It's 'parrothead.' She's a Jimmy Buffet fan."

Weber wrote in his notebook. "I'd like to go back to your apartment with you and check her computer for her address list. I'd like to review the computer history just to make sure she hasn't purchased a recent airline ticket or made other travel arrangements." He didn't want to tell Felix he wanted to search her e-mail messages for other clues that might shed light on her disappearance. "I'll also need the names of her doctors and dentist."

"Why her dentist?"

"When we put a person's name into the National Crime Information Center's Missing Persons file, we enter medical data such as physical handicaps and mental disabilities, as well as a complete chart of their dental history."

"You mean in case they find a body?"

"That does happen sometimes."

Weber made a few more notes, including Felix's mention of finding a body. "When we get to the apartment, you can check to see what Lillian may have taken, like her clothes, watch, jewelry, or overnight items. I'll need as good a description as you can provide. Her height, weight, whether she has any scars, tattoos, or birthmarks. We'll enter all that into her report."

"What else do you need?" Felix asked.

"It would help if you had some recent photographs, especially any that show her current hair color and style. And could you give us a list of all your joint credit card and bank account numbers so we can check to see if there's been any activity on them in the past seventy-two hours?"

Weber followed Felix back to the Wells' apartment, which was only three miles from the police station in a trendy area of upscale brick townhouses behind the Ballston Metro stop. But it was Friday rush hour, and in the bumper-to-bumper traffic, it took twenty minutes to cover the three miles down Wilson Boulevard. Once inside the apartment, Felix pointed out Lillian's room, and the two men opened her door and went in.

"Is that her laptop?" Weber pointed to a silver Sony Vaio on a small desk.

"Yes, but I haven't looked at it," Felix said.

"If you don't mind, I'd like to take it with me so one of our tech guys can check it out. I'll give you a receipt and return it immediately if Lillian shows up."

"Do whatever you need to do," Felix said as he walked over to Lillian's closet.

After looking through the shelves and racks of neatly hanging clothes, Felix said, "The only thing I know for sure that isn't here is her favorite pair of black leather boots. And it looks like her new brown leather jacket is missing. That's all I can tell you. I honestly don't pay much attention to the particulars of Lillian's wardrobe. As you can see, it's rather extensive."

"That's fine," Weber said as he noticed the bed was made up with gold decorative pillows carefully arranged on top of a light blue tapestry bedspread. When he walked into the bathroom, he immediately noticed an open cosmetics bag on the counter, as well as a comb and brush sitting next to a black hair dryer.

"Felix, I'd like to take your wife's hairbrush and this toothbrush, which I'm assuming is hers." The detective figured those items might be the best bet at getting the woman's DNA if it was needed, since her immediate family members were deceased.

"Sure, go ahead."

In the top left drawer of the vanity, Weber observed five different prescription containers. One bottle was labeled AZT; two others had exotic names, probably HIV drugs. He found one calendar pack of birth control pills and a tube marked Retin-A, which Weber knew was for the skin. It didn't look to him like Lillian Wells had packed to go anywhere.

"Detective Weber, I don't have a clue as to what jewelry Lillian owns. I know she always wears her wedding rings, and I don't see her watch here. It's a Vacheron—the kind with railroad numbers on it, you know, one, two, three. It belonged to her mother. Neither woman liked to stare at a watch to tell the time. Lillian also has a new pair of gold dangling earrings that she bought in Milan. I don't see them. I don't know if it's important, but her watch is worth about seven thousand dollars."

Weber made some more notes and continued searching through the rest of the apartment, his trained eye looking for any signs of a struggle, recent cleaning, or items out of place. He saw none. In the kitchen he noticed a stack of documents on the kitchen table and asked about them.

"Lillian made me a copy of our financial documents and credit card bills for our lawyers to review," Felix said.

"Well, why don't you copy down your account numbers and financial information while I sit in the other room and make some notes," Weber suggested.

Weber and Felix compiled a list with Lillian's descriptive data, medical information, car identifiers, bank and credit card data, and a list of friends with addresses and phone numbers.

"I think that'll do it for now," Weber said as he gathered up Lillian's laptop and a plastic bag in which he'd put Lillian's brushes. "Call me as soon as you hear anything. I'm going back to the office and will have all this put into our computer."

After handing Felix one of his business cards, Weber returned to his car. The first thing he would do Monday would be to contact Lillian Wells' doctor and dentist. As soon as he got back to the office, he intended to run a few checks on Felix Wells III. Some things weren't adding up.

The sun was setting. Thirty-nine miles away near Stafford, Virginia, off a gravel turnout at mile marker 141, Lillian Wells didn't know the day was ending. Her Vacheron Cortina watch said it was 5:57 p.m. It was still on the left wrist of her lifeless nude body.

CHAPTER 16

T he ringing of Bannister's alarm announced Friday's arrival. Last night he'd planned a four mile run for this morning, followed by a half hour of karate kicks and hand thrusts to the punching bags in the garage. He left at 5:30 a.m. despite the crisp twenty-nine degree temperature. He used the first mile to warm up and mull over the events of the day before. It had not been a good day.

Someone had gotten away with five million dollars belonging to Global Waters. But getting away and getting *away with it* were two different things. And then the Bureau had found Cal Williamson's car at DC's Dulles airport where someone, maybe his killer, had dumped it. Bannister was impatiently waiting to see if the lab guys came up with anything.

He kept up a steady pace as he ran past what used to be the old Lumpkin estate. He could only imagine what it had looked like back in 1843 when Martha Atalanta Lumpkin had changed the name of the city from Terminus to Marthasville. Fortunately for later residents, that name only lasted two years. The city's chief railroad engineer, hoping to bring some life to the economy, renamed the city Atlanta, using Martha's middle name—or most of it, anyway.

Bannister used the last stretch of his run to sift through what had happened so far. As he replayed the chronology of events, he remembered what an old homicide detective had once told him. Always follow three rules: Let the crime scene talk to you, work the facts, and trust your hunches. Bannister hadn't trusted one of his hunches yesterday when the theft was going down, and now the money was missing. Today he'd have to work the facts and get back on track. Right now his gut was telling him to identify the real Sean O'Brien. It was also telling him the subject must have had inside help.

Back at the garage he went through his routine of strength exercises, stretching, and powering through a series of sweeping kicks to the heavy bag. Hundreds of hours of repetitive movements had developed his muscle memory. His body remembered the moves but forgot the fatigue that went along with them.

He was almost through his workout when he again felt a jolt of pain near his right hip. For a second it took his breath away. Maybe he'd overdone it. In any event, the hot jets of the shower were a godsend and slowly massaged his muscles back to reality.

—❧—

At the office, Bannister put his cup of coffee on the desk and saw a note from Germaine White saying she had results of new records checks. He turned around to see her standing directly behind him.

"I see you've read my note," she said.

"Morning, Germaine. You've been busy."

"I knew you'd be pulled in a lot of directions today, so I thought I'd try and give you a head start." She smiled and tilted her head to the side.

"What've you got?"

"The name of the rental agent for Best Atlanta Company is Candace Miller. I ran her through ChoicePoint and other databases. I've got her home address, work address, and all her phone numbers, including cell."

"That's great, Germaine. What else you got there?"

"I remember both you and Ernie Gonzales said yesterday you thought Sean O'Brien was wearing a disguise for his driver's license photo."

"What's your opinion?" He knew Germaine liked to be asked what she thought.

"I agree. I took O'Brien's photo and used some new identification software to show what he'd look like clean-shaven, without glasses, and with a contemporary hairstyle. I know you didn't ask for these, but I thought they might come in handy later."

"You're always a step ahead," Bannister said. Germaine put the retouched photos on the corner of his desk and went back to her vault. Mercedes Ramirez sauntered over with a rested look about her, which was surprising, given the long hours she'd been working. She looked smart in a navy jacket, navy slacks, and white blouse.

"Nice effort last night," Bannister said. "Anything new?"

"It doesn't look like we're going to get much from the tunnel. I vacuumed the whole length in hopes we might pick up trace evidence. I'll have to go through the contents this morning." Mercedes leaned back against Ford Campbell's desk. "By the way, Derek looked at the dumpster out back. Did you know Derek has welding experience? Anyway, he said it looks to him like the guy with the torch was a novice. Something about metal fusing and the perimeter cut being too uneven. You know Derek offers his opinion on everything."

"At least you always know where you stand with him."

"We'll have to wait for the tool mark team to give us a definitive read."

"Did you get anything from the office search?" Bannister asked.

"You bet. The black landscaping plastic covering the windows has a Home Depot UPC sticker on one corner. The garden cart in the tunnel also has a Home Depot sticker on it. We'll probably be able to identify the store where they were purchased and work it from there."

"Maybe the stuff was bought with a credit card. If we can pinpoint the date of purchase, we can look at their surveillance tapes. We might get lucky."

"We also located stickers on the desks and lamps in the office, indicating they were rented from Easy Office Solutions. Campbell's going to check that out. One other thing: We got a couple of partial shoe prints in the dust in the parking area in front of the office. The search team says they look like New Balance running shoes. We should have a model and size by this afternoon. They might not belong to our subject, but none of our people were wearing tennies."

Bannister's cell phone rang. It was Robin.

"Ty, I know you're extremely busy, but I just had to call you. I opened my mail this morning and my orders were in it. I have to be at Quantico the second week of January." Robin couldn't keep the excitement out of her voice.

"That's fantastic. I'm real happy for you. Have you given your notice?"

"I'll let Adam know this morning. He knew it was just a matter of time. Next week is Thanksgiving, and with everything going on—I feel bad about hitting him with it now, but I want to give him plenty of time to get a replacement. Speaking of Thanksgiving, what are your plans?"

Bannister hadn't given it a thought. "I usually spend a quiet day at home," he said. "Cook something special, maybe watch a movie or something." He switched the phone to his other ear and leaned back. He felt a little nervous. "Hey, I've got an idea. If you haven't made plans, how about joining me for dinner at my place?"

"I'll only accept if I can bring something. How about a dessert? Could you go for something sinful?"

He knew she was flirting with him and he liked it. "You read my mind," he said.

"Okay, you've got a deal."

"I really look forward to seeing you. And I'll be at Global later today. I'm meeting with Adam after the SAC's briefing here this afternoon. We're reviewing your list of terminated employees and other possibles."

"Yes, I know. He said he'd like me to sit in, because every employee who was let go the past two years turned their company property in to me. It was always me and a security officer who escorted them out of the building."

"Then I hope my meeting doesn't run too late."

"Oh, one other thing."

"What's that?"

"About Thanksgiving. It doesn't count as the dinner you owe me. Bye, bye!" Robin laughed as she hung up.

Bannister was still grinning as he called Candace Miller. It was amazing, he thought, but with everything else occupying his mind, Robin could actually make him smile.

Candace Miller picked up right away and agreed to meet him at her office on Northside Drive in an hour.

The secretary at Best Atlanta pointed toward the back of the office, where an attractive woman with auburn hair was just getting off the phone. Candace Miller stood up and waved Bannister into her office. When they shook hands, he noticed she wasn't wearing a wedding ring.

"I've never met an FBI agent before," Miller said. Her smile seemed genuine even if her white capped teeth looked like they'd been done in Beverly Hills. "What's this all about?"

After he explained that one of her tenants, Sean O'Brien, might be involved in an extortion, she went to pull his file. Bannister asked her to bring the whole folder and not touch the documents.

"He called me at the end of June and said he'd like to look at the property. I drove over there, showed him an empty office, gave him a quick spiel about location, location, location, and he said he'd take it. We couldn't have been there more than ten minutes."

From a photo spread of six pictures, including Sean O'Brien's driver's license photo, she picked O'Brien out immediately.

"Can you describe what he looked like?"

"He looked like that picture. He had on a long-sleeved blue denim shirt and jeans. I remember what he was wearing because it was a scorching humid June day."

"Do you recall anything about his voice or what he said?"

"Naturally, I asked him about his business and if he anticipated any problems with a credit check, you know, because he was a graduate student."

"How did he respond?"

"He was very smooth. He gave me all the information I needed, and I wrote it down. I told him it would take a few days to process the paperwork, but everything would be ready for him by the end of the week."

"Did you see him again?"

"Yes, he made an appointment for that Friday and came to the office to sign everything. He sat exactly where you're sitting now."

"How did that meeting go?"

"Fine. No problems. We'd done all our normal checks and he came through okay. The paperwork was ready when he arrived. The only thing out of the ordinary was that he paid the first two months of the two-year lease and the thousand dollar security deposit in cash—$3,600."

"Did you ask him about that?"

"Sure. He said he was still in the process of setting up bank accounts and getting business cards and stationery printed. Made sense to me." Miller brushed her auburn hair away from her face and flashed Bannister with an electric smile.

"Is there anything you recall about his voice? Accent, stutter, or anything unusual?"

"I'm not good on accents. He wasn't foreign, though. I'm sure of that. He sounded educated. Confident."

"Did you notice any distinguishing marks? Tattoos? Scars?"

"No, nothing that I recall."

"Did he wear any jewelry? Ring? Watch?"

"He didn't have any rings. He might have had a watch on, but I didn't see it."

"Do you recall what kind of vehicle he drove when he followed you to the office?"

"Not exactly. I just remember it was a white car."

"Do you remember if he physically handled these lease agreements and other papers?"

"Come to think of it, he did do something odd with the papers. He took a pencil out of a briefcase and used the eraser end to move the papers around in front of him before signing them. I don't know if he actually touched them or not."

"I'd like to take these with me for forensic analysis." After putting on cloth gloves, Bannister slid the lease agreement and three other credit forms into plastic sleeves. "You can make photocopies of these for your file. I'll give you a receipt and we'll return the originals later," he told her as he made some notes. He wasn't optimistic about getting any prints.

"If there's anything else you remember, please call me right away. No matter how insignificant you think it might be." Bannister handed Candace Miller one of his cards.

"One question, agent Bannister. Do you think we're going to be stuck for the last eighteen months of his lease?"

"That I don't know. Right now, Mr. O'Brien is a person of interest to us. Perhaps when we locate him we'll get an answer for you." As Bannister walked out of the office she shouted back.

"I just remembered something. He was wearing Obsession."

"Pardon me?"

"He was wearing Calvin Klein's Obsession cologne."

"Yeah?" He sounded skeptical.

"It happens to be my favorite men's cologne," she said. "I didn't say anything to him, though. If you point something out like that to a guy, they get self-conscious and think they've put on too much foof."

"Thanks, Candace."

—◆◇◆—

Ford Campbell and two agents from the white collar crime squad identified two credit cards issued to Sean O'Brien and all transactions.

A mail box at a PakMail store was identified. They retrieved the original registration papers from the Secretary of State's Office for US Euro Trans-Consultants, which would be submitted for fingerprint checks and handwriting analysis. Campbell said computer checks for the firm showed no activity. He thought it was a front.

Agent Campbell and his team were efficient. They'd confirmed the rental of office furniture but struck out on getting additional information on O'Brien. Campbell asked the FBI in Charlotte to pursue the rental of a ground penetrating radar system. Interviews were underway at a tunneling equipment company in Dahlonega, Georgia, where Sean O'Brien had purchased drilling gear, pipe casings, and other equipment.

Records at a rental car company at the Atlanta airport showed that Sean O'Brien rented a Ford Taurus for a week—the same week he'd signed the lease for the office. Another company showed O'Brien had rented a white panel truck for six months. It was due back next week. A BOLO (be on the look-out notice) was issued for the van and its Georgia license plate. Campbell's team was also checking with ten companies that sold welding supplies. Later, they would scour Atlanta area wig dealers.

———⟞ʘʘʘ⟝———

Derek Barnes was handling the neighborhood investigation around Mike's Mini-Mart, but preliminary results weren't promising. Mercedes Ramirez announced she had found two hairs, possibly human, in the surface debris she vacuumed from the tunnel. That could be a break.

An hour later Ernie Gonzales, the technical supervisor, called. "Ty, we've got a signal."

"What?"

"Both transponders and the motion sensor from the money bag are working," Ernie said excitedly. "One of the guys was repairing some equipment in the shop when the signals went off. It's only been three minutes."

"Do you have a fix?" Bannister asked.

"Yes. It's coming from Piedmont Park. That's about six miles from here," Gonzales said.

"Get a team rolling, now! I'll call the radio room and see if we have any units in the vicinity."

Luck was on their side. Two agents were on Piedmont Avenue a half mile from the park. They responded to the call and were told to look for a white van or panel truck. SAC Brennan and ASAC Witt were notified of the development.

Bannister grabbed Mercedes and they headed for the park. Gonzales's team arrived at the same time as they did. Gonzales pinpointed the GPS signal, which was still working but hadn't moved. The signal was coming from a spot opposite a gazebo. Unfortunately, it was ten yards out into a lake. The bank robbery agents checked out the walking paths from the gazebo to the parking lots. They located a young couple pushing a baby stroller who had seen a man walking alone away from the gazebo in the opposite direction. They were unable to give a good description. The woman thought he was a white male. Her boyfriend said the man was black. No help.

Bannister and Mercedes were still on site an hour later when two of the office's dive-trained SWAT agents came out of the water holding a canvas mason's bag. Inside was the package of waterlogged hundred dollar bills with the hollowed-out center. The transponder, now visible, was still stuck in the middle of the package. Gonzales lifted a corner of the false bottom where the other transponder and motion sensor were installed. Both the transponder and the sensor were operating perfectly. Now they knew one of the subjects was still in the area.

While Bannister and Mercedes drove back to the office, they got a second break. A Transit Authority cop, remembering their BOLO notice, spotted a white panel truck in the long-term parking area of the Doraville subway station. The truck, without a license plate, had a VIN number matching the Budget vehicle rented by Sean O'Brien. Derek Barnes and an evidence team were dispatched to the lot, where they secured the truck and arranged for it to be towed to the FBI garage. The team was making progress.

Everyone was back in the office for SAC Brennan's briefing. Brennan started the meeting by saying he was pleased with their efforts and was confident they would solve the Global extortion. When the boss turned to the ASAC for his input, Witt warned everyone to make sure their paperwork was current and accurate. Witt reminded everyone the inspection team from Washington was arriving in ten days for their inspection of the office. He said he didn't want any heads to roll because of the Global case. A classic case of the carrot and the stick. They all preferred carrots.

Everyone briefed their part of the investigation. Additional assignments were made and they adjourned.

Bannister called Adam Kush at Global and checked to see if he had his list of discharged and disgruntled employees. He said he was ready and would be at the office late. Kush told him their insurance company agreed to reimburse Global for the five million dollars but was deferring payment for sixty days.

Before locking up, Bannister checked in with Doug Gordon in Washington.

"Hey Ty. I'm sorry we didn't get much from processing your friend's car. No real leads."

Bannister bit back a curse and said, "I know you're doing the best you can."

"The lab guys analyzed dirt taken from the tire treads. Surprisingly enough, the soil is almost identical to that found in the vicinity of the FBI Academy. Unofficially, it looks like the car may have been driven in an area that is parkland or Government reservation. I know it's not much, but it's all we've got right now."

"Thanks, Doug. Keep me posted. And if I don't hear from you, have a good Turkey Day."

Bannister hung up and immediately got another call.

"Special Agent Bannister? This is Candace at Best Atlanta. I just thought of something. I've got a recording of that Sean O'Brien's voice.

He left me a voicemail message on my office phone when he made an appointment to pick up the keys. I've still got that message on the machine."

"Candace, you're my new best friend. Can you stay at the office till I get there?"

"I'll be here, but I have a closing in an hour. Can you come before then?"

"I'm on my way."

Ernie Gonzales set him up with equipment for dubbing calls, either from a computer or phone, and Bannister was out the door in fifteen minutes.

Candace Miller welcomed him into her office. Bannister made two copies of O'Brien's message and secured the original backup tape as evidence. When they shook hands, Candice held onto his hand a bit longer than necessary. Bannister detected something inviting in her voice when she said, "If I can do anything else for you, Tyler, please give me a call."

He took the tapes with him and drove over to Global Waters for his meeting with Adam Kush. He was walking into the lobby right as the doors were being locked. He headed upstairs to the executive level where Adam and Robin were still working.

Inside Kush's office at his round table, the three went over a list of fifteen Global employees fired in the past two years. Bannister was looking for the inside link. Six of the employees were women; nine were men. One woman had worked in the payroll department as the assistant manager, had access to all personnel files, as well as Global's accounting system, and had managed to override a supervisor's authentication for overtime payments. She'd padded her own salary by five hundred a month. At the time of her dismissal, she had been overpaid five thousand dollars.

One of the men had been fired for lying on his application about credit-related scams, one of which involved bilking an older man out of $18,000 for a used truck. He'd been sued in civil court, and no arrests were on his record. Another guy was one of Global's computer trouble-shooters who had been arrested for stalking a topless dancer. When he was fired, he had threatened to get even.

Bannister told them about the recording of Sean O'Brien's voice. He took out the tape and played the call.

"Miss Miller, this is Sean O'Brien. Unless there's a problem, I'll be at your office this Friday at ten to pick up the keys. You have my number."

Adam Kush was the first to speak. "Sounds like a young guy."

As Bannister pushed the rewind button on his tape recorder, he looked at Robin. The pale expression on her face told him to stop and listen.

"I know him," she said slowly. "That's Terry Hines. The voice belongs to Terry Hines."

"Come to think of it, his voice does sound familiar," Kush said.

"How sure are you, Robin?" Bannister asked.

"Play it again, please." He played it two more times.

"It's him. I'm sure of it."

"Where's Hines now?" Bannister asked.

"On a cruise, I think," Kush said. "He went on vacation Wednesday and isn't due back until a week from Monday."

Bannister took out copies of the modified photo Germaine White had prepared and slid them on the table to Adam and Robin. They only needed a moment to glance at the photograph.

"That's him," Adam said.

"That's Terry," Robin said.

CHAPTER 17

"We've identified Sean O'Brien."

"No kidding. Who is it?" Witt asked.

"He's one of Global's current employees," Bannister said into his cell. "Guy named Terry Hines."

"Fantastic. How'd you make the ID? Where are you?" Witt asked.

"At the office. We still have a lot of checking to do, but it looks like he's their international marketing rep. The realtor who leased the office to him had saved a message from him on her voicemail. I took a recording of the voice and played it for Robin Mikkonen and Adam Kush. Robin's positive it's Hines. I showed her and Kush a computer-enhanced photo of Sean O'Brien. They say it's a match."

"Have you got enough for an arrest warrant?"

"Not yet. What I want to do first is compare his DNA from a coffee cup he had on his desk to the DNA from the hairs Mercedes recovered from inside the tunnel. We're processing the van O'Brien rented for the past five months. We may get something from that. I'm optimistic he's one of our subjects."

"Whadda ya mean, one?"

"We still don't know how many people are involved. It'd be damn impressive for one guy to pull this off. He'd have to procure or make his own ricin, secretly rent an office, and dig a sophisticated tunnel."

"Where's Hines now?" Witt asked.

"Three hours ago he boarded a cruise ship at Fort Lauderdale,

Florida." Anticipating Witts next question, Bannister pulled up the cruise line's web page on his computer and was staring at the planned stops for the Sunset Princess.

"How do you know that?"

"Kush pulled Hines's itinerary. He's leaving today from Fort Lauderdale on a nine-day cruise. His ship stops at Key West, Cozumel, and Grand Cayman. I got in touch with our Fort Lauderdale agent who handles liaison with the cruise ships. The security officer on board the Sunset Princess happens to be a retired agent out of Tampa. He said the passenger manifest lists our guy as having boarded."

"Do you think he has the money with him?"

"It'd be a helluva risk to carry around a suitcase full of money. More likely than not, he took a few stacks with him and stashed the rest. We should be able to get the DNA results soon. Mercedes took the evidence to the CDC since they agreed to do the DNA testing. They already have the ricin and understand we're dealing with a biological threat. We don't know if there's more ricin out there. I briefed Stu before calling you, and he's assigned four agents to come in tomorrow to run down leads on Hines. I'll put the details together for the US Attorney's office and see if we can get a search warrant for his apartment, car, and computer."

"Does the SAC know?"

"Not yet. I thought you'd want to call him with the news."

On Tuesday afternoon Bannister was sitting at his desk jotting down notes for a meeting with the boss. SAC Brennan wanted to hear the evidence against Hines. Bannister had taken a call earlier from the security director on board the Sunset Princess, informing him the ship had just left Key West with Hines still aboard.

Germaine White had drawn a timeline on the case, as well as a link analysis between Sean O'Brien and Terry Hines. It looked damaging to Hines. Bannister walked over to Stu Peterson's office where he was bent over his desk with some papers and a bottle of correction fluid.

"Witt's driving me nuts," Stu said. "He's obsessed with the inspection. I'm trying to manage investigations, and for the third time today I've had to revise this statistics sheet for him. He asked if I minded him calling you directly for hourly updates on the Global case. He was surprised when I said yes. I'm trying to keep him off your back."

"I appreciate that."

"He's wound up tight, concerned the inspectors are going to turn up something he'll get blamed for. Believe me, that's not what I want. None of the supervisors wants anything to delay Witt's promotion back to headquarters where they can keep him on a short tether."

Stu glanced at his watch and picked up his notebook. He stood and motioned for Bannister to head for the elevator. The two went down to the fourth floor to Brennan's office. Witt was already there. The four of them took seats around the boss's coffee table.

"What've we got so far?" Brennan asked.

"We have good circumstantial evidence pointing to Terry Hines. Robin Mikkonen is positive Hines's voice is identical to a call the real estate broker received from O'Brien. One of our techs is doing a voice analysis of that call and Hines's voice from a Global Waters training video. Physically, Hines and O'Brien are a match. Both Mikkonen and Kush said an enhanced driver's license photo of O'Brien looks like Hines. Since he's one of Global's corporate managers, he definitely has inside information. The original extortion package used an internal address for Kush that outsiders wouldn't have known."

"Any useful fingerprints?" Brennan asked.

"No. He's been careful. We've come up empty from the office, truck, and documents. We've tied the truck to the office and tunnel through concrete and soil samples found in the bed of the truck."

"Anything from the money bag?" Witt asked.

"No. We recovered $4,800 in torn bills and our three tracking devices but didn't get any other forensics. Gonzales believes the subject used some type of electronic shielding material to block our signals."

"At least we got our sensors back so we won't have to worry about accounting for missing government property," Witt said.

Brennan rolled his eyes.

Bannister's cell phone vibrated and he looked at the number. It was Mercedes. He excused himself from the meeting and stepped out to the secretary's office.

"We've got a match. The DNA from the hairs in the tunnel is the same as the DNA we got from Hines's coffee cup," she said.

"Hot damn!" Bannister pumped his fist through the air. "That's great, Mercedes. That's all we need. I'm in a meeting with the boss right now. I'll let him know."

Bannister walked back in and told them the news.

"Man. That's great!" Brennan said, pounding a closed fist into his open hand. "I knew you guys would solve this thing. Let's get the warrants."

"Your team's doing great work," Stu said, standing up and shaking Bannister's hand.

"Where're we going to pick him up?" Witt asked.

"No need to rush," Bannister said. "There's no indication the threat to poison Global's water products will be carried out. Their people are still on alert. We need to find out where the ricin came from and if there's any more out there. Hines thinks he's gotten away with it. He's confirmed on a Delta flight next Sunday from Ft. Lauderdale to Atlanta."

"Why don't we arrest him as soon as his ship docks?" Witt asked.

"We could, but it would complicate things. I'd like a shot at interviewing him as soon as he's arrested. We can control everything if we take him down in Atlanta. If he's arrested in Florida, extradition proceedings might drag things out."

"I know the US Attorney would prefer to make a press release on a case that will probably receive international attention. I'd like to call him and let him know we intend to make an arrest in Atlanta," Witt said.

Brennan nodded approval.

Witt put his cell phone on speaker mode and punched in three numbers. "I need the number for the US Attorney in Atlanta."

"Sir, this is not an emergency. You'll have to dial 4-1-1," the operator said.

After the laughing subsided, Witt, his face still red, said, "I'll handle it later."

Brennan looked in Bannister's direction with a grin.

"We can search Hines's apartment, office desk, and computer, and get more evidence while he's working on his tan," Bannister said. "I'll make sure he's under surveillance. We can have Ft. Lauderdale put an agent on the plane with him and search Hines's luggage when he arrives."

Brennan said, "Gary, let the US Attorney know we're all in agreement."

Stu said, "I want Hines arrested at Hartsfield as soon as he gets off the plane. Have him taken to the international concourse where Homeland Security has an office. You can take photos and prints, and interview him there. Unless he lawyers up, you might be able to find out if he's in this alone."

"I second that. I don't want to give him an opportunity to think. Catch him totally off guard."

—◦◦◦—

Search warrants and an arrest warrant were signed early Wednesday. Bannister drove out to Hines's apartment. One of Gonzales's lock guys and a computer tech met him in front of the complex. Derek Barnes and Mercedes Ramirez pulled into the complex and parked near the back entrance.

Bannister didn't notify the apartment manager since Hines was still on a cruise, and they didn't yet know if he had any accomplices.

His apartment didn't have an alarm, but Hines had installed a second deadbolt. It took the lock guy only two minutes to open both locks.

Hines had more mirrors on his walls than any apartment Bannister had ever seen. There was even a full-length mirror on the back of his entry door. Ramirez had to photograph every room, and it took her extra time to make sure she wasn't standing where her reflection would be in every picture. Hines had a large David Hockney print on the wall behind his couch. It showed a man, visible from the waist up, standing in a turquoise swimming pool. With its bright blues and yellows, the print was reflected all over the apartment through the placement of the mirrors. Bannister felt like he was standing outside of a beach condo. He knew Quantico's Behavioral Science people would find Hines's narcissistic decorating interesting.

As soon as Ramirez finished filming, Bannister and the computer tech went to the den. Ramirez was assigned to search the living room, kitchen, and bathroom. Barnes took the bedroom. The entire apartment was orderly, clean, and lacked the normal clutter of magazines and stacks of CDs one usually saw.

"Ty, come in here," Barnes yelled from the bedroom a couple minutes after they'd started. He pointed to the closet at an open wicker hamper. Piled in loose stacks were bundles of hundreds. It looked like they'd located Global's money, or what remained of it.

"Mercedes, come back here and give Derek a hand in counting and logging this," Bannister said.

"Sure." Mercedes carried a half dozen large plastic evidence bags into the bedroom and joined Derek in processing the money.

"I can't believe he'd leave all this money here," Barnes said.

"I'm sure he had a plan. Just not enough time to execute it," Bannister said.

The computer tech bypassed a couple of passwords and made a copy of Hines's computer hard drive. He then packed up the PC, disks, and CDs. One of the two desk drawers contained a cell phone and a telephone voice changer. Bannister took both items.

In a faux wooden box on the closet shelf, Barnes located two men's wigs and two pairs of eyeglasses with clear, non-prescriptive lenses. The box also had two unopened packets of latex gloves. A shirt, which resembled the one in Sean O'Brien's driver's license photo, was hanging in a dry cleaner's bag and was tagged, as was a pair of white New Balance running shoes, size ten-and-a-half.

After ninety minutes, the search team was ready to leave.

"Our unofficial count of the money, by tabulating the stacks, comes to $4,947,600.00," Barnes said. "Besides the pack with the sensor, which we recovered, it looks like only fifty thousand is missing. We'll do a bill-by-bill count at the office."

"That's fine. I called the office to have a car with SWAT guys come here. When we leave, you're going to follow the SWAT car back to the office. The tech guys will be following right behind you. Take the money straight to the valuable evidence vault and log it in. You can do the count later," Bannister said.

"No problem," said Mercedes. "I guess I'll feel what it's like to be an armored truck driver but without the armored truck."

"I'll make sure she doesn't try and stop off at the mall on the way," Barnes added.

After leaving a copy of the warrant and an inventory of everything they'd seized, the tech relocked the doors and they headed back to the office.

Bannister called Adam Kush and gave him the news. After listening to him whoop and utter a few excited expletives, Bannister asked him to tell only his company president and general counsel about the money's recovery. Kush asked if Robin could be cut in; Bannister had no problem with that. But Hines wasn't yet in custody, and they weren't sure he was the only Global employee involved.

Hines's computer was a prosecutor's dream. Everything he'd done was recorded in files on his hard drive. He had separate files for setting up the alias of Sean O'Brien; for ordering castor beans to make ricin; for purchasing cloth to shield power line transmissions; and orders for the telephone voice changer and tunneling equipment. Numerous documents were printed out by the team, and Derek Barnes was tasked with checking out leads to verify Hines's activities for the past year. They still needed to find out if anyone else was involved. Hines had a passport, but his only known foreign travel had been to Vienna last year. Barnes would try and learn if Hines had any contacts.

—❧—

It was after nine o'clock when Bannister got home. He'd stopped at the supermarket to buy what he needed for Thanksgiving dinner with Robin. Tonight would be a microwave frozen dinner. But first things first. He opened the fridge and grabbed a cold bottle of Mexican beer. He'd only had a couple of pulls on it when his home phone rang.

It was Gina Williamson, Cal's ex-wife. "I hope I'm not interrupting anything," she said.

"Not at all. It's good to hear your voice."

"I wanted to talk with you. With someone that understands."

Gina starting sobbing. Bannister waited, letting her cry.

"I'm sorry. I told myself when I called you I wouldn't do this. Even though we're divorced, Cal and I still love each other. I keep telling myself he'll show up and there'll be an explanation for all this. But inside I feel something terrible has happened to him."

Bannister didn't tell her he felt the same way.

"I don't know who I can talk to. I don't even know if I can trust the people he works with. Cal's always gotten along with everyone, and he never mentioned having any enemies. But I'm not calling from my home or cell phone just in case my phones are bugged."

"Where are you right now?" Bannister asked.

"In Leesburg, at a friend's house. She invited me to spend Thanksgiving with her, and I needed to get away. Do you think there's something wrong with me?"

"No, and I'm glad you called. Cal would want you to do that. What you're going through is difficult. Have you been sleeping?"

"Not really. Not well."

Cal said you're a strong person. If you weren't, he never would have married you."

"Thank you for that. Are there any developments you can tell me about?"

"No. I wish I had some information, any information about Cal I could share with you. But I don't. I'm totally in the dark, too. How's Dawn handling all this?"

"As well as can be expected. She's in her senior year of college. Even though she acts like a free spirit sometimes, I think she's always found comfort in structure and tradition. In a way, I think she's in denial."

"Right now that may not be all that bad."

"I think if someone told me Cal had been killed on a mission, I could handle it. He used to tell me his job was a lot safer than being in law enforcement, because people didn't know what he did. Even so, we always took precautions when we were outside the country. Back here in the United States, you just don't think something like this could happen. I never realized what people go through when someone they love is missing."

"I know. This whole situation's been eating away at me, too. I keep asking myself, what am I missing? Why Cal? What should I be doing to make sense of it?"

"Exactly. It's so frustrating. It's not something you can talk to your friends about." Bannister could hear Gina taking a deep breath.

"Thanks, Ty, for being there."

"Cal would do the same. I'll let you know when I hear something, okay?"

CHAPTER 18

ARLINGTON, VIRGINIA

Stacy DiMatteo couldn't wait for Christmas. Not for the usual reasons, but because she was getting married that week. Everything she was doing was centered on December 30. She was thrilled to see the malls and shopping centers festooned with Christmas decorations, though Thanksgiving was still a week away. Several of Stacy's friends who worked with her at the National Security Agency were having a bridal shower for her on Saturday. Even though she'd recently celebrated her twenty-eighth birthday, Stacy felt as giggly as a teenager. She had a whole new life in front of her.

Stacy was part of a new breed of intelligence analysts. A generation ago, when even the name of the NSA was restricted, an analyst would never have been at a nightclub Thursday evenings enjoying salsa dancing. So she never would have met her future husband, also a doctoral candidate at Georgetown University.

Stacy was careful never to divulge to outsiders that she worked for NSA. Besides her parents and fiancé, she told no one what she did for a living. She'd worked for NSA for five years and was extremely cautious about even giving her telephone number out to anyone. So when her cell phone rang, she was surprised she didn't recognize the number on the caller ID.

"Hi, Stacy? This is John . . . John Parker, Janice's brother?"

"Oh, hello . . ." Janice Parker was one of Stacy's best friends.

"She gave me your number. She said she was going to call you to let you know I was dropping off your shower gift—she couldn't bring it herself because of her broken wrist. I drove around but couldn't find your apartment. Right now I'm down in front of your clubhouse."

"Oh, thanks. A lot of us have complained to management about not being able to see the apartment numbers in the dark. Pizza delivery guys can never find the right unit. But Janice must have forgotten to let me know you were coming. You know, even though she's talked a lot about you, I don't think we've ever met."

"I'm in a blue Chevy parked in a space for new residents. I'm wearing a Redskins baseball cap. Do you mind coming down here?"

"Give me a couple of minutes. I'll drive over."

"Okay. I'll wait."

———✺✺✺———

It was going as he'd planned. He'd backed his car into the parking space and left his parking lights on.

The SVR was the Russian Federation's equivalent of the CIA. Most people were more familiar with its former name—the KGB. SVR officers assigned to Washington, DC, were some of Russia's best intelligence operatives. One of them had developed a source inside US intelligence with access to identities, home addresses, and contact telephone numbers for over four hundred intelligence personnel, including some in a specific branch of NSA. One of those numbers was a cell phone subscribed to by Stacy DiMatteo.

DiMatteo's phone number was programmed into an ES-Pro digital data intercept device. This let the SVR officer intercept signals from her phone. The ES-Pro could record any outgoing or incoming call, and there was no way for it to be discovered. The technology had been around for years. Presumably, it was used in 1998 when the former Speaker of the House Newt Gingrich had private cell phone calls intercepted and published.

Two weeks of telephone calls for Stacy DiMatteo had been recorded and reviewed. The SVR officer got the information he needed. Janice

Parker, one of Stacy's best friends, called to tell her she'd broken her wrist riding her mountain bike. The good news was that her cast would be off before Christmas and Stacy wouldn't have to worry about her maid of honor having a cast showing in wedding party photos. Janice and Stacy also talked about Janice's older brother, John, who was still an eligible bachelor. Janice had jokingly mentioned it was too bad Stacy had never met him. She might have ended up with John instead of her fiancé.

Five minutes after she'd spoken to him on the phone, Stacy pulled her Nissan Altima into the space next to a blue Chevrolet and stepped out into the dimly lit parking lot.

"You must be John," she said, extending her hand. He detected the fresh scent of jasmine as she leaned forward.

"It's a pleasure to meet you. Janice thinks the world of you," he said. "Her present is in the trunk. Can you give me a hand with it?"

"Sure," she said as he pressed the trunk release button on her key chain. He had previously disconnected the trunk light.

"It's kind of heavy and must have shifted to the back of the trunk," he said.

"Wow, I wonder what it is. It's really nice of you to bring it over."

As Stacy peered into the trunk of the car, fifty thousand volts of electricity from a stun gun smacked into her through the down vest she was wearing. The intelligence officer simply rolled her into the trunk. From inside his jacket, he deftly removed a hypodermic needle and plunged it into her right arm. In less than two seconds, the drugs were fully injected. Her eyes were staring up at him as he slowly closed the trunk.

He opened the door to Stacy's car and noticed she hadn't bothered bringing her purse or cell phone with her. He removed her keys and locked the door. No one noticed as the Chevrolet slowly left the apartment complex.

This wasn't an intelligence mission. It was an operation for himself alone—and his motivation was revenge. In 1987, his older brother, Dimitry "Dima" Kuznetsov, was one of the Soviet Union's best helicopter pilots. On the last day of that year, Dimitry was in Afghanistan piloting their newest version of the feared Hind Mi-24 helicopter. A Stinger missile, supplied to the mujahedeen by the CIA, found its target and sent Dimitry to a fiery death.

There was no military funeral for his brother because the war in Afghanistan was a war the Politburo never admitted was being fought. Andre stood there in freezing rain at Moscow's Sheremetyevo Airport when his brother's tin coffin was unloaded. It was taken to a simple cemetery, and along with several others, quickly buried. Mothers cried and asked questions, but received no answers. Friends whispered and under their breath swore at the Communist officials. No one came forward to acknowledge Dima's sacrifice, his heroism, and his love of the Motherland. Andre swore his brother's death would not be forgotten, and that someday he would get revenge against the Americans.

Andre didn't drive directly to the large storage locker he had rented in Springfield, Virginia. Instead, he took a circuitous route, all the while employing counter surveillance techniques or "dry cleaning," as intelligence officers called it. He only pulled in when he was sure he wasn't being followed.

The diplomatic license plates for his car were stashed in his briefcase. He knew seventeen US states issued and required only one license plate for their cars. For that reason, he had stolen the front license plate from a car with Maryland tags. With luck, the owner wouldn't even know it was missing for a few days. It really didn't matter, since the tag would be on the back of his Chevrolet for only two more hours.

Rolling the window halfway down to feel the cleansing breath of the cold night air on his face, he thought about how Stacy was different from his first two victims. Unlike the others, she was a complete stranger. He'd never seen her before. But she worked for US intelligence and that was enough. She fit nicely into his developing plan.

The other female victim, Lillian Wells, was a nice person. He hadn't lied to her eight months ago when he'd driven her to this same locker. He did have something to show her, as he had promised, something that had belonged to his brother. It was the second of two fifteenth-century Russian icons by Andrei Rublev. The two icons were supposed to have been retirement insurance for Andre and his brother. No one outside of his family was aware of their existence. The icons were believed lost for centuries until Andre's great-grandfather had helped one of the Romanovs when the Bolsheviks assassinated Czar Nicholas II and his family in 1918. In gratitude for saving his life, the man had given the icons to Andre's great-grandfather. They had remained a family secret since the revolution.

While assigned to Austria, Andre had made arrangements through a Swiss lawyer for one of the icons to be sold anonymously at auction. After fees and commissions, he still had $610,000.00 in a numbered account. He dedicated the use of that money to avenge Dima's death.

He turned his mind back to his last hours with Lillian Wells. He had driven her from Starbucks to the storage facility. No other cars were on the premises. He used his key to unlock the case hardened padlock and lifted up the rolling steel door. The locker was almost empty. Cardboard boxes were stacked alongside the corrugated steel walls. Resting on top of one of the boxes was a black artist's carrying case which held the icon.

Andre led Lillian a few steps to the rear of the fifteen by twenty foot locker. He slowly removed the Rublev icon from its case. In a voice revealing little emotion, he told her of its history. Lillian expressed her admiration for the object, but Andre guessed she was feigning interest. She'd been too quiet on the drive over. Something was bothering her.

A storage locker was an awkward place to talk about art and history. It was an even more unusual place to hear someone's confession, but when he asked Lillian if she had something she wanted to tell him, she'd burst into tears.

He remembered looking into her face, a pale portrait of sorrow and fear. In between biting her lip and sniffling, she managed to tell him she was HIV positive and begged him to be tested. As he carefully replaced the icon in its case, he smiled. "I've been tested," he said.

She seemed confused, but before she could say anything, he'd asked her if she'd thought about dying.

She didn't respond. But then, she didn't need to, because Andre had already thought about her death. As she reached into her purse for a tissue, Andre calmly removed from his coat what looked like a large black cell phone. He aimed it at her. In an instant, the stun gun's darts penetrated her skin, and her slightly vibrating body thudded to the concrete floor.

One Percocet pill, combined with other depressants, could lower one's respiratory system enough to be fatal. The amount he injected into Lillian was more than enough. Within a minute, she lost consciousness. She would then lapse into a coma and, perhaps six hours later, suffer complete circulatory collapse and cardiac arrest.

Her death had been quiet and painless.

He relived every detail of that day in February. He'd driven back to Springfield Mall where he moved Lillian's car from the coffee shop to the main shopping center parking lot. Later that same night, he drove back to the locker and checked Lillian for a pulse. It was barely detectable. He stripped all clothes from her body and placed her in the trunk of his car on top of a plastic drop cloth. Her clothes, purse, and cell phone, with battery removed, went into a double-wrapped plastic trash bag. He left her wristwatch, necklace, and earrings on her body to confuse the investigators who would eventually find her. Killing Lillian didn't cause him any excitement or remorse. He knew he'd think about her again, but right now he only felt relief she would no longer be in his life.

Weeks earlier, while rehearsing one of his operational missions, he had discovered several "official vehicles only" turnarounds off Interstate 95 north of the Marine Corps base in Virginia. He had previously checked out the turnaround at mile marker 141 after making sure no vehicles were following him. It was secluded enough so a car wouldn't be seen by any vehicle traveling in either the north or southbound lanes of the highway. He had stopped his car halfway through the turnaround. He opened the trunk and carried Lillian's body, wrapped in plastic, about five yards into the brush. He dropped it to the ground and unrolled her corpse from its plastic shroud.

As he'd walked away from the body, he snagged the plastic drop cloth on thorns from a bull brier vine. After unsnarling the material, Andre retraced the short distance to his car. The ground was hard and he left no footprints. His total time at the turnaround was two minutes.

During the drive back to his locker, he'd cruised through several apartment complexes, constantly looking in his rear-view mirror to make sure he wasn't being followed. He only stopped to throw the bag with Lillian's possessions into a half-filled dumpster smelling of pungent diapers.

Andre smiled as he stared at the car trunk concealing Stacy's body.

It was a bonus not having to dispose of Stacy DiMateo's car or other property. He had prepared her body the same as the others. She, however, would be the last one he would leave at the turnaround. When he got there and opened his car door, his nose detected the cheesy smell of fermentation. If a police officer stopped there, he'd probably assume a deer had been struck and was lying somewhere nearby. Andre carried the light body of Stacy DiMateo and laid her on the ground to the right of his male victim's remains. For a few seconds, he admired the diamond engagement ring Stacy had on her finger.

CHAPTER 19

Bannister expected Robin at any time. When he had told her he wasn't cooking a turkey, she said, "Great. Surprise me." His last traditional Thanksgiving dinner had been with Erin. He and his wife had only three months together. Three holidays—Thanksgiving, Christmas, and New Year's Eve.

The first Thanksgiving after her death, Bannister had worked as a volunteer at Turner Field, helping the Hosea Williams organization feed twenty thousand needy and homeless people. It made him feel good. He wanted to be surrounded by people who cared about others and were willing to give of their time. The last three Thanksgiving mornings he'd spent with two thousand other hardy souls—running the Atlanta half-marathon. Whether dishing out food from a tent or running down Peachtree Street, he found it refreshing to connect with positive people.

Robin called from the front gate exactly at noon, and Bannister buzzed her in. He met her out front as she parked her Jeep in the turnaround. The air was warm, and the sun threw splotches of bright light on the paving stones. Bannister's eyes followed Robin as she walked around to the passenger door. She wore a white sweater over tan slacks. The sun back-lit her golden hair. Her turquoise-blue eyes and brilliant smile were captivating.

"You look great," he said as Robin posed like a waiter, holding up a glass plate covered with foil. "What's the dish?"

"Dessert. It's a gateau. I got the recipe from a friend—he's a French chef—when I was in Paris. After I oo'd and ah'd over it, he told me his secret was using Belgian chocolate."

"You made it yourself?"

"Of course. It took me three hours!" Robin pouted, and he couldn't help but notice the mauve-colored gloss on her sensuous lips.

He showed her into the great room and offered her a drink. "A lot of traditionalists have cranberries on Thanksgiving," he explained. "The closest I come is cranberry juice and vodka on the rocks."

"I'm game," Robin said.

Holding her drink, she moved to the window and looked outside at his brick patio.

He could see her reflection in the window. She looked pensive, yet poised.

"I'm grilling some filets. I also have tuna steaks, if you prefer fish."

Robin turned around. "A steak sounds great. To save you from asking, I'll take mine medium."

"I set the timer for the corn soufflé and just finished making a spinach salad. And I'm gonna make some grilled asparagus."

"Sounds scrumptious."

"Are you excited about reporting to the Academy?"

"I really am. I've tried to follow the advice you gave me a couple of months ago, about getting into shape. There have been some positives and negatives. The positive is I'm up to doing forty pushups."

"That's impressive. That should put you at the top of your class, at least as far as the female trainees are concerned. What's the negative?"

"I'm now a bra size larger," Robin said grinning.

"I'm going to leave that alone. At least I know you won't have a problem with the running."

"I'm not nervous, Ty, but I don't want to do anything stupid."

Bannister motioned for Robin to sit in one of the tufted club chairs near the French doors leading to the patio. He sat in the one opposite her.

"Don't try to be someone you're not," he said. "Just be yourself. Take an interest in your classmates. Keep in mind, about three-fourths of your class will be male, and most of them will think they're overqualified. Guys also like to talk about themselves. Ask them questions. Stroke their egos. Listen ten times more than you talk, at least the first couple of weeks."

"Sounds like you're telling me to be manipulative," Robin said, tilting her head.

"Maybe a little bit, since you're going to be surrounded by competitive people. But don't lose track of the fact that you're all part of a team. Even though you want to build rapport, there's nothing wrong with having a little edge."

"I appreciate that. What should I expect from the women in my class?" Robin placed her drink on a coaster.

"The women are mostly worried about the physical program and how they're going to act in a primarily male environment. I'd take the same approach. Get to know them. They'll be your allies. Maybe one of them will become your best friend." As soon as he said that he paused for a second, remembering Cal.

"I just want to be successful."

Robin's comment brought him back to the present. He swirled the ice cubes around in his glass.

"You will be. Don't worry. I remember a few years back, I was visiting Temple University when Bill Cosby was being interviewed. One of the journalists asked him what it takes to be successful. He had a great answer. He said, 'I don't know what it takes to be a success, but I know one of the fastest ways to be a failure is to try and please everyone.'"

Bannister said, "You'll get over six hundred hours of instruction in everything from interviewing, crime scene processing, photography, and testifying. The teachers want you to succeed. They'll let you know what's important. Make sure you take good notes."

"Sounds like college."

"Sort of, but there's more interaction. Think before asking a question in class. You know they say there's no such thing as a dumb question. They're wrong; there are dumb questions. You don't want to come across as a dumb blonde nor do you want to be labeled a smart ass. If you don't know something, you can always look it up later."

"What about outside of class? Socializing? Will I have a life there?"

"Sure. Check out the Boardroom, that's what they call the beer hall. It's upstairs next to the cafeteria. It wouldn't hurt to have a beer or two with the guys. It'll make them think you're a normal person. Just don't forget about me," he added shyly.

"That's not going to happen. We'll still see each other, right?"

"During the first two weeks they encourage you to stick around. After that you can take off on weekends."

"Good. Something I've been worrying about—I've never fired a pistol before. Do you think that'll be a problem?"

"That may be to your advantage."

"How so?"

"You won't have to unlearn bad habits. The firearms instructors are some of the best in the country. They'll teach you everything you need to know. By the time you graduate, you'll be proficient with an automatic, the shotgun, and the MP-5 machine gun."

Bannister noticed Robin had finished her drink. "Would you like another Cape Codder or a glass of wine? I'm going to have a glass of Merlot. I've also got a Pinot Grigio from a small Italian vineyard. I really think you'd like it. Your choice."

"I'll try the white, thanks."

"So you're not a purist who says you have to serve red wine with steak and white wine with seafood?"

"I say drink what you enjoy."

"Me too," he said.

After pouring each of them a glass of wine, he suggested they go outside so he could get the grill going. "Ask me some more questions about the Bureau," he said. "I'm just getting warmed up."

"Okay. Have you ever had to shoot anyone?"

"Not in the FBI. I did when I served in the Marine Corps. During the invasion of Grenada."

"I'm not trying to sound nosy, Ty, but Adam told me you were wounded during that action."

"I was shot twice, but as you can see it didn't keep me out of the FBI." He thought about the two quarter-sized scars he still carried, one on his right shoulder and the other on his right thigh. He wondered if his recent bouts of pain might be related to those old injuries.

"The job does have its dangerous moments, but it's not like being a sheriff's deputy or a police officer who's routinely dispatched to handle drunk and disorderly people, or to arrest some guy flyin' high on drugs, or restrain someone who's mentally ill. They never know what they're getting into when they respond to calls of 'shots fired,' or who they're pulling over for a traffic violation. *They're* the ones with the dangerous jobs, other than maybe night clerks at liquor stores."

Fifteen minutes later they were ready to eat. He had set two places at the table in the formal dining room, using his Grandmother Stetson's china, silver, and Waterford crystal. He lit two candles in the center of the table and pulled back a chair for Robin.

"Gosh, Ty, you didn't need to go through all this trouble just for me. I'd be just as comfortable eating at the coffee table in your family room."

"I know that. I don't get to use this finery all that much, and after all, it is a special holiday."

The meal was first-rate. They both enjoyed the food and felt totally relaxed.

The bottle of Merlot was resting on a wine pedestal in front of Ty's plate. "Would you mind moving that bottle of wine so I don't have to curve my head to see you?" Robin asked.

"Sorry. Hey, I just thought of that country western song where the singer says I'd rather have a bottle in front of me than a frontal lobotomy."

Robin laughed and he did, too. They talked about all kinds of unimportant things. Like where they shopped for groceries, where they'd like to take a vacation, who were their favorite actors and actresses, and other topics young couples might smile about on a first date. He was grateful for everything he had and happy to share the day with someone with whom he felt so comfortable.

After dinner they went for a walk down Valley Road, with its tree-shaded walkway curving along a quiet stream. They returned to the house for coffee and her chocolate cake, which was so rich and smooth its flavor lingered after each bite. The time went by too quickly.

Finally Bannister walked her out to her Jeep.

"Ty, I want you to know I really appreciated you sharing this day with me." She turned to face him, holding her purse, and their eyes met. She leaned into him, and he pulled her close. Their lips met in a long, slow kiss. Just one.

They both knew the moment wasn't an ending, but a beginning.

CHAPTER 20

T he cruise ship, *Sunset Princess,* had docked an hour earlier and Terry Hines was back on US soil. For the third Sunday in a row, Bannister was at his desk. The FBI was not an eight-to-five job. He had seen Witt's car in the parking lot when he walked into the office, but he doubted Witt was there because of the Global Waters case. More likely he was schmoozing the two headquarters advance team agents who were getting things ready for the thirty inspectors flying in tomorrow.

Witt phoned him. "Am I interrupting you?"

"No, I'm upstairs at my desk," Bannister said.

"I didn't know you were in the office. Is everything all set for the arrest tonight?"

"Everything's under control. The Fort Lauderdale agents are following Hines right now. They'll tail him to the airport, watch him board his flight, and call us as soon as the plane lifts off."

"Aren't they putting an agent on board?"

"No, I didn't think it was necessary. It's a direct flight, and the weather for both Florida and Atlanta is clear with no chance of storms. There shouldn't be any diversion. I'm taking Mercedes Ramirez with me for Hines's arrest and interview."

"I'd feel better if you took one of the more experienced men with you, instead of a female rookie," Witt said.

"I've got confidence in Ramirez. She's done a helluva job already and deserves to be in on the arrest. Besides, how does an agent gain experience except by actually doing the work?"

"I don't want any screw-ups."

Bannister extended his arm, holding his cell phone straight out, thinking for a second how nice it would be to throttle Dim Witt. He put the phone back to his ear. "You're not planning to be at the airport, are you?"

"No. I'd like to, but I promised the headquarters guys I'd go out to dinner with them. You know, first impressions are important. Besides, I already spent two hours at Hartsfield earlier today when I picked them up." Even if Witt's priorities were ass-backwards, at least he was consistent.

"You're welcome to be there, Gary," Bannister lied. "If things work out right, we'll be able to interview Hines before slapping the cuffs on him. I'll make sure you and the boss are posted on all developments."

"Do you think I ought to get started on a press release?"

"I'd hold off on that. We don't have Hines in hand yet. Besides, there are still some unanswered questions. We're not sure he's in this alone or if there's more ricin out there."

"Yeah, I guess you're right. Who else will be at the airport?"

"I've got two task force agents who'll seize his checked baggage and bring it back to the office. I'll have another team at the gates as additional backup. If Hines parked a car at the airport, they'll take care of it. Ramirez and I will handle the rest. We'll take him to Fulton County Jail for booking."

"Okay. I'll wait until tomorrow morning to work on a press statement. We'll talk later."

Terry Hines arrived on the Delta flight from Ft. Lauderdale on time. Bannister and Mercedes had photos of Hines, including a recent copy of a Global Waters corporate identification badge. One of the Florida agents had called ahead, describing the clothes Hines was wearing.

Bannister walked up to him as soon as he came through the plane's jet way.

"Terry, I'm Special Agent Ty Bannister with the FBI. This is Special Agent Mercedes Ramirez. Adam Kush told us you'd be coming back to Atlanta on this flight. We need your help with a case."

"What case?" he asked, looking at Mercedes, then back at Bannister.

"It's important. We've informed the airlines you'd be delayed. Your luggage will be held for you."

"What's this all about? Does this have anything to do with the extortion?"

"I'd feel more comfortable talking in an office. I reserved us a room in the international terminal. Why don't we catch the tram?" Bannister smiled, trying to relax him.

"Sure," Hines said.

"So, Adam said you went to the Bahamas. Looks like you got some good rays," Bannister said cheerfully, careful not to ask Hines any questions.

"Yeah, the weather was great. I can't believe how hot the sun is down there, even at this time of the year. I guess the only people sporting tans in November are skiers and people coming back from cruises, like me." He grinned at Mercedes.

To add an air of informality, Mercedes said, "I've never been on a cruise. I think if I had a chance to visit the Bahamas, I'd buy some jewelry."

As they stepped onto the escalator, Mercedes commented to Hines, "I like your cologne."

"Thanks, it's Obsession."

Touché, Candace, Bannister thought.

At the bottom of the escalator, a crowd of tired-looking passengers waited for the tram to the main terminal and baggage claim.

They walked a few steps to the other platform where the door opened to an empty train going in the opposite direction to the international concourse. A few minutes later they were outside an unmarked immigration office. One of the task force agents was standing near the office, pretending to be looking at a magazine. Bannister signaled him with a quick nod.

The room was the basic four-wall cube painted a light blue, furnished with a gray, metal table, three standard desk chairs, and a small trash can. On a shelf along one wall, there was a fingerprint kit. On the ceiling was a small circular dome next to the light. It looked like a maroon-colored eye. It was actually a surveillance camera.

"Now can you tell me why I'm here?" Hines asked. He set a black leather carryall bag on the corner of the desk.

"You've seen lots of cop shows where they read subjects their rights, haven't you?" Bannister asked.

"Yeah, sure."

"Well, as I said, this is a sensitive matter. I'm going to read you your advice of rights before we even start talking. This is a formality, and I'd like to get it out of the way. I do it with everyone in this type of situation. You don't have any problem with that, do you?"

"No," Hines said, clenching his jaw and crossing his arms.

Bannister handed him a ballpoint pen and an Advice of Rights form. Hines studied the form as he leaned forward from the chair in front of the desk. Bannister and Mercedes just watched him, his forehead furrowed and his eyebrows arched as he stared at the paper. He picked up the form and held it in front of him, leaning backward in the chair, fidgeting, and crossing his wiry legs. He ran his left hand through his hair several times.

Finally, Hines signed the form and Mercedes witnessed his signature.

"So, you going to tell me why we're sitting here?" Hines asked.

"It's about the five million dollars extorted from Global Waters," Bannister said, looking him straight in the eye.

"You should know I went on vacation a day before the payoff was supposed to be made." Hines gave a smart-ass grin. "I haven't been in touch with the office, so I'm completely in the dark about what's happened."

"Aren't you Global's international business rep?"

"That's right, but I have a co-worker who was supposed to cover everything while I was gone."

"And did he?"

"How do I know?" Hines put both of his hands in the air like he was going to catch a giant beach ball.

"Did you call anyone at Global, or send any e-mails while you were on vacation?"

"No. I haven't had a real vacation in a long time, and I wanted to totally forget about work for a week. You can't blame a guy for that, can you?"

Bannister ignored his comment. "Do you know what happened?"

"No, as I said earlier, I haven't had any contact with Global, and I didn't read any newspapers or watch any TV the entire time I was gone. It was total relaxation." Hines's voice was growing louder and more defiant.

"Aren't you the least bit curious about what went down?" Bannister asked, moving his chair closer to the desk.

"I'm assuming one of two things—either you caught the bad guy and the case is solved, or you didn't catch him and think maybe I can help."

"What I know is that your vacation time started after close of business on a Wednesday. The five million dollar payoff took place on Thursday. On Friday you boarded the *Sunset Princess* at Fort Lauderdale for a nine-day cruise. Am I right so far?"

"So far."

"Who has access to your apartment?"

"Nobody. Just me. What's my apartment got to do with anything?" Hines's voice rose again.

"How do you explain this?" Bannister asked, sliding an eight-by-ten photo across the table. It was a close-up of the hamper in Hines's closet showing Global's millions.

Hines lowered his head, and his mouth hung open. He stared at the photo, his shoulders sagging. Without picking his head back up he said, "I'm going to be sick."

"Here," Bannister said, quickly turning and picking up the trash can. He passed it across the desk to Hines. Hines grabbed it with both hands and threw up into the can. Some of the vomit splashed off the back side. Neither Mercedes nor Bannister said anything. She put her notebook down on the desk and glanced at her shoes, which now had yellow splotches on both toes. Bannister stood up and grabbed a couple of paper towels from the fingerprint shelf and handed them to Hines. Mercedes took one to clean her shoes.

"Wipe your face," Bannister said. Hines looked stunned.

"We have the money except for what you took with you on the trip. We've searched your apartment and examined your computer. Please don't insult our intelligence by telling us you weren't involved." Hines stared at Bannister. His smirk had been replaced with a blank look, like someone who couldn't remember where he'd parked his car.

"Terry, you're in a position now where you can help yourself. We want to know who else was involved."

Bannister had gone over the details of this case a hundred times in the last week. It was possible Hines had carried out the entire scheme himself, but Bannister wasn't sure. No one spoke for a minute. Bannister and Mercedes continued to stare at him, trying not to let the smell of the vomit in the warm closed room distract them.

"Terry, this might be your last chance to give us your side of the story."

Hines remained silent, his eyes fixed on a blank wall.

Sensing he was now at his low point, Bannister said, "This whole operation was pretty damned impressive. Our experts think it took the work of at least three or four intelligent people to pull it off." He kept his eyes on Hines, trying to read his body language. Hines went through the motion of picking imaginary lint off his jacket, one indicator of a deceptive person.

After two minutes, which seemed like an hour, Hines grinned and said in a calm voice, "I want to speak to a lawyer. I'm not saying anything else to you assholes."

Mercedes bristled, but remained silent.

Hines looked at Bannister, then Mercedes, then back again to Bannister. "I'm sorry about that," he said, changing his tone and nodding his head in the direction of the trash can. "I need to wash my face."

"In a minute," Bannister said.

"If my lawyer says to talk to you, what would it get me?" Hines asked.

"That's not our decision. What we will do is let the United States Attorney know you cooperated with us. He'll have to take that into consideration."

"Well, I'm not saying anything more." Hines glared at both of his interrogators.

Whether someone was a master criminal, an opportunist, or a fugitive, they shared something in common. They refused to think about being caught. When they *were* caught, they responded in different ways. Hines's entire world had just crashed in on him. He'd fancied himself a successful thief returning from a cruise. A millionaire with the world for the taking. Now the only taking was being done by the FBI.

Bannister opened the door and set the trash can outside next to the concourse wall. He asked the task force agent to bring them three Cokes, and told him to make sure the airport sent someone over to clean the room as soon as they left. When the agent returned with the sodas, Bannister asked Mercedes to include in the log that they'd given Hines a soft drink.

Bannister told Hines, "Terry, you're under arrest for extortion and violation of the Patriot Act. We're taking you downtown. You'll be processed at Fulton County. We'll return in the morning when you'll have an initial appearance before a magistrate."

"What about a lawyer?"

"They'll assign you a public defender, or you can call your own lawyer when you get there. Now stand up and press your chest into the wall with your hands straight out to the sides."

While Mercedes finished writing up the interview log, Bannister handcuffed Hines's hands behind his back and searched him. Mercedes put her paperwork away, then searched Hines's leather carryall, removing the Atlanta Braves warm-up jacket the Florida agent said Hines had been wearing. As they prepared to leave the office, Bannister gave the task force agent the keys to Hines's car. It was probably in a long-term parking lot and would have to be located and towed to the FBI's impound lot. Mercedes draped the Braves jacket over Hines's shoulders as he was escorted through the airport. They walked directly out the exit, near the Marta subway, where the Bureau car was parked in a reserved spot.

Forty minutes later, Hines was in a clean orange jumpsuit with plenty of time to think about his future.

Bannister called Witt after they got back to the car.

"How'd it go?" He heard Witt's voice against the sound of glasses clinking in the background.

"He lawyered up," Bannister said. "We arrested him and booked him into Fulton County for the night. A magistrate's hearing is scheduled for ten tomorrow. How's it going with the inspection guys?"

"Fine. We're at Bones over on Piedmont. Fantastic meal. Did you know they're rated as one of the top ten steak restaurants in the United States?"

"No, I didn't." Bannister wasn't in the mood to listen to Witt's bullshit. "Well, enjoy your cigars. We need to get going."

"Good work, Ty. I told my colleagues we'd probably have a significant arrest tonight, and we'd give them details tomorrow. I'll call the boss at home. He'll appreciate the news."

After hanging up, Bannister asked Mercedes, "Guess what Witt was doing while Hines was puking on your shoes?"

"No clue."

"Kissing butt with the inspection team and enjoying a steak dinner at Bones."

"That's not as good as feeling an adrenaline rush working a good case," she said, grinning.

"I like your attitude, Mercedes. I'm thinking we'll go out for a really good meal when this case is over. How's pizza and beer sound?"

"Fantastic. If you're buying, it'll be even better."

CHAPTER 21

Virginia state trooper Jake Roberts had been with the Virginia State Police for eighteen months and had a good record. He also believed in premonitions. He didn't want people to think he was crazy, so he didn't share his hunches with anyone, especially fellow troopers. At the start of his graveyard shift that night, he suddenly felt certain something unusual was about to happen.

Roberts glanced at the clock on the dash of his patrol car. It was 3:01 a.m. There was a sliver of moon and no cloud cover. Tonight was particularly black. Since Thanksgiving, the temperature hadn't risen above freezing. Roberts liked it when he stepped out of the car and could see his breath. It left him feeling invigorated. He was heading north on I-95 to the patrol's post near the Potomac Mills Outlet Mall. He was halfway through his shift, and nothing out of the ordinary had happened. He wanted to check in at the post, replenish his supply of road flares, and make an urgent "head call."

The speed limit for most of the interstate section he patrolled was seventy miles per hour. As his own general rule, he didn't pull anyone over doing under ninety unless there was some other reason to stop them. Normally there was no shortage of cars and eighteen-wheelers screaming down the east coast's main north-south artery. Any officer could spend the entire shift writing speeding tickets. He'd just passed mile marker 148 when the post's dispatcher came to life.

"Station to one-one-seven."

"One-one-seven. Go ahead," Roberts said, recognizing his call sign.

"A citizen just called 9-1-1 saying she saw an SUV run off the southbound lanes of I-95 and flip over. When the operator asked for her location, the witness said she'd just seen mile marker 142, and the accident happened maybe a mile ahead of that."

"Ten-four," Roberts said. "I'm responding. I'll be on location in three minutes. Make a standby call to the paramedics."

Roberts flipped on his lights, snatched his gray Smokey the Bear hat from the passenger seat, and floored the Crown Vic. He loved the deep, throaty growl as the 429-cubic inch engine equipped with a "police package" roared to life. As he sailed up I-95, he was hoping the accident site was south of an "official vehicles only" turn-out in the median after mile marker 141.

Traffic was light, and the road conditions excellent. He was willing to bet whoever was driving had done one of three things: hit a deer, lost control after drinking too much, or fell asleep at the wheel.

Roberts braked as his lights reflected off mile marker 141. He saw the gravel access road and eased the patrol car into a U-turn back into the fast lane of I-95. Forty yards ahead, his lights spotted an upside-down vehicle facing southward in the median. Its red tail lights were still glowing.

Roberts hit his spotlight, illuminating the vehicle, a black Jeep Cherokee. He called Dispatch, telling them he was approaching the vehicle on foot. He grabbed a large, black flashlight from its holder under his seat and jogged across the slick grass and frozen churned-up sod, trying not to slip. When he got to the Jeep, he shined his light into both the front and rear seats. He saw no occupants. Assuming one or more persons may have been thrown free before the Jeep had reached its final resting place, he walked back along the median and spotted a prone figure lying in a depression about ten feet from the highway.

Out of habit, Roberts yelled, "Police officer. Can you hear me?" The only sound was a tractor trailer roaring past. A white male was lying on his stomach, his head turned at an awkward angle from his torso. As Roberts knelt down to feel for a pulse at the man's carotid, he already knew what he'd detect. Nothing. No pulse. Unofficially, the man was dead. Officially, pronunciation of death was up to the medical examiner.

It looked like the victim had broken his neck. The man's head had one long laceration near the hairline, and the left side of his face was abraded. Roberts didn't smell alcohol. The victim appeared to be in his early twenties. He was wearing a dark blue sweatshirt, blue jeans, and one white Nike tennis shoe. The other shoe was missing. Roberts patted the victim's rear pockets to see if he had a wallet on him but found nothing. He glanced around but didn't see the other shoe. It could be anywhere.

Using his shoulder-mounted radio, Roberts called Dispatch. "We have a possible ten-fifty foxtrot (vehicle accident with fatality)," he said. "Send an ambulance. I only found one person, who was ejected from the vehicle. I couldn't detect a pulse and believe he's dead. Call the Medical Examiner and send two backup units for traffic and crime scene. I'm going to look for passengers and mark off the area."

"Ten-four, one-one-seven," the dispatcher said.

"Two other things. Make sure one of the backup units has enough flares. And call E-Z Towing in Stafford and ask them to send a wrecker."

Roberts walked back to the Jeep and looked for signs it had skidded or braked but saw none. There was no vehicle debris on the road, which was common when a deer had been hit. As he crouched alongside the blown-out driver's door, he reached upward and turned off the ignition. He could smell oil and brake fluid, which had splashed on the hot manifold. He didn't think a fire truck was needed, but he knew one was responding to flush a possible fuel spill.

Roberts went to his unit, popped the trunk, and grabbed his last four flares. He heard radio traffic from two responding units. He walked back along the shoulder until he saw the victim's body, ignited the first flare, and placed it on the road. He then continued north in the grass median, lit the other flares and placed them in the fast lane of the interstate about fifty feet apart. As the last flare spewed its flame and pink smoke, two cruisers arrived.

Unit seventy-nine took the rear position for traffic control and began setting out more flares and cones. Unit thirteen, driven by Corporal Dwayne Higgins, pulled in at an angle behind Robert's car.

Roberts returned to the crash to do a quick inspection of the Jeep. There were no beer cans, bottles, or any other evidence the driver had been drinking. He didn't know the young man's identification. He assumed the driver's wallet was somewhere inside the vehicle but decided to wait for the wrecker. He figured if he reached in and opened the console, he'd have a shower of CDs and other items falling out. Roberts called in the Jeep's Florida license plate and vehicle identification numbers to Dispatch to get the registration and check for any warrants.

Corporal Higgins walked up to Roberts. Higgins had five years seniority on Roberts. He also carried twenty pounds more, not from equipment but from his midsection pushing against his Sam Browne belt.

"So, how do you read it?"

"My guess is this guy nodded off and lost control. It only takes a second at eighty miles per hour. It looks like he hit the berm head first when he was thrown out, snapped his neck."

"Looks that way," Higgins agreed. "Chalk up one more stat for those who couldn't be bothered with a seat belt."

"Yeah, it's a shame," Roberts said. He had just noticed the shield-shaped orange and blue UVA parking decal on the rear window of the Jeep. The driver was probably a student heading back to the University of Virginia in Charlottesville.

"Well, we're going to be here for a while," Higgins said, tapping a Marlboro out of his pack. "At least this wreck's in the southbound lane. Two more hours and the northbound's going to be a crawling parking lot to DC."

Dispatch called with the Jeep's registration and advised there were no wants or warrants.

"As soon as we get an ID, I'll phone it in," Roberts said to Higgins.

"I'll take pictures and measurements before the wrecker uprights the Jeep."

The flashing yellow lights of an approaching tow truck reflected off the pine trees.

"Did you have the car-cam running?" Higgins asked.

"Yeah. It's recorded."

"Hey guys," said the E-Z Towing operator as he oozed his enormous body down from his rig. He wore overalls and carried a 7-11 Big Gulp in one hand and was shoving the last of a sausage biscuit into his mouth with the other. He mumbled with his mouth full, "Stafford Fire and Rescue is behind me with a truck and ambulance. You want me to right this thing?"

"As soon as I finish a few measurements you can put it on all fours," Higgins said.

"Dwayne, if you've got things under control for a couple of minutes, I've really got to drain the lizard," Roberts said.

"Go ahead. I think we're good here." Higgins gave instructions to the E-Z tow operator as Roberts, using the beam from his flashlight, walked back to the gravel turn-around. He saw an opening in the brush and parted some small branches and briars, walking a few paces into the woods where he could take a piss. The last thing he wanted was a motorist observing his activity and reporting him. However, this call of nature couldn't wait. Roberts tucked the flashlight under his left arm. The odor from a dead animal hung in the air. He reached down to the zipper on his trousers. What his flashlight suddenly illuminated made him freeze.

"Sonofabitch," Roberts said aloud. "Sonofabitch," he repeated.

His flashlight was shining on a nude female body about a yard beyond where he was standing. He had almost pissed on her.

He grabbed his radio. "One-three from one-one-seven," he called to Higgins.

"One-one-seven, go ahead," Higgins said.

"Step back here to the gravel turnout. You need to see this."

"Ten-four."

"Follow me," Roberts said, retracing his steps into the brush when Higgins appeared. He pointed his light down to the ground for Higgins to see what he'd discovered.

"Sonofabitch," Higgins said, looking at the marble-like female body lying on the ground.

"That's exactly what I said."

"Damn it. We've definitely got us a crime scene here that's got to be secured. And I know one other thing," Higgins said.

"What's that?"

"For sure, that one's officially dead."

"I need to call the Lieutenant. How about getting some tape and roping off the area until the M.E. gets here?" Roberts said. He knew Higgins was the ranking trooper and would be in his right to give the orders.

"It's your call. You were the first responder," Higgins said. "I think we should keep outsiders in the dark about this. I'll pull the M.E. aside when he gets here and tell him he's got a two-for-one call. When you talk to the Lieutenant, ask him to get the Crime Lab team out here."

"Will do."

Roberts walked back to his patrol car. He thought about telling Higgins he'd had strong vibes that something weird was going to happen on this shift. But he only thought about it for a second before calling the Lieutenant.

CHAPTER 22

It was Thursday of week one of the office inspection. Bannister was sitting in Stu Peterson's office. A rotund figure occupied Stu's chair. He was a headquarters inspector conducting individual interviews with the task force agents.

"Stu said you were a .400 hitter," the inspector said. "From a review of your cases and statistics, I'd say he was right."

"Thanks, but I try not to lose track of the fact that an FBI investigation is always a team effort."

"Absolutely. Agents like you make all of us look good. That bioterrorism case definitely grabbed some headlines, and believe me, headquarters was glad to know a threat was neutralized."

"Sometimes you can be good or lucky," Bannister said.

"Your ASAC considers you lucky. He said he'd thought about moving in right away when you guys lost the signal from the money bag but held off because he had confidence in your plan," the inspector said.

What is he talking about? Bannister wondered. He was the one who had wanted to move in right away. It was Witt who'd ordered them to stand down for four hours while Hines crawled through the tunnel and slipped away with the money. But he wasn't about to explain that to the inspector.

"We're done. I've got all I need," the inspector said finally. "Unless you have any questions."

"I don't."

Let it go, Bannister thought. *Pick your battles. This wasn't one of them.* The inspectors had to talk with all the agents. At least his interview was over, all five minutes of it. He got up to leave.

Before he walked out the doorway, the inspector said, "If you're wondering why I'm not spending more time with you, it's because you passed my thump and flutter test."

"Come again?"

"I take an agent's cases and drop them to the floor. If they make a "thump," I know he's one of the worker bees. If they flutter softly when they land, the agent's a drone. I'll spend a long time going over every case with a drone." He laughed, and his whole body jiggled up and down.

Bannister thought about some advice Derek Barnes had volunteered to everyone before the inspectors arrived. Barnes had said, "Stay out of the office unless you absolutely need to be there. If you hear an inspector saying, 'We're just here to help,' run to the nearest exit." Bannister was stewing over what Witt had told the inspector and decided he'd go cover some leads for awhile and get some fresh air. Before he got out the door, Doug Gordon called.

"Ty, before you say anything, I've got a question. Do you know what kind of watch your friend, Cal Williamson, wears?"

"A Rolex Submariner. Why?"

There was a pause at the other end.

"We might have some bad news. I say might. Three bodies were discovered this morning by a Virginia State trooper."

"Three bodies?" Bannister repeated. He turned around and headed back to his office.

"Everything's preliminary right now. We don't have a positive ID on any of them. Here's what we know. Early this morning a trooper responded to a traffic fatality on I-95 South, not too far from the Marine Base and the FBI Academy. The trooper spotted a female's body in the brush. He called it in."

"What about Cal?" Bannister asked.

"Stay with me a minute. The paramedics and troopers waited for the medical examiner to arrive. He pronounced the accident victim dead, and then the troopers took the M.E. into the brush to show him where the female's body was lying. The M.E. had a field spotlight with him. He discovered the remains of two other victims right near the unidentified female. They're working the crime scene now."

"So why'd you ask about Cal's watch?"

"The remains of the victims still had their jewelry on. One had a Vacheron Rotina. That's a woman's watch. A man's Rolex was still fastened around the wrist bones of the other one. "

"So, what are you telling me, Doug? They found one female's body and the possible remains of a second female, and a male?"

"That's right."

"Were the victims killed there, or did the trooper stumble on a dump site?"

"It looks like they were dumped there. And they weren't killed at the same time. The M.E. said the remains with the woman's watch may have been there a year. The male's remains maybe a few months. He fits the time frame when your friend disappeared."

"What about the other female body?" Bannister asked.

"She's intact. The temperature's been below freezing the past two weeks. Her prints were sent digitally to our identification division in West Virginia. We should know who she is any minute now," Gordon said.

"What else can you tell me?"

"The female they took the prints off had a diamond engagement ring on her hand. Nothing else."

"And the other two bodies had watches? What were they wearing?"

"Nothing. There was no clothing or shoes on any of them."

"Any signs how they were killed?"

"None."

"What do you make of there being no clothes but the killer leaves identifiable jewelry on each body?" Bannister asked.

"I don't know. This is a new one for me. It doesn't look like theft was a motive. Whoever did this wasn't concerned with the bodies being identified once they were found." Bannister heard Gordon take a deep breath.

"Where are you now?"

"I'm at the Academy. We're using one of the offices in the Violent Crime Analysis Unit. One other thing, Ty. We're trying to keep a lid on this as long as possible. We don't want the press clamoring all over the place. You're the only person outside our team I've called."

"Yeah, it could turn into a giant grab ass like the DC sniper case."

"There are a couple of reporters sniffing around because they know something's up. A news chopper was in the air earlier and showed the kid's jeep. The skycam guy was speculating something else was going on because of all the activity at the turnaround."

"Hopefully the bodies will be identified before the press makes a serial killer deduction."

"Let me sound you out on something. Would you be interested in a temporary assignment to our squad? The boss wants to add three more counterintelligence agents to our flyaway squad—we're the ones who have to be ready to fly out of the country with two hours notice to handle espionage cases. In addition to investigating your friend's disappearance, we've got a couple of spy cases, which are burning manpower like crazy. We could definitely use someone with your background for a couple of months. What do you think?"

"If Cal's one of the victims, I'll do it in a heartbeat."

"I'll be straight with you. My gut tells me the John Doe's your missing friend. I hope I'm wrong. But, if that's the case, I'm sorry."

"The day you interviewed me, I prepared myself for the worst. Call me when you get an ID."

"You got it," Gordon said.

Bannister grabbed his notebook and left the office. He had to stop at a trucking company to get some documents and conduct an interview for one of his cases. He knew the best way to block out bad news was to concentrate on the job at hand. Three hours later as he was pulling into the FBI parking lot, Gordon called back. Bannister turned off the ignition and sat in the car.

"What'd you find out?"

"I'm sorry. The male victim is your friend."

"Ah, jeez." Bannister slumped back in his seat. "How sure are you?"

"One hundred percent. Our lab made a positive DNA match. Before we even got the DNA results, we checked the serial number of the watch with the Rolex Company. It maintains records whenever an authorized dealer works on one of their watches. The watch on the body had numbers on the watch face retouched four years ago in Vienna, Austria. The listed owner was Cal Williamson. You okay?"

"Yeah. It'll probably hit me later. Right now, can you grease the skids to get me assigned up there?"

"I already did. I figured you'd want to be a part of the team, so before I called you, I asked our Assistant Director if he'd put a call in to SAC Brennan. Our boss did ask if we had eliminated you from any involvement. I want you to know I'm not holding anything back. After we left Atlanta, we checked you out for the weekend Williamson disappeared. You got a clean bill. It's not that anyone really doubted your story. That's just the way we work."

"I would have done the same thing if the roles were reversed."

"The Agency's going to handle notifying his family and ex-wife in the next couple of hours. Let me know when you plan to head up here."

"Will do. Thanks."

—⋘∽∾∾∽⋙—

Later that afternoon, Brennan called Bannister to let him know his temporary assignment to DC was approved, effective immediately. Bannister made a few calls. He let his housekeeper, Amelia, know he was leaving. He let Doug Gordon know he'd be arriving late Friday, and they agreed to meet at the Academy offices on Saturday.

Bannister phoned Robin.

"I was just about to call you," she said. "Washington called and asked if I'd be willing to report to the Academy in ten days rather than in January. I told them yes. Did I make a mistake?"

"Absolutely not. Once you're there it takes Murphy's law out of the equation."

"I talked to Adam, and he said to go for it. I feel bad about the short notice, though. I guess you'll have to pay off your dinner bet in DC."

"Yeah."

"Ty, what's wrong?"

Bannister took a deep breath, then told her about Cal.

CHAPTER 23

I t had been two years since Bannister had seen Washington, DC. Even though his temporary assignment could last sixty days, he only packed two suitcases. Normally the drive from Atlanta was fast and boring—Route 20 to I-95 north and follow your hood ornament. Leaving at 3:00 p.m., he hoped to be in Fredericksburg in nine hours. He had reservations for three nights at a bed and breakfast in the historic downtown section.

In deference to the discovery of his friend's remains, he decided to listen to some blues. He put in the CD *Worrying You Off My Mind* by Big Bill Broonzy, a classic Chicago blues artist of the Thirties. The Thirties was that era before freeways were built, when every gas station had an attendant to pump your gas, check your oil, and clean your windshield. As Bannister glanced off to the right of the highway and saw the first billboard advertising "Only 99 miles to South of the Border," his phone rang. It was Gina Williamson.

"Gina, I'm so sorry about Cal."

"I know. An Agency representative and one of your guys, Special Agent Gordon, came to the office a couple of hours ago to tell me. Ever since Cal went missing I told myself to prepare for the worst, but inside I held out hope he'd show up somewhere and there'd be an explanation." Bannister heard her sigh.

"What did they tell you?"

"Agent Gordon said Cal's body was found near the interstate in Stafford, Virginia. He told me they found two other bodies."

"Anything else?" he asked.

"Yes. He gave me a telephone number and said if anyone asked about Cal to tell them to call that number. He said there's going to be a lot of news interest, and the less said, the better."

"He's the case agent working Cal's disappearance. You can trust him. I'm meeting him tomorrow."

"Are you coming here?" Gina asked.

"I'm on the road now. I'd like to see you later tomorrow if that's okay."

"Oh, yes. Please. I need to talk to someone who can help me make sense of all this."

"Does Dawn know?"

"Yes. I called her from my office. This may sound strange, but she and I talked about this a week ago. I mean . . . we went over the 'what ifs.' We both started crying at the same time."

"Sometimes you just need to let it out," Bannister said.

"We did. Then we had a long talk about our lives together and what Cal meant to her as a father, and what he meant to me as a husband. We let our hair down and the words gushed out." Gina stopped talking. Bannister waited.

"Cal was always saying you need to have contingency plans. I can still hear him saying 'good planning reduces stress.' I can't believe he's dead."

"I understand."

"Dawn's in Hartford with Cal's parents. I'm picking them up at the airport on Sunday. Cal's parents are devastated. He was their only child."

"It has to be tough. No parent wants to outlive his own kids."

"Did I tell you the CIA Director called me?"

"No."

"Agent Gordon and the other guy were still in my office. The

Director was sensitive and seemed sincere. He offered to help with funeral arrangements and said he's sending his protocol officer to the house tomorrow morning with a check for twenty thousand. Something about Cal listing me on a line of duty death form."

"The Agency takes care of its own. I'm glad their Director called." As Bannister thought of what else to say to Gina, he had to tap his brakes as a pickup passed and cut back too quickly in front of him.

"There are so many people to call. I'll have my phone with me tomorrow, and I do want to talk to you. Promise me you'll call," Gina said.

After hanging up, Bannister thought about how a memorial service for Cal would be different. Not because Bannister hadn't been to a friend's funeral in many years, but when you knew someone had died in an accident or from natural causes, there was a sense of normalcy to everything. People could accept what had happened. When you realized the person you were talking about was murdered and the killer or killers were still out there, it was different. He would be looking at the people who attended, trying to figure out who didn't fit. Asking himself whether the killer was one of the mourners.

Bannister continued to listen to the blues greats. *Tell-it-like-it-is* lyrics by Mississippi John Hurt, Robert Johnson, and John Lee Hooker helped the time and miles fly by. Finally he was pulling into the white gravel drive of the Samuel Hayes Inn, a four-star bed and breakfast built fifty years before the Civil War. It was dark and quiet when he parked his SUV in a guest parking space. He carried his black leather overnight bag down a lighted brick pathway curving around to the inn's main entrance. He set his bag down on the step and rang the buzzer. About a minute later, a man appeared behind the leaded glass front door, balancing a brandy snifter in his right hand and turning the door latch with his left.

"Please come in and watch your step." The man switched the snifter to his left hand and extended his right. "I'm Bradford Alden—owner. Welcome to our inn. You must be Tyler Bannister," he said. Alden's voice was smooth with clipped diction. He sounded British. As he turned, he walked toward the front desk with military precision. "Of our six guests for the night, you're the only one who hasn't checked in." Thin, perhaps six-two, but with an extremely firm handshake, Alden looked like an innkeeper. He had on light gray flannel slacks and a long-sleeved white shirt with a dark-gray sweater vest. High-arched black eyebrows pointed toward his full head of black hair. His inch-thick speckled gray beard was neatly trimmed. Thick black-framed glasses completed the look.

"After you're checked in, feel free to stop in the library and have a glass of brandy. Breakfast is served from seven to nine in the dining room."

Bannister's room had a queen-sized bed covered with a heavy burgundy bedspread and a half-dozen striped pillows. He preferred a historical inn to a hotel chain with cookie cutter rooms, but he could have done without the lace canopy. Opposite the bed was a gas fireplace with a cream-colored marble mantle. The fire glowed behind a glass screen. The ten-foot walls were dark blue with white trim. Directly over the fireplace mantel hung a large gold-framed portrait of a young woman standing with an open book in her hands. Bannister could almost feel the light evening breeze softly blowing her long hair over her shoulders as she gazed off into the distance. The painter had captured a mystical, almost sensual look. He thought of Erin. And he thought of Robin. Both women would have loved this room.

The persimmon-colored floor, which had a scent of fresh wax, was covered by a Persian carpet. He went into the bathroom to splash some cold water on his face, and found a large, white pedestal sink beside an elaborate-matching white tub with gold claw feet.

After unpacking, he took the stairs down from the second floor to the library. There was no sign of Mr. Alden. A bottle of Remy Martin cognac stood on a tray along with a half dozen snifter glasses. He poured about an inch into one and took it back to his room. A comfortable arm chair and ottoman near the fireplace beckoned him. Before collapsing into it, he turned on the small portrait light above the painting, turned off the other lights, and adjusted the fireplace to its lowest setting. Soft flickering hues of yellow and orange flames danced upward, drawing his eyes to the young woman in the picture. He held his glass in front of him and stared at the slow swirling amber liquid before tasting its warmth as it glided down his throat. It'd been a long day. Tomorrow the work would start.

———

After badging his way past Marine guards at the Quantico entrance and FBI police at the Academy's checkpoint, Bannister drove a half mile down Hoover Road and found a parking spot opposite the Jefferson Building. Doug Gordon had left his name with the receptionist, who issued him a temporary badge. He proceeded to a conference room not many people knew about, located above the back of the main auditorium. He had attended an undercover conference there once.

He walked down the aisle through the empty auditorium and past the stage. As he climbed the back stairs, he heard voices. Doug Gordon and Steve Quattrone of the Washington Field Office were at the entrance to the oak-paneled room, talking to a woman Bannister didn't know.

"Ty, you're timing's perfect. Steve just arrived with donuts," Doug said as he pumped Bannister's hand. "Since we're all here, we may as well begin. Sit wherever you want. I'll do the intros. Otis Huggins is with homicide in DC, and Roger Bell is a Sergeant with the Virginia State Police. Spencer Crum is with the Office of Security, CIA. Steve Quattrone works with me on the flyaway squad at the Washington Field Office. Ty Bannister is on loan from our Atlanta Division. And Natalie Fowler is assigned here at Quantico with the Behavioral Science Unit."

Everyone gave a quick smile during Doug's introductions and, in the usual conference room tradition, either nodded or stuck their hand up as their names were called.

"I know you have questions, and we'll have plenty of time to go through them. Right now I'd like to cover what we know." Gordon got up from his chair and walked over to a large white board at the end of the conference table. "To put your minds at ease, each of you has a top secret security clearance. Information will be discussed, which outsiders don't have a need to know."

"Our department heads will want progress reports," Otis Huggins said. Huggins was pushing two-fifty and looked like he might have played guard in football. He had massive shoulders and no neck. His round, ebony face housed eyes with raised irises, which gave him a sleepy look. Detective Huggins, however, had risen rapidly through the ranks and was now a Detective II in DC. He was street-savvy, still operated numerous sources in the District's gangs, and was a man of few words. He let his statistical accomplishments speak for themselves.

"We have a media agent who will coordinate all releases, those restricted to the various departments as well as what's released to the press. You remember the problems you had to deal with during the DC sniper case, right?" Gordon looked down the table at Trooper Bell.

Sergeant Bell was the only one at the table in a uniform. During his fourteen years with the State Police, he'd worked rapes, kidnappings, drownings, and murders. Not only was he an experienced interviewer, he was an outstanding tracker who knew the forests around Quantico and the Blue Ridge Mountains as well as someone who had lived there all his life.

"After the first four sniper shootings," Bell said, "we had at least a dozen officers fighting to get in front of a microphone. Hearing from so many spokespersons caused fear in the suburbs and temporary setbacks in moving our investigation forward."

"I don't intend for us to have that problem with this case," Gordon said. "We have three apparent homicide victims—two females and one male. They've been identified. The oldest remains are those of Lillian Wells, the thirty-three-year-old wife of a State Department officer. A missing persons report was filed with the Arlington PD by her husband nine months ago. The second victim is Caleb Williamson, a forty-three-year-old career CIA officer who disappeared the day before he was supposed to report to CIA headquarters. He, too, went missing from Arlington. The third victim, Stacy DiMatteo, went missing from her apartment complex in Arlington. She was an analyst with the National Security Agency. All three victims lived in Arlington and all are Caucasian."

"Any idea how they were killed?" Spencer Crum asked. Crum worked with Carl Holmquist in the CIA's security office. He was the shortest person in the room, including Natalie Fowler, who had him by at least two inches. He was attired in a maroon sweater and rust-colored corduroys whose color matched his buzz-cut hair.

"It's too early," Gordon replied. "DiMatteo's body had no signs of sexual assault or physical abuse, and the autopsy couldn't determine cause of death. The toxicology results won't be available for a couple of days."

"What did you learn from the crime scene?" Detective Huggins asked.

"The normal physical evidence wasn't there. No clothes were found on or near the bodies," Gordon said.

"Can we assume all the bodies were nude when dumped?" Sergeant Bell asked.

"Yes. The only physical items at the scene were jewelry. Williamson's remains had a Rolex on the left wrist. Wells' body had a watch on her left wrist. A pair of earrings and a necklace were found near the skull. DiMatteo was wearing her diamond engagement ring."

"Why would the killer leave expensive jewelry on the body?" Bannister asked.

"Doug, if I could interject here," Natalie Fowler said. Fowler was one of the Bureau's profilers. She had a doctorate in abnormal psychology from Johns Hopkins and five years experience working serial offender cases. She had a reputation for bringing a no-nonsense approach to her work. At Quantico, they referred to her as "Agent Friday" for her "just the facts, Ma'am" style. Fowler was lanky, about five-ten, trim, with wavy, shoulder-length brown hair. She used makeup sparingly and had a long, shiny face with high cheek bones and thin lips. She wore a navy blue FBI polo shirt over beige slacks.

"Please realize my remarks are preliminary only," she said. "Leaving jewelry on multiple victims after removing their clothing is something we haven't seen before. What it tells me is that the killer is organized, methodical, and he—since most serial killers are male—killed for satisfaction. At this point, we know nothing about motive."

"What do you make of the fact that Williamson and DiMatteo both worked in the Intelligence Community?" Crum asked, looking down the table at Agent Fowler.

"That's something we'll have to explore," Fowler said.

Gordon said, "After I make the team assignments, we'll definitely focus on that, in addition to addressing the questions of means and opportunity."

"Does everyone know Williamson's car was discovered at Dulles Airport?" Bannister asked, leaning forward and looking at Gordon.

"That's right," Gordon said, looking at the faces around the table. "Williamson was a good friend of Ty's. Presumably the killer drove Williamson's car to Dulles Airport two weeks after his disappearance. Its license plate had been replaced with a stolen tag. Wells' car was found in the Springfield Mall parking lot, about twenty miles from her apartment. DiMatteo's car was located outside the manager's office at her apartment complex. All were locked. A search of the cars was unproductive."

"It looks like the killer snatched DiMatteo from her apartment neighborhood," Detective Huggins said.

"It appears that way," Gordon agreed.

"And Williamson had been in the Northern Virginia area for less than forty-eight hours, right?" Huggins asked.

"Correct," Gordon said.

During the next hour, Gordon went over the information known about the victims. He answered questions and made assignments. He had previously discussed his decision to have Bannister work the

Wells case since she was the first victim. Gordon reasoned if there was a connection between Wells and Williamson, Bannister would find it. Bannister told Gordon he didn't have any heartburn with the decision.

"Ty Bannister and Steve Quattrone are assigned Lillian Wells. Spencer Crum and Sergeant Bell will work Stacy DiMatteo, and Detective Huggins and I will concentrate on Cal Williamson. There will be three funerals next week. I want them all covered. Our tech guys will install equipment to discreetly film the ceremonies. We can look for possible subjects and study the reactions of people close to the victims. We'll meet every day at our Washington Office. Any questions before we adjourn?"

"I don't have a question, but I'd suggest you keep in mind there will probably be more victims until the killer is caught," Agent Fowler added.

But that thought had already entered Bannister's mind.

CHAPTER 24

Bannister spent Sunday morning going over and over all the similarities and differences of the killer's victims. After realizing he didn't have any answers, he decided to spend the afternoon exploring some of the forty blocks of downtown Fredericksburg. Just down from his B&B was Dr. Mercer's Apothecary Shop built in 1742 to sell medicinals and herbs to the colonists. Plaques on walls of some of the adjacent brick buildings marked where Union cannonballs over a century later smashed through the mortar. Hours later, after filling his head with historic trivia and satisfying his hunger with an Italian dinner, he returned to his room to rest up for the week ahead.

———✦✦✦———

Doug Gordon told Bannister they had a rental car for his use, so he caught the 6:05 a.m. train from Lafayette Street, a ten minute walk from his B&B in Fredericksburg. At the station, he bought a copy of Monday's *Washington Times* to read during the fifty-five mile trip. One of the articles in the Metro section was captioned "Victims of Serial Killer in Stafford Identified."

The article was sketchy, but said the remains of three bodies discovered last week by a Virginia State trooper had been identified. Next of kin were being notified, and authorities had mounted an intensive investigation. The account said the bodies were believed to be homicide victims killed at different times. Bannister was glad specific details were absent.

The train pulled into DC an hour later. Bannister tossed the paper into a trash bin on the railroad platform and rode two escalators to the exit. Outside Union Station, fifty flagpoles standing in a semi-circle, each flying a different state's banner, made him think of the United Nations—but they were the flags of the fifty states. The temperature was thirty-eight degrees, and the cloudless sky was a robin's egg blue. He decided to walk the five blocks to the FBI office.

People were streaming out of a subway stop. Government workers were strutting to work. Several women in long coats and athletic shoes walked by, purposely avoiding eye contact. Students in windbreakers lugging knapsacks shared the sidewalk with businessmen in topcoats carrying briefcases. Bannister crossed the street toward the entrance of the Washington Field Office (WFO), set back a hundred feet from the main road. The building was the first FBI office built with special security measures to withstand a terrorist car bomb. Behind the façade of this green- and gray-marbled government building, which looked like it housed a successful law practice, was the heart of the Washington office.

After showing his credentials and badge twice, and signing in on two different logs, he was issued a temporary access badge and told to wait in the lobby. Five minutes later, his escort, Doug Gordon, came bounding through the doors to the right. Gordon was wearing his customary white shirt with a tie that looked like a Jamaican beach scene—all pale blues, yellow, and green.

"The weekends go by fast, don't they?" Gordon said, extending his hand.

"That they do."

"Come on up and I'll show you where you'll be camping out for the next few weeks."

They took an elevator up four floors and passed through two additional access doors before arriving in a large bay of modular desks.

"This is the Flyaway Squad's area. The agents are assigned cubby holes here to my left," Gordon said, pointing to a labyrinth of gray walls over which Bannister could make out the agents' individual pods.

Gordon indicated an office behind a glass wall. "That room's for anyone's use and has three large tables where you can spread out your reports, photos, and paperwork. You and three other team members have desks in the glass-walled area right next to it. Our conference room is behind your work station. Squad members have to walk past your desk area to enter the conference room, so be discreet about what you leave lying on your desk. I had the secretary leave orientation packages for you, Otis Huggins, and Roger Bell. Yours also has current FBI directories and numbers for everyone at headquarters and Quantico."

"So you think I'm going to be spending a lot of time working the phone?"

"I hope not. That's why the brown envelope has maps for DC and Northern Virginia. Your rental car is in a garage two blocks from here."

"You've gone through a lot of effort," Bannister said.

"No problem. I know when I hit a new city, or at least one I haven't been to in awhile, I hate spinning my wheels trying to figure out how to get where I need to go."

Gordon took another fifteen minutes familiarizing Bannister with the office layout. He pointed out the wing housing the executive offices and showed him where the breakroom, restrooms, and computer room were located.

"Stop by the secretary's office and give her five bucks. Tell her to put your name down for the coffee fund. I'll see you in the meeting in a half hour."

Bannister walked into the office Gordon had pointed out. On one of the three desks was a white cardboard name plate that read, BANNISTER. He settled in.

—⟋⟋⟍—

Ellen Kaminsky, WFO's Special Agent in Charge of National Security, was introduced at the start of the meeting. Kaminsky's light brown hair had a few blonde streaks. It was hard to tell if it was natural or if she'd had it done professionally. In any event, with her dark gray jacket, skirt, and white blouse, she looked every bit the professional she was. She gave a quick nod to everyone seated in the room.

"Each of you has some unusual expertise," she said. "Collectively, I think we've put together a great team, and I'm confident you'll solve these murders." Kaminsky put her hands down on the glass top of the conference table and leaned forward. "Even though the FBI is providing space and resources, this is a task force operation. Right now five agencies are involved and it may grow. Because of this, a lot of rumors and misinformation will be flying around. Communicate with each other and keep me in the loop. I'll do the same. Refer options to me for decisions, not problems. And I don't like working in a vacuum. That said, rest assured that you have my complete support. And the CIA is assisting us with costs." She looked over at Spencer Crum and winked. "One other thing. I dislike surprises, especially hearing them first from reporters. I have a meeting at Justice with the Deputy Attorney General. So, unless anyone has any questions, that's all I have."

No one raised a hand. Kaminsky looked over at Gordon. "Carry on, Doug. It's your show." She walked briskly out of the room.

Gordon took the cue. "It's been forty-eight hours since we met at Quantico. Here's what's new. Everything's complete on the autopsies except the tox results. There's no obvious cause of death for any of the three. DiMatteo's body was in excellent condition. She had three pinhead-sized marks on her body, two evenly spaced above her left breast, and one on her right arm."

"Does that mean she could have used drugs, or may have taken injections, like a diabetic?" Sergeant Bell asked.

"We won't know that until we pull her medical records and talk with friends and relatives," Gordon answered.

"Could the dual marks on her chest be from a stun gun?" Detective Huggins asked.

"That's possible. The other two bodies were too decomposed for a comparison. If the killer used a stun gun, it might explain how his victims were incapacitated. Today I want us to focus on developing connections among the three victims."

"Although there are anomalies, it looks like all three victims were specifically targeted," Quattrone said.

"I agree." Gordon swiveled his seat toward his colleague. "The victims weren't chosen randomly. Two of the victims, DiMatteo and Williamson, worked for US intelligence. I don't know if all of you know this, but they worked against the Russians. The first victim, Wells, although not connected to US intelligence, was married to a career foreign service officer."

"What about funeral plans for the victims?" Sergeant Bell asked.

"DiMatteo's service and funeral will be in Woodbridge on Wednesday morning. At the same time, at a Presbyterian church in McLean, there'll be a memorial service for Williamson. Lillian Wells' funeral is scheduled for Thursday in Arlington. We're going to cover all three." Gordon picked up his notebook and stood up.

Bannister was paired with Quattrone. They'd drawn the ticket on Lillian Wells. Bannister knew she was the key. She had been the first victim, at least the first victim they knew of, and her death had preceded the other two by five months.

Gordon had pulled the missing persons report and a database dump on Lillian Wells and left it on Bannister's desk. Bannister had read through all of it before riding with Quattrone over to Arlington PD to talk with Detective Alvin Weber, the officer who had taken the report nine months earlier from Felix Wells when Wells had reported his wife missing. Bannister wanted Weber's read on Wells before they interviewed him tomorrow at the State Department.

"Was Washington your first assignment?" Bannister asked Quattrone in the car.

"Yup. Been here ten years. Worked counterintelligence the entire time. Doug and I volunteered for the squad when it was set up six years ago. It's been great work, and I've learned a lot. I've had a chance to work cases in Denmark, South Africa, and Greece."

Quattrone pulled into an *official vehicles only* space behind the Arlington Police Department, pulled down the visor with the blue lights, and put an FBI Vehicle sign on the dashboard. When they got inside, Weber was already waiting and had reserved an interview room. They were shown into a bare-walled room with a wooden desk and three chairs.

"Sorry about having to use one of these, but all the offices are occupied this afternoon unless you want to talk outside. There are a couple of concrete benches and umbrellas set up out there. It's where we grab a smoke," Weber said.

"This'll do just fine." Bannister noted Weber smelled like he'd just finished a cigarette. "We'll only need a few minutes."

"So I got word this weekend one of my missing persons was no longer missing. I reviewed the report this morning. Figured someone would be calling," Weber said. He crossed his arms in front of him and rocked back on a steel, gray chair. "But I didn't expect the first call to be from the Bureau." He looked at Bannister and Quattrone.

"I guess you could call it a police cooperation case, about now," Quattrone said.

"We're certainly willing to cooperate. How can I help?" Weber asked.

"Do you think the husband had anything to do with your missing woman's disappearance?" Bannister asked.

"I don't know. Do I think he killed her? No, but that doesn't mean he didn't hire someone to do it."

"So what was your read on him?" Bannister asked.

"Initially suspicious. Hey, the guy takes two major hits from his wife. First, out of the blue she tells him she wants a divorce and second, she insists he gets a blood test right away."

"We know the results."

"Exactly. He comes back HIV positive, and then she tells him she's got the virus, too."

"So, who gave it to whom?" Bannister asked.

"Don't know," Weber said.

"So, what's he got to gain by killing her?" Quattrone asked.

"Maybe only revenge. As I said, we don't know who got infected first. It's possible only one of them was playing the field and infected the other. Or maybe both of them were screwing other people and got infected independently. In any event, they both had to face reality. They were both given a death sentence."

"After he filed the report, did Wells ever call you back?" Bannister asked.

"Yeah, once. After his wife's Lexus was towed to an impound lot, he called me for my help in getting it released so he could turn it in to the leasing company."

"That's it? He never called to see how the investigation was going?"

"Right. Real sensitive guy."

"Did you think she might have been suicidal?" Bannister asked.

"I explored that possibility but basically ruled it out. I checked with her gynecologist and informed her that Lillian was missing. I told her the police had been informed by her husband that Lillian Wells was HIV positive."

"What did she say?"

"Initially she cited confidentiality and all that bullshit, but I simply asked her if she thought we should be concerned with suicide as a possibility. She said no, she didn't. The Wells woman seemed to be handling things okay. She'd been to a lawyer to file for divorce, and she paid him a three thousand dollar retainer. That's not something you normally do if you're going to take a header off a bridge or something. She had a net worth of maybe five or six million. So she had megabucks to spend on medical treatment and the works. She'd already met with a counselor that Dr. Connie Bradford recommended and was making plans to meet one of her girlfriends who was coming from Chicago to visit," Weber said.

"The obvious signs weren't there," Bannister said.

"And even the not-so-obvious. All her medication, clothing, and cosmetics were in the apartment. She'd been grocery shopping the same day she had appointments with her doctor and lawyer. And her car was found at one of the busiest shopping centers in the state. It wasn't pointing toward suicide."

"What about the husband's whereabouts at the time she went missing?"

"The concerned husband waits seventy-two hours before filing a report, and only after his wife's lawyer urged him to do so. He said he was at their apartment Tuesday, Wednesday, and Thursday nights the week his wife disappeared. He didn't notice she wasn't home; he didn't go out, didn't have anybody over, and simply stayed home watching TV in his bedroom."

"So, he doesn't have a verifiable alibi, right?" Bannister asked.

Before Weber could answer, Quattrone leaned forward and asked, "Do you think he'd take a polygraph?"

"I don't know. You'll have to ask him. My guess is he'll lawyer up. Not because he's shrewd or anything like that, but just because he comes across as an insensitive, gutless, self-serving guy who'll be too scared to make a decision by himself."

"This is helpful," Quattrone said.

"I also made a CD of all her e-mails I copied off her laptop."

"Did you review them?" Bannister asked.

"I did six months ago when I opened the case, and I looked over my notes before you guys got here. Wells had a separate e-mail address open for six weeks after getting back to the United States and only received two messages. One was unsigned; the other was signed, 'Andre.' The IPC addresses for both messages were from cyber cafés—I think one in Geneva, Switzerland, and the other one in Moscow. I never interviewed her husband about anything on her computer, so that's something you might want to explore. I also have a printout, which lists all her credit cards, balances, and telephone numbers. The names of her lawyer, dentist, and gynecologist are on there also. Thought you guys could use it."

"Thanks. You saved us a lot of work."

"No problem. By the way, I don't think anyone interviewed the victim's friend in Chicago. Let me know if there's anything else I can do."

Back at the office, while Quattrone typed up his notes, Bannister mapped out a list of people to interview. Working the phone, he set up appointments with Dr. Connie Bradford and Homer Vinson, the attorney who was one of the last people Lillian Wells had seen before she disappeared. Felix Wells was scheduled to work a half day at the State Department tomorrow. They'd try and surprise him in the morning. His wife's funeral would be twenty-four hours later. Bannister set out a lead for the Chicago office to track down and interview Mary Claire Vines, Lillian's best friend. He'd already made arrangements to attend the service for Cal Williamson. Quattrone and other team members would cover Wells' funeral.

Doug Gordon stopped by Bannister's desk. "I'm off to Quantico for a meeting with our lab people and the State Police, so I'll see you in the morning. Here are the keys for your rental car. It's a silver Pontiac Bonneville parked in the Colony Parking garage at the corner of 7th and F Streets."

Bannister stayed at the office another three hours, trying to find a connection among the three victims. When he left the building later that night, he was reminded that the District was not alive at night like New York or San Francisco. It was more like downtown Detroit, quiet and dark with graffiti-covered steel curtains rolled down the fronts of businesses shuttered until daylight. A few street people were slowly emerging from hidden hideaways. Although it was cold, he walked with his topcoat open as he always did at night. If necessary, Bannister wanted quick access to his Bureau-issued Sig Sauer nine-millimeter.

Approaching the entrance to the four-story Colony garage, he glimpsed two shadows for a second before they disappeared. The car was on the second floor, parked along the outside wall. As Bannister swung the door open to the staircase, the pungent smell of urine hit his nostrils. He walked up the dank, slick steps and pushed the door open to the second floor. Standing next to the elevators were two black males. The taller one spoke first.

"Hey, Mack. Got the time?" He wore a purple Lakers jacket and a black doo-rag on his head.

Without looking at his watch, but keeping his eyes directly on the young man, Bannister said, "It's eight-thirty."

"Since you're so smart, put your mutthafuckin hands in the air and give it up." The Lakers fan pulled a silver-plated automatic from behind his back and grinned.

His partner, who was about six inches shorter and looked to be maybe fifteen, stood behind him, appearing innocent enough with his black Reebok baseball cap on backwards. As Bannister glanced at the first guy's gun, he saw the smaller one was holding a knife down along his right side. Bannister slowly raised his hands but only to shoulder level.

In a fraction of a second, his left hand flew forward, grabbing the barrel of the automatic, jerking it rapidly to his side as he violently twisted the barrel in toward his assailant. Just as quickly, Bannister snapped his attacker's gun hand and arm back toward the left. At the same time as the bone of the assailant's index finger snapped, Bannister's right fist smashed into the side of his nose with a quick punch, and his right knee buried itself into the guy's groin.

As the blood gushed from the mugger's nose, Bannister swung him down to the pavement on his right. Bannister pivoted to his left and whirled a right leg kick to the jaw of the short partner standing a few feet away. He never saw it coming. The heel of Bannister's wingtip caught the guy flush on his mouth and jaw. Bannister heard the crunching of breaking teeth and bone, followed by a dull thwack as the younger man's head bounced into the concrete floor as he fell backward. Bannister thought the subject was probably unconscious before he hit, and his accomplice lay curled up in a fetal position, moaning on the cold, gritty concrete.

Bannister searched both assailants for other weapons, then called 9-1-1 and told them he was an FBI Agent who'd just been assaulted by two subjects, both of whom he'd disarmed. He asked them to send a black-and-white as well as an ambulance for the two subjects who needed medical attention. It had all happened so fast his pulse wasn't even racing. Bannister had just reacted.

Three minutes later he heard sirens. This time Bannister was glad to hear them. Four officers responded, along with an ambulance. It turned out that the larger of the two subjects was wanted for parole violation and questioning in two gang-related shootings; the smaller guy had a warrant for two armed robberies.

Forty minutes later, the garage was quiet as Bannister familiarized himself with the controls of the rental car and adjusted its mirrors. Soon he was on I-95 South, heading for Fredericksburg.

Bradford Alden had to let Bannister in at the B&B. He asked him to join him for a brandy. Bannister agreed. They each found a comfortable chair in the library.

"So, how was your first day back in DC?" Alden asked.

"It was a full day, but it ended well," Bannister said, again relishing the warmth of the brandy going down his throat.

CHAPTER 25

"**D**oug told me about the close call you had last night. How you feelin?" Quattrone asked.

"Fine. I'm lucky those gang bangers thought I was just a schmuck businessman."

"From what I hear, they're going to be sipping prison food through straws."

"They're lucky they didn't get shot."

"Yeah. Luck is relative."

The four lanes of Shirley Highway, as the locals called I-95, was a red ribbon of tail lights for the forty miles from Fredericksburg to DC. Traffic moved, and it took only an hour to arrive at the Watergate Hotel. Bannister checked in, and ten minutes later he and Quattrone were crossing the Potomac River into Arlington, ready to interview some of the last people to see Lillian Wells alive.

Homer Vinson had agreed to meet them at his law office before he saw any of his scheduled clients.

"I'll tell you what I know, which isn't much." Vinson put his large forearms on top of his desk and leaned in their direction. "It's a real shame when a nice person's taken from us. You know, in my career I've only had one other client die a violent death. In that case, the cops arrested the perpetrator at the scene."

"Well, we're not that fortunate," Quattrone said.

"I only had that initial meeting with Mrs. Wells. She retained me to represent her in her divorce, and I never talked to her again."

"Did she say why she wanted a divorce?" Bannister asked.

"Her husband had been unfaithful. She'd been diagnosed with HIV the week she saw me."

"Is that right?" Bannister said. He didn't think it was necessary to tell Vinson what Detective Weber had already told them.

"Yes. Her doctor is Connie Bradford. She has an office two blocks from here. You may want to talk to her."

"We have an appointment with her," Bannister said, glancing at a note card.

"Anyway, after Lillian found out she was HIV positive, she demanded her husband be tested. He came back positive, and she came to see me."

"Did she mention she and her husband had been living in Vienna, Austria, for two years before she visited you?" Bannister asked.

"Yes. She said her husband was assigned there, and that he had admitted sleeping with prostitutes in Amsterdam." Vinson straightened a couple of papers on the end of his desk. "I read where her body was discovered with a couple of other victims. Are you at liberty to tell me if there's a connection among them?"

"We're looking into that," Quattrone said. He glanced down at his cell phone, which was buzzing.

"I got a call yesterday from Felix Wells," Vinson said.

"What did he want?" Bannister asked.

"It was strange. He asked if I'd be the executor of his wife's estate. He said he knew an attorney or a bank normally handled that task, and since I'd already met with Lillian, he assumed I'd be interested."

"That's a little unusual, isn't it?"

"It is. But, hell, I had no ethical problem with it, and told him I'd handle it. I'm still holding his wife's retainer payment in trust. During the call, Wells sounded sad. The last thing he said was, 'I feel so guilty. I can't believe I'm burying her this week.'"

"Did you read anything into that?" Bannister asked.

"Not really. But who knows? I've met a lot of good actors."

As they walked out of Vinson's office, Quattrone said, "Doug sent a team message that lab results are in for Victim Number Three. The meeting's at 4:00 p.m."

They drove two blocks to the office of Dr. Connie Bradford. She saw them right away, and because her patient was deceased, she could confirm what they'd already found out. She dropped a name they'd need to identify. Lillian Wells had confided she'd had sex with another man besides Felix. The guy's first name was Andre. No last name. Dr. Bradford said Lillian had mentioned he was handsome and an excellent tennis player. She said the liaison with Andre had taken place in Vienna.

Bannister recalled that one of the deleted e-mails from Lillian's laptop had come from a sender named Andre. In the message, Andre had mentioned that he was in Moscow but was coming to Washington, DC.

He decided to review those printouts before discussing them with anyone.

Shortly before noon, Bannister and Quattrone went to the State Department to interview Felix Wells. After walking past a dozen concrete barriers and several giant flowerpots, they checked in at reception and were issued visitors badges. Felix Wells III came down and led them past a wall of international flags to a main floor briefing room usually reserved for the press.

Wells turned one of the blue-padded media chairs around to face the others. "Make yourselves comfortable," he said as he sat down. Maybe Wells was trying to impress them. He presented a good appearance. He was impeccably dressed and looked like he'd be comfortable in front of a camera.

"We're sorry for your loss, Mr. Wells. We're doing everything possible to identify who was responsible," Bannister said, moving his chair to give Quattrone a little more elbow room.

Wells answered all of their questions and made good eye contact. His voice showed no emotion. His words were well-chosen, and he didn't in any way act like a man whose wife's funeral was the next day. His tone and body language during the interview gave no indication of deception. Despite his apparent sincerity, he couldn't shed light on anything. Wells agreed to take a polygraph exam.

"One last question, Felix. Did Lillian have any male friends we might be able to talk to?"

"Male friends? No, she had girlfriends, but no male friends as far as I know."

So much for his knowledge of an Andre connection.

Doug Gordon and Detective Huggins interviewed Gina and Dawn Williamson. They also re-interviewed Cal Williamson's replacement at CIA headquarters, who had taken over handling the Russian desk the week Cal had disappeared. Interviews in Atlanta failed to develop any new leads.

The team of State Trooper Bell and CIA Security Officer Spencer Crum interviewed Mark Wattling, Stacy DiMatteo's fiancé. They also talked with Janice Parker, who would have been Stacy's maid of honor, and several of Stacy's co-workers and friends. Both investigators had to loan out their handkerchiefs. Everyone associated with DiMatteo expressed shock or broke down in tears.

DiMatteo's fiancé hadn't seen Stacy the day she disappeared. Wattling had called her at NSA during her lunch hour to let her know he and a friend were going to a Washington Wizards basketball game. Although Wattling didn't have an alibi for after 11:00 p.m., the interview team was satisfied with his answers. He denied any knowledge of the other two victims. He also agreed to take a polygraph if asked.

Wattling said he and Stacy had dated for three years before he'd proposed to her earlier that summer. To his knowledge, she didn't have any serious former boyfriends or lovers. She was on good terms with everyone at work. It troubled him that her car had been found at the manager's office. If the killer had driven it there, it didn't make sense. And if Stacy drove to the office, knowing how paranoid she was about being out alone at night, it had to be for a good reason. For someone to lure her there, Wattling believed it had to be someone she knew or someone in a position of authority who could convince her to drive there. All the tenants knew the office closed at 6:00 p.m. during the week. It didn't make sense to Wattling. Sergeant Bell made a note.

———◦◦◦———

On the drive back to the office, Quattrone glanced over and said, "You're deep in thought."

"I've been focusing on the victims' cars and telephone calls," Bannister said.

"Come up with anything?"

"Look at the telephone calls. Williamson didn't receive any, either on his home phone or cell phone. Lillian Wells received one unusual call the night before she disappeared. That call was traced to a phone booth in Arlington. Stacy DiMatteo received a call to her cell phone the night she disappeared. It came from the coin phone outside the apartment manager's office. Whoever called Wells and DiMatteo knew their cell phone numbers."

"So someone knew both women," Quattrone said.

"Exactly. If the unknown caller is the killer, he somehow gained access to their cell phone numbers."

"So what about the cars?" Quattrone asked.

"Lillian Wells probably wasn't abducted at the shopping center where her car was found. I think she met the killer nearby and left in his vehicle. My guess is they met at a restaurant or someplace within walking distance of the Springfield Mall. Maybe at one of the adjacent strip malls. The killer then returned later and moved her car. He may have moved it before disposing of her body."

"That's plausible."

"The big question for me is: Where was Williamson's car between the time he was abducted and two weeks later when his Infiniti was found at the airport parking lot you guys already searched the week before?" Bannister asked.

"That's bothered Doug and me, too. The easiest way to stash a car is to do what bank robbers do: Steal a car and leave it at some large apartment complex for a week. If it's still there a week later, it's clean and you can use it for a getaway."

"Could be," Bannister said.

Quattrone waited for the steel gate to be lowered before driving into the FBI's subterranean garage. "Or maybe the killer had access to a storage facility," he said.

"Exactly. My money's on a storage facility. The killer is smart and knows something about police work. He knew leaving Cal's car at the airport would throw the investigation off in different directions."

"And the killer used his vehicle to transport DiMatteo away from her apartment, right?"

"Probably."

"So, where're we going with this?" Quattrone asked.

"I think we should identify storage locker facilities in Virginia, say in a twenty-mile radius from where the bodies were dumped. Later on, if we get a suspect's name, we can check rental records."

"Let's see what Doug and the others found," Quattrone said as they headed toward the conference room.

———

"Stacy DiMatteo's body had a lethal dose of oxycodone and barbiturates. Our lab said the dosage would have been sufficient to kill ten people," Gordon said to the task force assembled around the table.

"What about the other two bodies?" Sergeant Bell asked.

"Trace amounts were detected in the tissue of Caleb Williamson. There wasn't sufficient soft tissue left on the first body to analyze," Gordon said.

Gordon then went around the room and asked for updates from

each two-person team. Natalie Fowler, sitting next to Bannister, was the next to last to speak.

"I'll hand out a copy of our profile at the end of the meeting. This is a work in progress. We entered all the data we had about the victims, the crime scene, dates, location, manner in which the bodies were found, etc. Here's what we got: The killer is a white male, single, between 38-48 years old, right handed, athletic, educated, and financially stable. He's had some type of formal disciplinary training, maybe in law enforcement or the military. He's employed in a job where he can control his hours or location. Are you with me so far?"

They nodded.

"Based on the victimology of Williamson and DiMatteo, we need to examine what drove the offender to choose them as victims. We think our killer has well-developed social skills, but his background will show he's been detached in his relationship with his parents and siblings. He has a high IQ, avoids intimate relationships outside of the so-called one-night stands, doesn't trust anyone, but is extremely convincing to other people. Finally, he holds himself to a high standard of authority."

"I've got a couple dozen questions, but I think I know what you'll say," Detective Huggins said, smiling.

"If you're implying that I probably won't be able to give you simple answers, you're right. But you can trust me that based on the totality of the facts, combined with our modeling, what I've given you might point in the right direction." Fowler gave a quick smile and passed out the profile.

"Ty, you're up," Doug Gordon said.

"We came up with a name, 'Andre,' who is of interest. Williamson and Wells had both been assigned to Vienna. Andre had a sexual relationship with Lillian Wells in Vienna. He sent her an e-mail that said he was in Moscow, and that he would be coming to Washington, DC. That e-mail was sent three weeks before she was killed. He's a possible link and needs to be identified."

"I agree," Gordon said. "Why don't you and Steve continue working the Vienna connection. Do a computer dump, using the keyword 'Andre,' of all State Department visas from the day Lillian and Felix Wells returned to the United States until she disappeared. Spencer can help you run his name against all international airline manifests for the same period. Everyone write up your interviews. We'll meet again Thursday after all the victims have been laid to rest."

Driving to the Watergate, Bannister thought about what he'd wear to Cal's memorial service in the morning.

Thirty miles away, in an apartment off Beauregard Street in Alexandria, Virginia, Andre had already picked out the dark-blue blazer he intended to wear to Cal's service.

CHAPTER 26

Bannister got to the church early, not to get a seat near the front, but to make sure he had a good seat in the rear. Gina and Cal's parents, Millie and Frank Williamson, had invited him to sit with the family. Because he was working, he had to decline. The FBI had made arrangements to take photographs at all three churches where services for the murder victims were being held. The systems installed would result in time-lapse still photos, as well as videotaping. A surveillance team outside each church would record vehicle information.

Carl Holmquist came into the church. Eyeing Bannister, he walked over and extended his hand. "This is a tough day for a lot of us. I know you and Cal were friends. These memorial services are supposed to bring closure, but this one won't," he said.

"I know. It's amazing how many people have been affected by Cal's death. His family, co-workers, neighbors, and friends."

"So true," Holmquist said. He took a seat on the opposite side of the church.

Most of those attending came as couples. A few groups of conservatively dressed men showed up about the same time, probably having driven over directly from CIA Headquarters. Their arrival was preceded by a man in a blue blazer and dark, gray slacks, who quietly took a seat two rows in front of Carl Holmquist.

—————

Andre sat down in the church pew. He had come to observe the pain and suffering he had personally caused. He had come to witness his blow against American intelligence.

Before the service began, Andre closed his eyes and relived Cal Williamson's last day. It was two months after killing Lillian Wells when Andre had decided there would be additional victims. He wanted all of them to be members of US intelligence. He'd met the CIA's new chief of the Russian desk three years earlier when Williamson had attended a diplomatic function in Vienna. He recalled the officer's rugged appearance and confidant air. He'd been impressed with the way Williamson dressed and the easy way he'd asked him questions. When Andre, in response to one of those questions, explained his last name, Neff, was Swiss, he noted a slight gleam in the CIA man's eyes, as if he knew *Neff* was a cover name.

Through one of the Russian's intelligence sources, Andre discovered Williamson's new address in Arlington and confirmed Williamson had moved into his townhome on a Saturday. Andre assumed correctly that Williamson would report to CIA headquarters the following Monday.

Andre's plan had been simple. He had parked his car early Monday morning near a "kiss and ride" bus stop close to the Forest Hills area where his target lived. Dressed in a business suit and carrying a briefcase, he had merely waited across the street from Williamson's townhome. As soon as he saw the garage door opening, he moved quickly.

Andre walked up to the driver's side door as Williamson's car was halfway out of the garage. When Williamson stopped his car and lowered his window, Andre smiled and said, "Mr. Williamson, I know who you are. I met you in Vienna. I am a Russian SVR officer, and I wish to defect. Please, may I talk to you inside?"

Williamson said "yes" and pulled his Infiniti back into the garage. After Andre showed him his official identification and said he wanted to arrange a longer meeting at a safe location, Williamson closed the garage door. When asked if anyone else was in the house, Williamson said no. Andre said he had documents in his briefcase that would establish his *bona fides* with the CIA. However, he reached in and pulled out a stun gun instead. Williamson had reacted quickly, leaping sideward, but the darts had found their mark. Andre bent over his target's helpless body and injected a fast-acting drug directly into his neck. The amount of drug used was sufficient to render his subject unconscious, but it was not fatal.

After removing a plastic drop cloth from his briefcase and popping the trunk release to Williamson's car, Andre spread the plastic inside the trunk. He removed a pager and cell phone from Williamson's belt and took out the batteries. He glanced inside his victim's briefcase and put it back on the passenger seat. He lifted Williamson's body into the trunk.

Andre noticed the alarm panel next to the door leading from the garage to the home was activated. He didn't plan on entering the house. He pressed the garage door opener, backed out the car, and drove to his storage locker in Springfield. He then left the storage facility on foot and walked a half mile to the nearest bus stop. He rode the bus back to the "kiss and ride" near his target's home, retrieved his own car, and arrived at work at the National Press Building in Washington, DC, at 9:30 a.m.

That evening, Andre had checked the Internet for any information identifiable with Lillian Wells or the discovery of any Jane Doe bodies in Northern Virginia. Satisfied, he returned to the storage locker to finish what he'd started. Andre spread a second drop cloth on the floor and removed Williamson's body from the trunk of the Infiniti. He stripped off the clothes, leaving only a watch on his victim's left wrist.

Williamson's briefcase had a secretariat wallet with $350 in cash. Andre kept the money. In the briefcase, he'd found a CIA identification badge, two passports, and other documents. Monday's copy of *The Washington Post* was folded neatly on top. Andre examined everything, then put the wallet, documents, pager, cell phone, and other items inside a double-plastic garbage bag. He wrapped his victim's clothes around the briefcase and shoved the bundle into a separate bag.

Andre had replaced Williamson's body on the drop cloth in the trunk of the Infiniti. He drove his victim's car, with a stolen Maryland license plate on the back, to mile marker 141. He carried Williamson's body to the spot where the remains of Lillian Wells were located. He unrolled Williamson from the plastic, placing his body on its back, five feet from Wells' remains. He injected a second needle into his victim's neck. Death would occur within hours.

He drove the Infiniti back to the storage locker where it would remain until he moved it two weeks later. On the way back to his own apartment, Andre had stopped at the adjacent apartment complex and threw two garbage bags into a partially filled dumpster.

Andre opened his eyes, stood up in the pew, and let a young couple squeeze by him. Within twenty minutes, four hundred people were packed into the sanctuary. The minister stood, said a few words, then introduced a Defense Department representative who stepped behind the pulpit and gave the eulogy. His delivery was polished—not surprisingly, since this was mostly a gathering of professionals. Except for the family, there was no sobbing and little talking. No one mentioned how Cal Williamson had died. Everyone in the church knew.

As the eulogy ended, Andre reverently bowed his head, perhaps to hide the slight smile on his lips.

―◦◦◦―

Forty-five minutes later, the service concluded with a piano rendition of *Beautiful Aisle of Somewhere*. Bannister wasn't thinking of *somewhere* but tried to focus on *someone*—the person responsible for this. He swore to himself he'd do everything he could to make the killer pay.

―◦◦◦―

At Friday's team meeting, Gordon passed out photos taken inside the churches. The teams would show these to designated family members and co-workers of the victims. All strangers needed to be identified.

Spencer Crum said a review of visas as well as airline and ship manifests had identified almost three hundred "Andres" who'd entered the United States during the critical time period. The team determined ninety-three were possibly still in the country. Natalie Fowler, using special software, reduced that number to fifty-one men who fit the profile. Each of them would be further investigated. Additional leads were given out to the teams before the meeting ended. It was four days to Christmas.

Bannister placed a call to Vienna for Kelly Owens, one of his fraternity brothers who had been on Dartmouth's tennis team. Owens was with the World Bank, and had been working in Vienna for the past three years. Vienna was five hours ahead, and Bannister reached him at home.

"Kelly, this is Ty Bannister."

"Ty! How the hell are you? Where you calling from?"

"DC."

"Did the Bureau promote you?"

"No, I'm working a case here. Hoping you could help."

"I'll do what I can. What do you need?"

"Is your tennis game still sharp?" Bannister asked.

"I might have lost a step in the past ten years, but my serve and volley are as good as ever. Why the tennis question?"

"We're trying to track a guy who's supposedly a good tennis player, and until about nine months ago, he was probably working in Vienna. His first name is Andre, and we believe he's a foreign national, probably thirty-five- to forty-years-old. Could you discreetly check with some of the clubs and teams there and see if you can locate any possibilities for us?"

"No problem. Can I assume this guy played competitively, or is good enough to give lessons?"

"Yes, I think that's probably a safe assumption. E-mail me with your results, okay?"

"Sure thing."

"Great. Next time we get together, the drinks are on Mr. Hoover."

Bannister had one more call to make. He dialed Robin's room

number at the FBI Academy. Although they'd e-mailed each other, he hadn't talked to her during her first two weeks there.

"So how's my favorite student doing?" he asked.

"I was just thinking about you. I'm stretched out on my bunk in my running gear. The last time I had this outfit on was when you and I ran that 10-K in Atlanta."

"So, did you make the right decision?" Bannister asked.

"Absolutely. I'm so excited. As a matter of fact, I'm so pumped up I'm having a hard time falling asleep. Of course, having a roommate again takes some getting used to."

"Are you getting along with your roomie?"

"We're like sisters. But not the kind that fight. You'd like her. She was a pharmacist before signing up."

"No kidding? That's unusual."

"We just had our first physical fitness test. I ranked second among the women. We have thirteen women and twenty-seven men."

"I guess I've got some competition."

"No you don't. Trust me."

"What's your schedule for the holidays?"

"We have the week off. For Christmas, I'm meeting my parents in Colonial Williamsburg. My sister's staying in California. I think I told you my father's an executive with the National Preservation Trust, right?"

"You mentioned it."

"Well, for Christmas my parents always go to some historic area and celebrate. Last year they were in St. Augustine."

"What about New Year's?" Bannister asked.

"I don't have plans. I'll be here in the dorm unless someone gives me an invitation I can't turn down."

"Why don't you be my guest for New Year's Eve? I have a two bedroom suite here in DC. I could pay off that dinner I owe you, and maybe we could take in some of the sights."

"I'd love that, Ty." There was a pause. "Could that create any problems for me?"

"No. When you sign out, just put my name and number down as a contact."

"Gosh, I'm looking forward to seeing you. Now I'll have something to look forward to. And what a great way to start the new year."

"Merry Christmas, Robin. Enjoy Colonial Williamsburg and your visit with your folks. I'll see you for New Year's." Bannister closed his phone and smiled. Finally, a bright spot.

CHAPTER 27

Victor Ivanov was leaning back in a black naugahyde office chair in the cramped office space of the Washington Bureau of Russia's ITAR-TASS news agency. The view from the two windows on the tenth floor of the National Press Building wasn't spectacular. Ivanov looked over the tops of his shoeless feet propped up on the corner of his desk. All he could see was another office building directly across 12th Street. If he had wanted to, he could stand up and look upward into the sky and tell what the weather in DC was doing. Ivanov wasn't interested in the weather right now. It was exactly twelve noon and time for his daily ritual.

Andre Kuznetsov, the other TASS correspondent, walked into the office just as Ivanov was removing his socks.

"V-chome dela snogami? What's wrong with your feet?" Andre asked, pulling out the chair at his desk, watching Ivanov as he slowly removed his socks, turned each one inside out, shook it, and put it back on.

"Nyet problemi. There is nothing wrong with my feet."

"Well, I've walked in before and seen you shaking your socks. I thought maybe you had athlete's foot," Andre said.

"My feet always get hot, whether it's summer or winter. When I was in the Army, I learned to turn my socks inside out to keep the skin dry. I got in the habit of giving these piggies some air each day. I always do it at noon so I don't have to remember."

"Well, I'm going to remember not to come into the office at noon,"

Andre said. "You're lucky we're not permitted to have visitors in our space. Maybe you might want to think about getting some shoes that breathe better than those Bulgarian toe stompers."

"*Kak Italiani?* Like those Italian models you wear? Besides you, the only people I see wearing those expensive shoes are *gomodseksualisti.* Homosexuals."

"Hey, I didn't mean to upset you. Besides, I happen to appreciate quality shoes. You spend about a third of your life on your feet. You may as well wear a well-made product."

"Well, I spend hundreds of hours on my ass, too. You got a suggestion for that?" Ivanov removed his feet from the end of the desk and swiveled around to face Andre.

"Try getting out and doing some work," Andre chuckled.

Victor smiled. They always ribbed each other the first time in the day they saw each other.

"Did you hear about that CIA officer who was found murdered?" Victor asked.

"That was strange. I bet CIA Headquarters is trying to figure out if the guy was a traitor, or the victim of a homosexual lover, or some conspiracy."

"One of my contacts said two female bodies were found with him."

"Maybe it was a *ménage a trois.* You know how the Americans always seem to be involved in kinky sex," Andre said.

"Do you remember that American guy, Adrian Block, who worked as a diplomat for thirty years and then got fired as a suspected spy?"

"Vaguely." Andre picked up a copy of *The Washington Post* and glanced at the headlines.

"Supposedly, he was a KGB agent. One of my friends used to visit a prostitute in Vienna who was friends with the whore who serviced Block. Guess what kind of sex he supposedly was into?"

"No clue," Andre said, continuing to look through the newspaper.

"His whore used to get completely nude except for a plastic see-through raincoat and spiked heels. She had him push a dog bone across the tiled floor with his nose, buck naked with a dog leash around his neck. If the bone moved off course, she whipped him with a riding crop. You've got to admit, that's pretty weird."

"Yeah, and that's probably a good seminar topic for the shrinks. I just stopped in to check my messages and review the mail. I've got to stop by the embassy later, but first I have an appointment at a congressman's office. He just came back from break and agreed to see me."

"You working on that article about US, British, and Russian Navy cooperation?"

"It's an excellent excuse to see the congressman. He's actually piloted a mini-sub. He's on the Armed Services Committee, which could be useful to me. I think I'll finish my article regardless of what develops. I have my cell phone if anything comes up." Andre tossed the newspaper on the desk and turned to leave the office. *"Do svidanye,* Victor."

In the three months Andre had been assigned in Washington to the world's fifth largest news agency, Victor had called him only once, and that was during his first week on the job, just to make sure he had the right phone number. As Andre drove through the streets of downtown DC, he thought about his two appointments that afternoon. Only one concerned business.

At the Defense Intelligence Agency's (DIA) Intelligence Analysis Center, Sparky Gillespie prepared to meet a reporter who was dropping off a load of toys for Christmas. Sparky, the DIA's representative to the Marine Corps' Toys for Tots program, had received a call from a journalist who said he was collecting toys from other reporters. He wished his donation to remain anonymous. Sparky, whose real name was Francis, agreed to meet the reporter in the parking lot of the main complex at Bolling Air Force Base. Sparky left the reporter's name with the guards at the main entrance so his visitor wouldn't have any problems when he arrived at 1:00 p.m.

—◦◦◦—

Andre called a taxi to pick him up at a parking lot two blocks from the old Smithsonian Building. As a green and white Capitol City cab pulled to the curb, Andre walked around to the driver's side.

"I need to deliver a bunch of Christmas toys to Bolling Air Force Base," he told the driver. "Can you give me a hand? They're in the back of my car. I'm afraid the alternator is dead. I've got a tow truck coming here later."

A thin, dark-skinned man with a long nose got out of the cab and walked to the back of Andre's open trunk. The cab driver was wearing a Washington Nationals baseball cap, black slacks, and a long-sleeved white shirt. "No problem," he said. "We can handle. But I must charge extra loading." The cab driver grinned.

"That's okay. There are about two dozen boxes." Andre pointed to the dolls, robots, and other toys he'd bought at Toys R Us. The four hundred dollars he'd spent gave him satisfaction, knowing it was for a good cause—his own.

"Are these for party?" the cabbie asked.

"For Christmas. For kids without parents."

"That is nice."

Andre called Sparky as they pulled into the visitor's line at the entrance to the base, letting him know he had come in a cab. The guards checked the identification of the driver as well as the passenger in the back seat. While the cabbie produced his registration and popped the trunk, Andre, carrying his false identification, showed a District of Columbia driver's license with the name Andre Neff. The guard checked his clipboard and saw his name opposite Gillespie's.

After giving the cabbie directions, Andre arrived at the front of the DIA complex. You couldn't miss the modern silver and gray buildings.

Even the five-story attached parking garage looked like a wing of the main structure. A man was standing outside, waiting for him.

"I'm Sparky Gillespie." He extended his hand as Andre emerged from the cab.

"Andre Neff."

"I can't believe what a godsend you are," Sparky said. "Your gifts will put us over the top. This will be the fourth straight year we've exceeded our goal. You're going to make a lot of kids happy."

Andre noticed two things about Sparky. The first was that his red hair contrasted with his cream-colored complexion. The second was a port wine stain on the upper left side of Sparky's forehead. It reminded Andre of Mikhail Gorbachev, the former President of the Soviet Union. He tried not to stare at it.

"These aren't just from me," Andre said, "but also from a bunch of other guys in the press pool. I hope you understand why we wanted to downplay our contribution."

"Sure. Everyone's got their own reasons. What's important is what you're feeling in your heart. I wish you could be there to see the smiles on the kids' faces and hear their excitement when they open their gifts."

"I'll take your word for it. That's good enough for me," Andre said.

It only took two minutes for the two of them to transfer the gifts from the taxi to Sparky's SUV.

"My understanding is you're involved with collecting food for the Nathaniel Gospel Mission, is that right?" Andre asked.

"You seem to know a lot about me. Who's your source?" Sparky asked. "Do I know him?"

"I'm sure you do, but I know you appreciate we newspaper people always protect our sources." Andre laughed as he thought about the mole who had identified Gillespie as a shrewd Russian intelligence analyst. Sparky smiled and didn't pursue the questioning.

"After the holidays maybe I can arrange to meet you and drop off a few cases of soup, cans of fruit, and boxes of pasta," Andre said. "What do you think?"

"Sure. That sounds great. Give me a call and we can make arrangements."

"I'll do that," Andre said. "My cab's running up my tab, so I've got to get back."

Andre reached over and gave Sparky a quick bear hug and pat on the shoulder. He hated this show of familiarity, but it was part of the act. "You're doing a wonderful thing. God bless you. And all the other Santa's elves. And happy holidays," he added. He smiled and walked back to the cab.

"I'm finished here. Take me back to my car, please," Andre said to the cab driver.

CHAPTER
28

One more Christmas had come and gone. The investigation had slowed, and the task force members were home with family or relatives. A "polar express" had plunged the nation's capital to seventeen degrees. Bannister spent the morning working out of his hotel room. It wasn't so much working as it was networking. He called a lot of friends, both in and out of the FBI, to wish them a happy New Year, good health, and prosperity for the coming year. Not surprisingly, none of the people he called were at work, so Bannister left messages. A few of his acquaintances could talk anyone's ear off, so he was okay with that. There were other things on his mind.

Bannister spent the week working, poring over reports. Finally, it was December 31. Robin had agreed to meet Bannister in the reception area at the FBI Academy. All the separate sections at the Academy were connected by glass-enclosed walkways. He looked down one hallway through double glass doors and spotted her from fifty feet away. She was carrying a red garment bag and a small duffel. He couldn't help but notice her tight-fitting jeans. She walked right up to him, dropped her duffle, and gave him a hug. She stepped back smiling.

"Do I look any different?" she asked.

"You look gorgeous, as always."

"Since I started here, I've lost five pounds and gained a lot more strength and agility."

"Shazamm ma'am! That's impressive." Bannister slung the duffel's strap over his shoulder, and they walked out the door to his car, which was parked in front. Robin grabbed his hand. Hers was warm.

Once they were underway, he asked, "How was your Christmas?"

"It was nice. I actually enjoyed touring Colonial Williamsburg with my parents. They were really jazzed about all the things I'm learning at the academy. They went back to California yesterday. How was your Christmas?"

"I'd like to say it was eventful, but it wasn't. Mostly quiet."

"Did you put up a tree?"

"No. I always do, but this year I didn't think I'd be back. Amelia left a little artificial Christmas tree on my kitchen counter so I could feel the spirit of the holiday."

"Did you get to open up anything nice?"

"Only a stack of junk mail." Robin scrunched her nose at that comment. "I watched a couple of Christmas specials and . . . thought about you."

"Good thoughts, I hope."

"What if I said they were bad?" He laughed and drew a pinch from Robin.

"So you only had a couple of days in Atlanta?"

"Yeah, I had to put some paperwork together for Witt to take to the US Attorney. You heard Terry Hines is out of jail, didn't you?"

"No. How could he be? He's charged with a terrorist act."

"Apparently he appealed the denial of his bond, and a judge agreed to set his bail at a million. Hines surrendered his passport and can't leave Atlanta. His parents put up their Long Island home as collateral."

"Do you think he's dangerous?"

"The poison he mailed can kill on contact. I'd feel a lot better with him behind bars."

"Me, too." Robin changed the subject. "So, where are you taking me tonight?"

"You said you like seafood, so I made reservations at the Oceanic. It's got a good menu and one of the best wine cellars in town."

"You're not going to try and ply me with liquor, are you?"

"You bet I am," Bannister said, and got another pinch.

—⟡⟡⟡—

They arrived at his suite, and he showed Robin to her room. She went to hang up her garment bag.

"I have a special drink for you to try. Are you game?"

"Sure. What is it?" He heard her voice from the other room.

"It's an interesting aperitif wine, especially when you add a twist of orange." He poured each of them a glass of Lillet Blanc on the rocks.

"Thanks, James Bond. You know I prefer my drink shaken, not stirred." Robin came around the corner with a playful grin. He handed her the drink as they eased into the sitting room.

"Cheers."

They sipped their drinks.

"This is good," Robin said, swirling the ice cubes.

She talked about the academy, describing her classmates and their diverse backgrounds. One of the other females was a chemist who was also a professional potter, with several pieces in museums. One of the guys, who had his doctorate, had been a corpsman in Afghanistan and recently published an article on post-traumatic stress syndrome.

"Sorry," Robin laughed. "I didn't mean to rattle on and on."

"I don't mind." He smiled.

"I can't tell you how much I appreciate the advice you gave me, especially about getting into good shape before reporting. I still have energy after class when a lot of the other students are wiped out and too tired to study."

"Well, you're only going through there once. You may as well give it your best shot."

"That's what I'm trying to do."

They chatted for another half hour before Robin excused herself to take a shower and dress for the evening.

Later, when she stepped into the kitchen, Bannister drew a breath.

She was stunning, draped in an ivory silk dress accented with a gold necklace and matching dangling earrings. That Nordic blonde hair cascaded down to her shoulders, making her look like she was ready to walk down the red carpet at some awards ceremony.

"You really look beautiful." Bannister sincerely meant it, and he could tell by her smile she was pleased with his compliment.

"I didn't want you to be disappointed. You look great, too." She brushed a piece of lint off his double-breasted jacket.

After a short drive to the restaurant, he handed the keys to a valet. They checked their coats and were escorted to a table by one of the wait staff. The ceiling was a multi-colored, stained-glass oval.

Robin's eyes turned upward. "I love the lighting," she said. "It's so soft and subdued. And did you notice the ecru damask on the chairs and booths match the table linens?"

He grinned sheepishly. "I don't know what damask is, but the color combo is nice."

Centered on each table was a hurricane shade with a large candle whose flame sent light dancing through the room. The entire dining area had a sense of openness but with enough privacy they didn't have to worry about the people nearby hearing their every word.

Robin ordered the signature dish of lobster with ginger, lime, and Sauternes sauce, while Bannister stepped out of the box and agreed to try a pecan-encrusted sturgeon filet. To hell with calories, they said, when their waiter pronounced the golden matchstick fries the best he'd ever had anywhere.

Over a glass of chilled Chardonnay they chatted, laughed, and smiled, totally caught up in the warmth of each other's presence. A soothing piano muted the sounds of a restaurant at work on the last day of the year. Their meal arrived, beautifully presented.

"It's like a work of art. I'm almost afraid to eat it," Robin said.

"Let's hope it tastes as good as it looks."

They were not disappointed, and the service throughout the evening was outstanding. Robin's napkin slipped off her lap, and before she could reach down to retrieve it, a waiter discreetly replaced it.

An hour and half later, they topped off the meal with cups of rich coffee and a poached pear stuffed with a bourbon mousse nestled in a phyllo shell.

The night was still young when they left the restaurant. Bannister drove around the Capitol grounds, past familiar Washington landmarks. "I like the way the monuments are lit," he said. "I think seeing them at night makes people think more about what they memorialize."

"For me, I just like their stark, simple beauty," Robin said.

As he drove down Independence Avenue toward his hotel, Robin said, "Ty, stop here at the Lincoln Memorial. Let's walk up the steps."

He pulled over and they got out.

"You know it's freezing tonight," he said as they started up the stairs. "Is there something special for you about the Lincoln?"

"I just remember that scene from the Clint Eastwood movie, *The Line of Fire,* where he's sitting on the top step watching the female Secret Service agent he likes walking away. He says, 'If she looks back, it means she's interested. Come on now, take just a little look back.'"

They arrived at the top step and turned around, gazing at the lights bouncing off the frozen Reflection Pool.

"And what happens? In the movie?" Bannister asked.

"She looks back at him." Robin reached for his gloved hand. "I thought it was so sensual."

"Sensual, huh? One little glance?"

"They end up in bed together."

"Is that right?"

"Yes, that's right."

"Maybe I should send you down these steps and see what happens. But I'd rather you didn't walk away from me at all."

They slowly descended the steps and walked arm in arm back to his car. Robin shivered as she settled against the cold leather.

"Thank God for heated seats," he said.

Five minutes later they were at his suite.

Robin moved around the room, silently dimming the lights, creating a warm and intimate atmosphere while Bannister poured champagne. He had just put two glasses on the counter when she walked up behind him. She put her arms around his waist, resting her head on the back of his shoulder. He could smell her perfume, a refreshing hint of tangerine. He turned slowly and looked into her eyes. He kissed her softly once, then again, and again. His hand caressed her hair as he felt her mouth hot on his.

Robin pulled away, smiling. "It's your call. Your room or mine?"

"Whatever's closest."

As he kissed her deeply, his hands gently slid the zipper down the back of her dress. Her hands were busy tugging at his belt. She led him to the bed. He kissed her neck and the curve of her shoulder. He kissed her firm breasts, listening to her quick breathing. His tongue twirled slowly around her nipples, teasing a response. His hand glided slowly between her thighs, arousing her to a new level. Her hand reached his pulsing hardness and caused him to shudder. In their hunger to caress, to taste, and to feel, they moved from finesse to animal lust.

"I want you so badly, Ty. Let me feel you now." Robin guided him to that moist pleasure spot and rocked her hips upward to meet his thrusts. They rode waves of pleasure Bannister had only imagined. As black stars exploded before his eyes, Robin let out a loud, prolonged moan. Her legs wrapped themselves around his back as her arms pulled him deep inside her. She held him so tightly he almost couldn't breathe.

He lay there on top of her, still inside, for a long time. Their hearts were beating hard as their chests rose and fell as one, their warm glistening bodies entwined. As he softly rolled to her side, he heard a quiet whimper, then another, and then Robin started sobbing. He kissed salty tears flowing down her cheeks.

"You're wonderful," was all he could think of saying.

"Oh, Ty, I've dreamed of being with you like this." She placed her fingers across his lips. "Don't say anything. Just hold me." He gathered her into his arms and hugged her gently.

"I've never met anyone like you," Bannister said finally. "I hope the New Year is starting off the way you wanted," he added. "It is for me."

"I'm just so happy. I couldn't wait to see you again. I never told you this, but on that first day when you came to Global Waters and looked at me, and spoke to me, I thought, this guy is sexy and would be great to go out with."

"So why'd you wait a year to go out with me?"

"Me, wait! I practically had to take out an ad for you to ask me out." Robin lightly punched his arm, then hungrily kissed him again, harder and harder as her hand reached below and they both shared an urgency to explore each other's body again.

Some time later he got up, returning with two of the hotel's thick white terry cloth robes and their neglected flutes of champagne. As they finished their drinks, they heard fireworks exploding in the indigo sky over DC.

"It's midnight," Bannister said. "Happy New Year, Robin." He kissed her. "Do you want to get up and watch the fireworks?" he asked.

"Maybe later. I'd rather see you get up and help me *feel* the fireworks again." Her smile was inviting as she wrapped her arms around him once again.

Andre followed certain foreign customs, like making New Year's resolutions. Two weeks ago, he had made a resolution that would be checked off his list tonight.

Sparky Gillespie seemed surprised to be getting a phone call so soon from Andre Neff. He told Andre that unlike his work with the Toys for Tots program, his food bank efforts went on throughout the year. He was delighted to get a jump start on contributions for January and February, the two coldest months in the DC area. He and Andre agreed to meet at Armand's Chicago Pizzeria on Wisconsin Avenue at 8:00 p.m. Sparky had given Andre his cell phone number and told him to call him when he got there.

Andre had already stopped by the Rezidentura at the Russian Embassy, where an intelligence technician had signed out an untraceable cell phone to him. After driving around Washington for an hour to make sure no one was following him, he parked in the back of a bank parking lot next to the pizza restaurant. He looked over and saw Sparky's vehicle pull into the adjoining lot, taking one of the two empty spaces on the side. Another car pulled into the remaining space next to Sparky.

Andre called him.

"I'm at Armands," said Sparky. "Where are you?"

"I'm next door in the bank lot. It's empty, and the restaurant spaces were filled when I got here. Do you want me to drive over there so I can unload this food?" Andre waited to see if Sparky would take the bait.

He did. "Let's make it easier on both of us," Sparky said. "I'll drive over to the back of the bank."

"Great. After we unload this stuff, I'll buy you a pizza and pitcher of beer. How's that sound?"

"For free beer, you've got my attention," Sparky said.

Andre had scouted out the parking lot the week before. He knew the only exterior surveillance camera the bank had was the one trained on the ATM and teller machines on the right side. He would drive out the left side, the same way he came in.

Sparky backed his Ford Explorer next to Andre's car. Andre popped his trunk and both men stepped to the rear. Sparky looked down at two open cardboard boxes filled with canned vegetables.

"Sparky, do you mind giving me a hand with these boxes? I don't know if the bottoms are strong enough." Andre pointed inside the trunk.

"Not a problem," Sparky said as he reached into the trunk.

Just then Sparky felt all his muscles pulsing and going into spasm. He lost his balance and fell forward toward the trunk. His head struck the trunk latch of Andre's car. His limp arm crumpled as his shoulder struck the wheel well. He saw Andre smiling and felt his legs being pushed into the trunk. Sparky saw the hypodermic in Andre's gloved hand just before he felt a hot burning sensation in the side of his neck. He wanted to scream, but couldn't move his mouth. His hands and arms wouldn't work. His face scraped the carpet on the bottom of the trunk. The last thing Sparky saw was the orange and yellow neon sign of the pizzeria before the lid closed and his world turned dark.

In less than thirty seconds, one of DIA's unselfish public servants was lying unconscious in the trunk of Andre's car.

Andre took Sparky's keys and drove his Ford Explorer back to the pizzeria, parking it in the rear of the restaurant where the employees' vehicles were located. He pulled his Washington Redskins ski cap down over his forehead and got out of the car. After locking the doors, he casually walked to the front of the restaurant. No one bothered looking at him. Two minutes later he was in his own car headed toward downtown DC. He crossed over the 14th Street Bridge into Arlington and fifteen minutes later turned off the interstate and followed the now familiar road to the storage locker.

After lifting Sparky Gillespie's body out of the trunk and placing it onto a plastic drop cloth, Andre stripped the body. He was surprised to find Sparky wearing two identical Seiko watches. One read 9:05 p.m.; the other read 5:05 a.m. Why two watches? Then it occurred to him: Sparky was an intelligence analyst. The second watch showed current Moscow time. Well, Sparky wouldn't need either one now. He rolled several loops of plastic around the body and lifted it back into the trunk.

Andre had planned Sparky's next stop in advance. The route included two areas where motorists could pull off the road, and two rest areas. Andre stopped at all four spots to make sure he didn't have a tail. He didn't use his previous dump site—though he had considered it, just to flaunt it at the investigators. The new location was in Maryland, past the Patuxent Research Refuge and about two miles from the headquarters of the National Security Agency. He turned off Bald Eagle Drive to the three-mile Wildlife Loop. He didn't expect any other vehicles on this back road.

When he saw the familiar mile marker, he pulled over. He cut the engine and listened for any sounds. There were none. Andre slid on the oversized pair of work boots he'd bought at a local Wal-Mart. He dragged the bound plastic roll containing Sparky's naked, but still-warm body across the bare dirt ground of a small clearing. He unrolled his victim. Blank eyes now stared upward at the tar black sky.

Andre carried the plastic back to his car and placed it and the boots in a garbage bag to discard later in a trash dumpster he'd used before.

—⁓⁓—

Walking to the conference room for the Friday briefing, Bannister took a call. It was Robin.

"Ty, you're very sweet. Thank you for the roses."

"I knew you had a big test this week, and I think today's the day you're supposed to get your orders."

"You're right. I'm so excited. When the flowers came, I had to stare at the card that came with them for just a moment . . . I was thinking, who is Secret Service Agent Frank Horrigan? But then it hit me—Frank Horrigan was Clint Eastwood's character in *The Line of Fire!* Tricky. But *I loved it.*"

"If someone would have recognized my name on the delivery card, it would have set the rumors flying. I wasn't sure if you were ready for that."

"So, the flowers were because of the excitement of this week?" Robin asked.

"Let's say they were for the excitement of last weekend."

"They're beautiful. The other female trainees think I've got a secret admirer. Hey! Guess where I'm being assigned to my first office?"

"No idea."

"Washington, DC. Isn't that great?"

"There's really good work here, Robin."

"Oh, I know. I'm on a high right now. I nailed that exam yesterday, and combined with my orders and your flowers—I don't know what to say. I do know I can't wait to see you again."

"Me, too. Keep plugging away. I'll call you soon."

Bannister hung up as he walked into the conference room and grabbed a seat near the middle of the table. The other task force guys filed in behind him.

Doug Gordon asked Otis Huggins for an update on surveillance from the funerals.

"We had excellent video coverage of the church and graveside services for all three victims. The service for Wells was small. Everyone has been identified. The services for DiMatteo and Williamson were heavily attended. Only one couple at DiMatteo's service is still unidentified; thirteen people in the church for Williamson's service are unknown."

"Have you made photos of the unsubs yet?" Spencer Crum asked.

"We have multiple sets. Of the unknown subjects at Williamson's service, four males fit the profile. However, two were there together and might be lifestyle partners. I based that on the fact that they were holding hands." Huggins grinned widely, showing his gold tooth.

"What about the other two?"

"I've got copies of their photos for each of you," Huggins said.

Trooper Bell asked about vehicle coverage.

"I was getting to that," Huggins added, hesitating. "We screwed up. We didn't film the cars, just noted their tag numbers. In hindsight, we should have filmed the vehicles. One of the Maryland tags taken from a vehicle at Williamson's service came back as stolen. It wasn't reported until two days later, but was a 'hit' by the time we ran the plates. We already queried the surveillance teams. No one remembers it."

"The bottom line," Gordon said sarcastically, "is that *maybe* the killer was at Williamson's service." No one spoke for a moment.

"Sergeant Bell has a rundown on storage lockers," Gordon said.

"As you recall," Bell said, "something that's bothered us is that we don't know where Williamson's Infiniti was stashed before it showed up at Dulles Airport. We made the assumption it wasn't hidden at an apartment lot, and the killer would not have risked putting it in his own garage. That leaves us with the probability it was in a storage unit for a week or so."

"And there's a shitpot full of them," Quattrone said.

"Exactly. Not counting vertical storage facilities like Public Storage, we identified 168 businesses within thirty-five miles of downtown DC. The key criterion we looked at was that you had to be able to drive a vehicle up to the rental locker, or be able to drive a vehicle into it."

"How far did you get with that?" Gordon asked.

"Right now, we're checking the name of Andre LNU (last name unknown) against all rental records and will match the Andre rentals to exterior lockers large enough to conceal a car."

"Ty, what have we got from State Department and the airlines?" Gordon asked.

"I'll let Steve go first," Bannister said.

"I handled liaison with State, and Ty covered the airlines. Wells got an e-mail from Andre LNU saying he was in Moscow but would be arriving in D.C in three weeks. Sometime during the fourth week after that e-mail, Wells disappeared. We're operating under the assumption that Andre, if he is the killer, flew into the United States during that time frame and has been here since then. Ty, give them the numbers," Quattrone said.

"Sure. We focused only on the airports in New York, Newark, Washington, and Baltimore. Steve concentrated on foreign nationals. I handled US citizens. First we looked at the total number of 'Andres' who flew into the United States last January. Then we determined how many are still here. We compared their bios against Quantico's profile, which looked at single white males between 38-48 years old. There were still fifty-one possibles. We then cross-checked those names with the CIA's databases to find out how many either entered or departed from Vienna in the last three years. We ended up with five."

"That's a manageable number. Anything else, Ty?" Gordon asked just as a huge thunderclap sounded, and a pounding, driving rain mixed with hail slammed into the conference room windows. The lights flickered but stayed on.

"We're pulling out all the stops on the fifty-one possibles. However, I made a call to one of my fraternity brothers assigned to Vienna for the last three years. He's an outstanding tennis player. I asked him to check with his sources for good tennis players whose first name is Andre. He came up with two. Both happen to be in DC. Andre Deverville, a French national, works at the World Bank, and Andre Kuznetsov is a reporter assigned to the TASS News Agency here in DC. Kuznetsov, by the way, is also on the Russian Embassy's roster with the rank of Second Secretary. Both guys were in Vienna when Lillian Wells and her husband were there."

As Otis Huggins excused himself to take a call, Gordon continued. "We're making progress. Let's see if we can get good photos of Deverville and Kuznetsov, and compare them to the unsubs at the funeral services. We need to keep pushing. We want to get this guy before he strikes again."

"We may be too late, Doug," Otis Huggins said as he walked back into the conference room. "My commander just called. The mother of a DIA analyst filed a missing person's report this afternoon. Her son never called her last night as he always does. He didn't answer his phone this morning. A call to DIA confirmed he never showed up to work."

"Well, there may be an innocent explanation to that," Gordon said as they all turned to look at him.

"Yeah, but the DIA people said this guy hasn't missed a day of work, sick or otherwise, in three years."

CHAPTER 30

Doug Gordon called an emergency meeting of the task force Sunday afternoon. Gordon showed up wearing his customary white shirt with tie, while the rest of the team were still in their weekend clothes. "Some of you may have gotten my page while in church, and I'm sorry about the short notice," Gordon began. "Three hours ago, Otis Huggins took a call from one of his buddies with the Maryland State Police."

Huggins nodded.

"Early this morning a body was discovered at a nature preserve a few miles from NSA Headquarters at Fort Meade. An elderly couple, up early to see if they could photograph some kind of bird they were looking for, spotted the nude body of a male at Patuxent Wildlife Refuge."

"Is it the DIA guy?" Steve Quattrone asked.

"There's a good chance it is. A trooper in the area was the first responder. His initial description said the body was a white male, approximately thirty years old, with red hair and a birthmark on his forehead."

"That matches the description we have of Sparky Gillespie," Otis Huggins said.

"Any jewelry on the body?" Bannister asked.

"Yeah. Two watches," Gordon said. "Gillespie's supervisor at

DIA gave us a description and said the guy had a couple of quirks. He always wore two watches so he'd always know the correct time in Moscow." Gordon let that sink in. He leaned forward, putting both hands on the end of the table. "AFIS should be able to match his prints before we're out of this meeting. I think we should assume our killer has struck again."

"Will the victim being in Maryland complicate things?" Spencer Crum asked.

"We'll factor that in. Since the body was found in a national park, we dispatched an evidence recovery team from our Baltimore office. Our team and officers from the Anne Arundel Sheriff's Office have been there for two hours. The road into the area is sealed off. A metro reporter for the *Baltimore Sun* is the only one making calls about a possible murder victim. He's been given the 'no comment' comment."

Looking at Bannister, Gordon said, "I'd like you and Quattrone to meet Gillespie's supervisor at DIA at four o'clock. So far, he's only been told we're working the missing person angle. But the possibility of espionage has probably popped into his head."

Gordon saw everyone was staring in his direction. "Let's go around the table. If you've got anything new since Friday, share it. If you have anything you want to ask, fire away." He pointed at Steve Quattrone, who was sitting closest to him.

"Are they still cutting the heat back in this building on the weekends? It's freezing in here," Quattrone said, hearing a quiet "Hooahh" response from one of the guys.

Quattrone pulled out a stack of photos. "My contact at the Office of Foreign Missions obtained visa photos of our two main suspects, Andre Deverville and Andre Kuznetsov. I got the photos after hours Friday, and our lab made copies yesterday. Ty and I compared them with surveillance shots from the memorial services. We think a guy sitting in the third pew from the back at Williamson's service is the Russian. Give us your opinion."

Quattrone passed out the photos. The room was silent for a minute while everyone studied the pictures.

"Looks like a make to me," Trooper Bell said. There were no dissenters.

"He's a newspaper guy, right?" Huggins asked. "Maybe he was on assignment."

"Or he might have been operational," Crum added.

Gordon asked, "Do we know if he's a known or suspected intelligence officer?"

"We're carrying him as a suspected IO, assigned to their science and technology branch," Quattrone said.

"Remember, Kuznetsov's paperwork indicates he's a Second Secretary with the Russian Embassy. He's a diplomat," Bannister said.

"Ah, shit," Crum said, smacking a fist into his hand.

"You mean if he's good for these killings, we can't touch him? He's got immunity?" Bell leaned backward and threw his hands up in the air like he was under arrest.

"It looks that way. We've only got two options. If he's our guy and State confirms he's a diplomat, we can declare him *persona non grata* and kick him out of the country. Basically, he goes free unless the Russians want to put him on trial in their country. Or we could ask the Russians to waive immunity and let us prosecute him here," Bannister said.

"What's the chance of that happening?" Bell asked.

"It's possible," Huggins said. "I was here in January of 1997 when the number-two man in the Georgian Embassy crashed a red light downtown, injuring four people and killing a sixteen-year-old girl. The guy's name was Makharadze. He was drunk. The accident reconstruction team said he was going at least eighty miles per hour when he hit. We had to release him from custody because he was a diplomat. Our government asked the Georgian government to waive his immunity and they agreed. Makharadze was tried and convicted here of manslaughter and got a seven- to twenty-one-year sentence."

"First, we've got to make sure Kuznetsov's our guy," Gordon said. "Anything else, Ty?"

"We'll run his license and see if it shows up on the list of vehicles at Williamson's service."

"Right," Gordon said, looking back down the table.

"And if it's not on the list, we should be asking, how *did* he arrive there? Maybe in the car with the stolen tag."

"Good point," Gordon said.

"We had some luck with the mini-warehouses," Bell said. "We identified two drive-in storage lockers rented by 'Andres.' One locker's in Reston; the other's in Alexandria. The names are Andre Cloutier and Andre Neff. Both signed six-month rental agreements this spring. We're working on trying to ID them."

Huggins raised his hand as he spoke. "As you all know, I'm with Metro PD. Bell and I are the only non-feds on this team. Right now I'm not worried about one of my people getting whacked, but if I were the Bureau or one of the other intelligence agencies, I'd be wondering if one of my own employees might be next on our killer's list."

"You care to comment on that, Natalie?" Gordon looked at Special Agent Natalie Fowler.

"I agree with Otis. You don't have to be a profiler to see that whoever's responsible for these murders seems to be picking a victim from each of the major intelligence agencies."

"Do you have any suggestions?" Gordon asked.

"Just that I'd put the security offices at every intel agency on notice the killer might be targeting their personnel and to have their employees report any unusual requests or incidents right away," Fowler said.

"I'll get that out," Gordon said. "I want a full court press on Andre Kuznetsov. Let's do a complete workup on him, and while we're at it, rule Andre Deverville in or out. Bell, I want your team to keep digging on the two Andres who rented the lockers. And Ty, you guys find out everything about Gillespie's contacts and activities. We'll meet here tomorrow."

——⟨❦⟩——

Sitting at a small dinette table in his apartment kitchen in Alexandria, Virginia, Andre had spread out sections of the Sunday *Washington Post* on the table. The smell of Hoppes gun solvent hung in the air like a sour dish towel. He had cleaned and was now re-oiling all the parts of his recently acquired nine-millimeter Walther P99 automatic.

He wanted extra protection while carrying out the rest of his plan. At a gun show a week earlier in Fredericksburg, he'd gotten lucky. A widow was there with her son, selling off her late husband's collection of handguns and pistols. On the table were eighteen guns, all collectors' editions. A commemorative model Walther P99 was still in the original box with leather case, manual, and two 10-round magazines. The price tag said $1,150. When the widow agreed to take $1,100, Andre handed her eleven hundred-dollar bills. Sale by a non-dealer meant no waiting, no fingerprints, and no records checks.

Andre had the new gun with him when he'd met Sparky Gillespie. He didn't know if he'd ever have to use it, but he was prepared to, if necessary. After target practice at an indoor shooting range the previous day, he was pleased with the gun's action. He was surprised to find he shot better with it than with the Makarov pistol he'd been trained with, and which Soviet forces had carried for almost fifty years.

As he reassembled the pistol, Andre thought of the week ahead. If things went well, he should be identifying his next target by the end of the week.

**CHAPTER
31**

Doug Gordon was correct about the fingerprint check of the body. By the time Bannister and Quattrone walked to the car, they'd gotten word that the body had been identified as that of Francis "Sparky" Gillespie. Ten minutes later they pulled into the empty parking lot at DIA. Gillespie's supervisor and a guard were at the entrance. They showed their badges and followed the supervisor, who had introduced himself as Dave Miller, into a silent lobby. The only sound was four sets of heels echoing across the marble floor. The guard turned away and walked to a console in the center as they continued toward a bank of elevators.

"I have some bad news. Francis Gillespie's been killed," Bannister said.

"Ah, shit! I was afraid of something like this," Miller said, shaking his head side to side. They took the elevator to the third floor where Miller pointed out Gillespie's cubicle. "I've got a bunch of people who need to be notified. Does his mother know?"

"One of our agents and a deputy are at her house right now."

"She called me yesterday from Sparky's home to let me know there weren't any signs someone had been in his place. She's got a key to his condo. She said his stereo was playing. It was on low volume, like maybe he'd stepped out temporarily."

"She say anything else?" Bannister asked.

"Just that she had a sick feeling. Said it wasn't like her son to take off without letting her know. Oh, she fed his fish before locking the door."

The air in the DIA was warm and stuffy, unlike the refrigerator atmosphere of the FBI conference room they'd recently left.

Bannister and Quattrone took off their jackets. They spent the next hour going through Sparky's desk and files. His space was clean and lacked the dust you normally saw on the tops of cabinets or on the computer; his space was organized with nothing lying out in plain view. He didn't have the usual office props, like photos of a dog or cartoons or quotations pasted on the wall. But nothing at his work station seemed out of the ordinary.

"A lot of analysts are neat freaks," Quattrone said, as he pointed to all the tabs on Gillespie's files that had been typed and centered.

"I give them credit for being organized. The ones who've worked for me have been able to put their hands on information fast. Not like agents who stockpile excuses why they can't find something," Bannister said.

He continued with his examination, copying telephone numbers from Post-It notes stuck on the top edge of Gillespie's computer monitor. A Day Timer was lying on the right side of the desk. He looked through it and saw it had the current year's calendar, as well as the daily pages for last December. One appointment jumped out. Bannister read the lone entry for December sixteenth: "Andre Neff 1330."

The supervisor returned.

"Do you guys think Sparky was a victim of this serial killer?"

"It's a possibility," Bannister said. "Any inquiries should be directed to our Washington office. I'm taking Gillespie's appointment book." He handed him a receipt.

"He's a . . . I mean was . . . a helluva nice kid. Quiet, smart, polite. A hard-working analyst. I've only been in charge of this section four months, but I was impressed with his work."

"You'll have to prepare for the reactions of his colleagues when they return tomorrow. Would you do me a favor and call the guards at the front gate to see if they have the visitor's log for December?" Bannister asked.

"No problem."

———⟨◊◊◊⟩———

As the supervisor escorted the agents out of the building, he made the call to the guard house and was told the log book was there.

After the guard was assured they were conducting an official investigation, he produced the log. Two names were matched to a taxi that had entered at 12:55 p.m. on December 16. The cab's plate was recorded, as were the driver's name and that of his passenger—Andre Neff.

———⟨◊◊◊⟩———

When Robin returned to her Quantico dorm room, her room phone was ringing. She thought it might be Ty, but it was a Washington agent named Lisa Jessup.

"Your counselor, Stan, and I worked together in San Antonio," Jessup said. "My husband, Dwight, and I are agents here in Washington."

Robin kicked off her tennis shoes and stretched out on her dorm bed, plumping two pillows behind her head.

"The reason I'm calling is that we're looking for someone to rent our townhouse for six months while we're both on a temporary assignment to Los Angeles. Do you think you might be interested?"

"I was actually thinking about getting an apartment for a year while I scouted out a good place to buy."

"We'd really prefer to rent to an agent. It's a nice two bedroom, two bath townhouse, completely furnished. The best thing is that it's one block from the Ballston Metro stop in Arlington. Your counselor thinks highly of you and thought you might jump at the chance."

"That's nice to hear." Robin got up and reached over to her desk to grab a notebook and pen. "Tell me more."

After they had discussed the details, Robin said, "Well, I'm definitely interested. I'd like to come up as soon as possible to look at it. We have night training this week, so I'm afraid I won't be free until Friday night or Saturday."

"What about Saturday? I have a commitment earlier in the afternoon, but would four-thirty work?" Lisa asked.

After the two women exchanged contact information, Robin called Ty.

"It's me, Robin. Where are you?"

"I'm at Capitol City Cab."

"Did something happen to your car?"

"No, I'm working."

"On Sunday night?"

"Yeah, I just tracked down a taxi driver I hope can ID a photo. Dispatch said he was due back at the barn in five minutes. What's up?"

"Things may be falling into place. Remember how I said I wanted to get an apartment close to downtown?"

"Uh huh."

"Well, an agent couple from WFO is looking for someone to rent their townhouse for six months while they're both in LA. It's in Arlington, and they're offering it to me at a decent price."

"What are their names?"

"Lisa and Dwight Jessup. Do you know them?"

"I don't know him, but she works on one of the Russian squads."

"Super. Maybe I can pump her for some information. I don't have a squad assignment yet, but I was told all of us are either going to counterterrorism or counterintelligence."

"You might want to check her place out before committing. You know, location, parking, and shopping."

"I am. I'm going to look at it Saturday afternoon."

"What about Saturday night?"

"It's open. Do you feel like hanging out with a trainee? Their place is supposed to be right near the Ballston Metro stop."

"I know of some restaurants near there you might like. Give me a call when you're done with the tour and I'll meet you."

"Fab. You know I miss you. I think training intensifies everything."

"Hmm. I believe I've been a witness to that."

"You're being nasty, but I love it. See you next week."

As Bannister was trying to think of someplace different to take Robin, the cabbie pulled into the garage. The driver stepped out, introducing himself as Desta Iskinder, formerly of Ethiopia. Extending his hand to Bannister, he said, "I am now American and would be full of happiness to help the American FBI."

CHAPTER 32

Wednesday was known as hump day. Today the task force would go over the hump. Ellen Kaminsky, WFO's Special Agent in Charge, ordered all team members to report to the field office's windowless command center. Located directly one floor beneath the room where the team usually met, the conference room was an upgraded space with light cherry paneling and the latest communication bells and whistles. When Bannister got there, multiple conversations were taking place. The talk was animated and team members were smiling. For a change, there was an air of excitement in the room. One of the agents had turned on the big screen to CNN.

"Let's take our seats and get started," Kaminsky said, walking in purposefully. She had what was referred to in the Marine Corps as "command presence." She strode halfway around the table, grabbed the remote, and switched off the TV. The talk stopped, and a dozen leather chairs swiveled as the task force members took their seats. All eyes were on Kaminsky.

"Before we start, I'd like to thank all of you for your tireless efforts in this case. We still have a lot of hard work ahead of us. Doug will talk about the breakthrough and what needs to be done." Kaminsky put her notebook down and acknowledged Doug Gordon, who was sitting at the opposite end of the table. Gordon was wearing his black camel-hair sport coat and customary white shirt. You couldn't help but notice his bright, diamond-patterned Italian silk tie. He took his cue and stood up.

"We finally have a subject," Gordon said. "In front of you is a sheet of photos with four different shots of Andre Kuznetsov. The top two photos are from his visa and passport. The other two are surveillance pictures taken this summer, and that's how he looks today. We're fairly positive he's our guy."

"Bring us up to speed, Doug," Kaminsky said, folding her arms and leaning backward.

"I'll trace what we know about Kuznetsov. One of our attachés showed his photograph to a landlord in Vienna. The guy picked him out and remembered him as the person who rented a flat in Vienna for three years. However, the landlord said he went by the name Andre Neff. By the way, that apartment cost twice what the Russians authorize for one of their officers. We don't have an explanation for how he swung it, but we'll look into that later. Anyway, we now know Andre Neff is an alias used by Andre Kuznetsov. I'd like Spencer to take a couple of minutes and tell us what the Agency's learned."

Spencer Crum remained seated, looked left and right, and nodded to Kaminsky. "He's a forty-three-year-old intelligence officer with the rank of Captain. He's Ukrainian by birth and has no family we know of. His father died of a heart attack in 1970. Kuznetsov had an older brother, Dimitry, who was a top Russian pilot, and was shot down in Afghanistan in 1987. Kuznetsov's mother died the following year.

"The KGB recruited him when he was in college. We know he's never been married, is fluent in English and French, and is a skilled tennis player. His cover has always been as a reporter. Before coming to Washington at the beginning of the year, he had assignments in Vienna, Brussels, and Algiers. Our file says he received the Order of the Red Star for recruiting someone pretty damn important. We hope it wasn't an American." Crum frowned and pointed back toward Gordon.

Gordon continued, "Kuznetsov and Caleb Williamson's assignments to Vienna overlapped. We don't know if they met while they were there, but Kuznetsov certainly would have known Williamson was CIA. He was still in Vienna at the beginning of this year when Felix

Wells and his wife, Lillian, rotated from Vienna to Washington. He returned to Moscow, probably for updates and some refresher training before being posted here in February. Two weeks after his arrival, Lillian Wells disappeared. Six months later, Williamson disappeared. Two months after that, DiMatteo was killed. And last week, Gillespie was killed. There's no information Kuznetsov was anywhere but in the DC area when all four people disappeared. We still have to prove he's responsible. Natalie, has Quantico revised its profile?"

The question caught Special Agent Fowler just as she had taken a chocolate kiss from the cut-glass dish on the table and popped it into her mouth.

Fowler smiled, embarrassed, and brought her hands together as if to say she wasn't going to take any more candy. "He fits our profile almost to a 'T,'" she said finally. "Assuming he's the killer, we still don't know what precipitated the violence. Why this year? Of course the death of his older brother would always be simmering beneath the surface. And early in his career, Kuznetsov's hatred for the United States would have been constantly reinforced by the KGB. And even though relations between Russia and the United States have changed, the KGB's successor organization, the SVR, still considers the United States a major enemy. One thing we're concerned about is the time between the killings, which is rapidly decreasing. We don't know how the victims are being selected, but I wouldn't be surprised if there's not another one within two weeks, if we don't stop him first."

"Could he have killed other people before this year? Perhaps in Brussels or Algiers?" Kaminsky asked.

"I think I can answer that," Spencer Crum interjected. "The answer is no. We checked in both cities. One American died in Brussels when Kuznetsov was there. A graduate student was killed by a hit and run driver. There was an American couple killed in Algiers when he was assigned there. But they were missionaries who had their throats slit along with four Arabs. We believe they were victims of Islamic radicals belonging to the opposition's political party."

"Thank you." Fowler continued, "Obviously, something happened, which triggered the outbreak of killings. We believe that whatever the catalyst, it was probably connected to Lillian Wells."

"It might be HIV," Bannister said. Everyone turned and looked in his direction. "We know Lillian Wells had a relationship, maybe an affair, with a guy named Andre while she was in Vienna. That same Andre e-mailed her that he looked forward to seeing her in Washington. Soon after she got back to the United States, Lillian Wells saw her gynecologist. She was told she was HIV positive. Her husband, Felix Wells, found out a couple of days later that he also had the virus. It's possible Kuznetsov got infected from Lillian Wells."

"And when he found out, he went ballistic? Is that what you think?" Kaminsky asked.

"It's speculative, but it's an explanation," Bannister said.

"Natalie, have you figured out why he strips the bodies and leaves only a watch or item of jewelry?" Quattrone asked.

"My guess is he wants to minimize forensic trace evidence but still rub our noses in it. Sort of like with the twenty-one kids believed strangled by Wayne Williams in Atlanta in the eighties. Their naked bodies were dumped in the river so the water would wash away any evidence. By leaving jewelry on the bodies, our killer communicates he isn't doing this for monetary gain, but for some other reason. The fact the bodies aren't displayed in any way, but simply left naked also mocks our capabilities. When he's caught, I'd be interested in finding out whether he kept any trophies from his victims."

"Thanks, Natalie," Gordon said. "This week we obtained three search warrants. One for the locker rented by Andre Neff, and the other two for Kuznetsov's car and apartment. We have ten days to execute these warrants.

"Yesterday we searched his locker at the mini-warehouse in Alexandria. We told the owner of the warehouse we needed entry to the premises to follow a suspect believed involved in interstate thefts. She gave us the access code to the gate without any questions.

Coincidentally, the DC driver's license Kuznetsov used to rent the locker was a fake. The home address on the license turned out to be the Shoreham Hotel in DC. That same license was also recorded by guards at Bolling Air Force Base when he signed in for an appointment with Francis Gillespie.

"Our team completed a forensic search of the locker but didn't take anything. We left it the same way we found it. We didn't want him to know we were there. It was pretty much empty, except for a coffee table, a few boxes, cleaning supplies, and a plastic bin of clothes. The usual stuff. The unusual item was a case holding what appears to be an antique Russian icon," Gordon added.

"What would he be doing with an icon?" Kaminsky asked.

"We don't know the significance. But we took the photographs of it, along with a description, and had them sent to a Smithsonian expert late yesterday. He worked most of the night and called me a half hour ago. It was his opinion that if the work is original, it may be an icon painted by Andrei Rublev, one of two icons that were missing for a hundred years. The other icon surfaced in London two years ago at an auction house where an anonymous seller sold it for $750,000."

"Can we charge Kuznetsov with smuggling or dealing in stolen art?" Quattrone asked.

"We don't know if the icon is stolen. All we know is that it's been missing. Its last known owner was Czar Nicholas, the emperor of Russia," Gordon said. "It's anyone's guess how it came into Kuznetsov's possession. He may have been the anonymous seller of the other one."

"What kind of coverage do we have on him now?" Kaminsky asked.

"Our Special Operations Group is surveilling him. They installed a GPS beacon on his car last night. We're physically covering him eighteen hours a day—6:00 a.m. to midnight. If his car moves during the six hours we don't have agents watching it, an alarm will be activated here in the center, and a team will be scrambled to get on site as soon as possible," Gordon said.

"Any other technical coverage?" Kaminsky asked.

"We're authorized to install microphone and video coverage in his car, but the weather isn't cooperating. To do the installations, we have to borrow his car and replace it with a duplicate while our technicians do their work. We didn't have enough time yesterday. Tonight and tomorrow there's a possibility of snow. We can handle the odometer adjustment if we move the car, but we can't replace snow and ice on the car or cover tracks in and out of his outdoor parking space."

"Under normal circumstances, would we have enough today to arrest him?" Kaminsky asked.

"Not yet. If this were a normal criminal case, I'd recommend bringing him in for questioning and try to sweat out some incriminating statements. But we don't have enough to successfully prosecute. And this isn't a normal situation. The lab is going over everything we vacuumed from the locker. That'll probably take two days. We plan on doing a covert search of his apartment Monday. If we're lucky, we'll find enough to pursue legal and diplomatic options," Gordon said.

"Okay, then. Keep me informed. Let's continue keeping a tight lid on this. I briefed the Baltimore SAC, and his people will follow our lead. We'll all meet here at the same time Monday." Kaminsky adjourned the meeting.

The team members weren't smiling as they filed out of the room.

Doug Gordon pulled Bannister aside. "I'd like you to supervise the search of Kuznetsov's apartment Monday. I feel I owe you that."

"I appreciate it. I'll draft a plan and make assignments this afternoon," Bannister said as his cell phone buzzed. It was ASAC Witt from Atlanta.

"Ty. Gary Witt. How are things going?"

"We're making progress. I'm optimistic."

"Good, I hope you'll be able to maintain that attitude."

Bannister waited for Witt to get to the point.

"For your information, Terry Hines jumped bail this morning. The marshals received a signal when the alarm from his bracelet went off.

Because it was rush hour, their team couldn't get to his apartment for forty-five minutes to check on the problem."

"What'd they find?"

"No Hines, that's for sure. It looks like he used bolt cutters to snap the ankle bracelet. He left a note." There was a pause.

"And?" Bannister tried to keep exasperation out of his tone.

"The note said, 'The FBI will pay for ruining my life.' I know you have ten days left before you're due back in Atlanta. Would you be interested in coming back early to help search for him?"

Bannister didn't need long to think about that. "The marshals have been under a fair amount of heat lately. I'm sure they'll move a domestic terrorist to the top of their list. If they catch Hines fast it would be great publicity for them. Up here we're at a critical juncture on the murders."

"Right."

"Any indication Hines had help escaping?" Bannister asked.

"It doesn't look that way, but the marshals are checking it out. Since you were instrumental in Hines's arrest, I wanted you to know right away. I called SAC Kaminsky to advise her you might be a target."

"Thanks for the concern. I'll take precautions, but I don't believe Hines knows I'm in Washington. If he did, he'd have a helluva time finding me."

———✦✦✦———

A mile away inside the Russian Embassy on 16th Street, Andre was reviewing precautions. He was in a secure, soundproof room with two wooden desks and two office chairs. A faded red area rug covered the rough-textured concrete floor. Illumination came from two fluorescent lights. There was nothing else in the room—nothing taped to the wall. Not even a picture of Vladimir Putin, the current Prime Minister of the Russian Federation. No phone, no lamp, no outlets, no ashtray, no trash can. The desks didn't even have drawers.

This room was reserved for intelligence officers to write reports and plan operations. Andre liked the nakedness of it. It reminded him of his victims. If everything went according to his evolving plan, there would be two more before the weekend was over.

CHAPTER 33

On Friday afternoon, Bannister met with the supervisors of Washington's technical and computer squads. He thought the search of Kuznetsov's apartment should take only an hour. Bannister was satisfied with the plan and had all the assignments made when Doug Gordon returned shortly before quitting time.

"How's it look?" Gordon asked, glancing down at all the paperwork.

"Good. We'll stage at our offsite in Alexandria. The entry to his apartment will take place at 9:30 a.m. if all goes well."

"When's our guy usually go to work?" Gordon asked.

"Kuznetsov's a creature of habit. According to surveillance, he leaves exactly at eight and gets to his office in the National Press Building a few minutes before nine. We'll follow him downtown. Teams will be in place to alert us if he leaves his office or if anyone approaches the apartment. We'll use our Cable TV truck as cover. Once the entry team is inside, they'll radio the other team members in the van."

———∞∞∞———

The weather forecast for Saturday predicted an overcast sky with a high of thirty-four degrees. Bannister decided to run eight miles in Rock Creek Park. He needed to work off some nervous energy, not to mention a couple of excess holiday pounds. The streets and sidewalks were clear of snow and ice. The usually grassy areas were still covered with two inches of frozen snow with a hard sheen. He dressed in layers, knowing he'd be out a long time.

As he jogged under the Kennedy Center he came to a point where runners and walkers had a choice. If they turned left, they'd be at the start of the Chesapeake and Ohio canal path, where a narrow brick sidewalk continued to an iron footbridge spanning the twenty-foot wide waterway. Once you crossed to the other side of the canal, there was a dirt-packed road, closed to all vehicles, that wandered along the edge of Georgetown. You could stay on that path for 164 miles to its end in Cumberland, Maryland.

He ran through the park and along the serpentine path, toward the National Zoo. The return would be slightly downhill with whatever wind there was at his back. After running in solitude for half an hour, he saw the sign for the National Zoo and, reaching the only water fountain still running in the winter, he stopped and took in a few mouthfuls of cold water before heading back.

He was in the zone this morning, alternating between listening to his shoes hitting the asphalt and letting his mind wander to whatever thoughts it wanted to worry over. Massachusetts Avenue was now on his left, and he glanced over at the wrought iron fence separating the park from an old Georgetown cemetery. He slowed for a few seconds and stared at the trail near where the remains of the congressional aide, Chandra Levy, were found in 2002. Her murder, like those he was investigating, was senseless. Her killer, Ingmar Guandique, wasn't caught for seven years. Bannister didn't want the families of their victims to go through the same anguish as Levy's. The killer of his friend needed to be caught. He mentally swore under his breath he'd do everything he could to make sure it was sooner rather than later.

When he reached Virginia Avenue, he stopped and used a stone wall to stretch. The same excruciating pain he'd felt last week had returned to his right leg. He rubbed his leg and slowly walked back to the Watergate, using the three blocks to cool down. After a hot shower and change into comfortable clothes, he felt better. He drove back to Georgetown for a casual brunch at Mr. Young's on M Street. All three fireplaces were going as he walked through the entrance. The aroma of fresh cinnamon rolls, was in the air. He ordered eggs, fresh orange juice, a couple of their hot rolls, and two cups of dark coffee. Saturday's *Washington Times* had an article about the victims of the serial killer. Its speculations were pretty much on point. Bannister vowed that when they next wrote an article about the killer, it would include news of his capture.

—◦◊◦—

At 1:00 p.m. Andre Kuznetsov left his apartment. He was a man on a mission. He drove the speed limit for fifteen miles before arriving at Main Street in Clifton, Virginia. He constantly checked his rear-view mirror for signs of cars following him. He'd repeated this drill dozens of times and knew what to look for. He slowly circled through a park on his way back toward Arlington. He then drove through the park a second time in exactly the same manner. When he arrived at Lake Barcroft in Arlington County, he pulled over two separate times, and each time he waited five minutes before starting up again. He was a careful man. He was a professional.

At 3:00 p.m. he pulled into the parking garage at the Ballston Common Mall on Wilson Boulevard and got out of his car. The mall was crowded with after-holiday shoppers looking for deals. Andre blended in with the shoppers in his jeans and leather jacket, hiking boots, and Redskins baseball cap, but he was carrying a Walther automatic secure in its shoulder holster, and a large knapsack slung casually over his left shoulder. It contained the items he would need in one hour.

—◦◊◦—

Bannister went to the office mid-afternoon to double check the assignments for Monday's search. He figured Robin would be calling around five o'clock after her townhouse tour. He walked downstairs to the operational center to see if anything was going on with their subject.

He was surprised to see Trooper Roger Bell in the office.

"I'm impressed," Bannister said.

Bell turned around from the computer monitor he was staring at. "I was reading the file on Kuznetsov. You guys sure burn hundreds of hours following these clowns around the capital."

"Part of the spy business."

"If the State Police could have the money you spent this year following this guy, we could have bought a dozen new patrol cars. Out of curiosity, how often do you think he makes you?" Bell unscrewed the cap from a bottle of water and took a couple of gulps.

"Every now and then. Sometimes if one of our agents knows he's been spotted, he'll just smile and wave at him."

"Why the hell would he do that?"

"Just to make him a little paranoid. He'll wonder, why am I being followed? How long have they been on me? How many times has the Bureau followed me and I failed to spot them? You know, things like that."

"Well, anyway, I had some extra time and I'm trying to learn as much as I can about our subject. Besides, my wife is out of town with her sister who just had a baby girl."

"Congratulations on being an uncle. If you need me to explain anything about our reports, I'll be here for another hour." Bannister walked over to one of the empty desks and punched in the technical supervisor's home number. He wanted to make sure there hadn't been any substitutions for the search team.

"Ty, glad you called. I was just going to call Doug. Something's happening with our target."

"What do you mean?"

"He's temporarily out of pocket."

"Where?"

"The Ballston Common shopping center. Our guys have been on him like flies on shit since he left his apartment at one o'clock. He spent two hours dry cleaning himself all over Northern Virginia. We're pretty sure he's operational."

"How'd you lose him?"

"I didn't lose him. The surveillance team inside the mall lost him. He pulled a slick maneuver. First, he got in one of the elevators inside the mall, along with a couple of baby strollers. When they reached the second level, he stepped out and got right back in with a couple of ladies going down to the first floor. He immediately walked over to the up-escalator, and when he got to the top, he rode it right back down. About two stores down from the escalator is a hallway leading to the restrooms. Our tail walked past the hallway and glanced down. The target was standing at the end of the hallway, looking back."

"So then what happened?"

"A few seconds later another foot team member looked down the hallway and didn't see him. He thought the target might've ducked into the men's room, so he went to check it out. Nothing. The guy had vanished. At the end of the hall there's an exit to the outside. There's no alarm on the door, but it only goes out. No way to get back into the mall if you go through that door."

"So where's he now?"

"Don't know. We've got two units circling the perimeter of the mall but haven't spotted him. Our guess is he'll return to his car in a little while, so we're sitting on it."

"Thanks. Do me a favor, call my cell phone as soon as he surfaces, okay?"

"You bet."

An hour went by before Bannister's phone rang. It wasn't the technical supervisor. It was Germaine White calling from the Atlanta office.

"Don't tell me you're working," Bannister said.

"As a matter of fact, I am. I apologize for not working on your case sooner, but ASAC Witt pulled me off my regular analysis to do some stupid assignment involving all the visits Chinese delegations made to Georgia last year. He wanted the information by close of business last night so he could include it a report he has to send to headquarters in thirty days. Thirty days! I don't think he understands the definition of the word *priority*."

"You may be right about that. What have you got?"

"Well, I found a document with a list of intelligence community personnel who had worked on a National Intelligence Estimate for the White House. It involved the economic impact on the United States from Russian organized crime. The document was dated eighteen months ago. So here's the thing: The names of the all the intelligence victims are on the list. It doesn't include Lillian Wells" name, but she wasn't working for any of the agencies."

"Can you tell me the names on the list?"

"Sorry, Mr. Bannister, but it's classified. I think it's important, so I need to send it by secure fax to you at the office. I don't want to send it unless I know you'll be there to receive it."

"We're in luck. I'm in WFO's operational center right now."

"One other thing, Mr. Bannister. I know this list might just be a coincidence, okay? But you know I'm not a big believer in coincidences. And if it's not a coincidence, then I think we've got ourselves a mole somewhere."

Bannister let that thought sink in. "I think like you, Germaine. I don't believe in coincidences either. Send me the list right now."

"Will do. And there's another thing. Derek Barnes finished going through all of Terry Hines's contacts. He doesn't think there's any foreign connection or co-conspirators, but Hines did send several e-mails to an Andre Neff in Vienna, Austria. Derek couldn't dig up anything on him. Since Hines is still a fugitive, it's possible he could reach out to anyone. Do you want me to research this Neff character?"

"Yes," Bannister said. "It could be important." Was it possible the Andre Neff they were investigating was identical to this Andre Neff that Hines had contacted? Another coincidence? "Would you call me immediately with your results?" he asked.

"For you, absolutely."

Bannister gave Germaine the office number and waited for the fax. In five minutes he held in his hand the list of names. One of the two CIA representatives was Caleb Williamson. From the NSA was Stacy DiMatteo. One of the two DIA representatives was Francis Gillespie. If a mole had given this list to Kuznetsov, it might explain how he was selecting his targets.

His eyes traveled to the name from the FBI.

Special Agent Lisa Jessup. He had to look at it twice. He knew Lisa Jessup—she worked on one of the Russian squads. And she was meeting Robin that afternoon to show her the townhome she hoped to rent to her while on assignment in Los Angeles.

—⚭⚭⚭—

Andre didn't know if he was being followed, but today he wasn't taking any chances. He used all his training inside the mall. He looked at reflections from store windows. He walked into a bookstore and went to a far corner where he picked up a book. Looking over the top of it, he tried to see if there was anyone inside the store who wasn't browsing. He left the bookstore and entered a women's lingerie shop and casually looked at intimate apparel for ten minutes before leaving. He'd carefully planned his exit from the mall.

When he ducked out the mall's side door, he immediately walked fifty feet to the entrance of the parking garage. Glancing back, he saw no one was following him. He walked through the dimly lit lower level of the garage and out a side entrance near Glebe Road. He walked briskly one block to Wilson Boulevard. He timed it so he caught the light green with the walk signal flashing.

A half block further on the opposite side of Wilson Boulevard was Christophe's Florist. Andre walked in and looked out the front window. Seeing no one following him, he ordered a dozen roses. Andre declined the clerk's offer of a box. He paid cash for the flowers, pushed open the large glass door, and went to his left. As he turned the corner, he put his knapsack down on the top of a newspaper box, using it as a table. He took out a Macy's Department store shopping bag he had picked up the week before when scouting his route. The flowers fit neatly inside. So far, so good. It was 3:55 p.m.

Five minutes later he was at the entrance to Keystone Mill Commons where there were sixteen townhouses, eight on each side. His target's home was the last one on the left. He walked down the sidewalk until he came to the end. He stopped briefly, placed the Macy's bag by his feet, and looked around. He saw no one outside. He reached into his knapsack and pulled out a brown baseball cap, which had FTD in yellow block letters. He'd had the lettering done at a tee-shirt store the previous weekend. He switched this hat with the Redskins baseball cap he'd been wearing and stuffed that one into his knapsack. He lifted out the bouquet of roses and folded the shopping bag, putting it, too, inside his knapsack. He unzipped his jacket, felt his gun, and adjusted his cap. Satisfied, he walked up the six brick steps of the end unit and rang the bell.

—◊◊◊—

"I couldn't find the office directory listing the agents' phone and pager numbers," Bannister said. Roger Bell was still glued to the computer monitor.

"This must be your lucky day. It's right here. I was just using it."

"You going to be here a little longer?"

"I was planning on leaving at five. Why?" Bell asked.

"Maybe I'm getting a little paranoid about this case, but I've got to check something in Arlington. If everything pans out, I'll call you in half an hour."

"Sure thing."

The numbers for both Dwight and Lisa Jessup were listed. First,

Bannister called Lisa's cell number and got her voicemail. He then called the home number and got their answering machine. She might not be home yet, he thought. This wasn't going as smoothly as he wanted. And the more he thought about it, the less he liked it. He decided to drive out to the Jessup's residence. He wanted to talk to her about the list and the intelligence assignment Germaine had faxed.

Before leaving the office, Bannister called the technical supervisor for an update. Their subject was still unaccounted for and teams were watching his car. Bannister copied down phone numbers he might need and headed downstairs to the office's underground garage. He'd call Doug Gordon after meeting with Lisa Jessup.

—◦◦◦—

During the past eight days, Andre had intercepted and recorded a dozen cell phone calls to Lisa Jessup's number. He knew her schedule for this Saturday. He knew she would be expecting a visitor within thirty minutes. That visitor was the second half of his plan.

The townhouse door opened a crack in response to his knock. Andre saw the brass security chain, and peering from behind it, a white female with short, brunette hair. She had an expressionless look on her face and quickly took in Andre's appearance, her eyes shifting upward for a second at the yellow "FTD" on his baseball cap.

Andre smiled. "Afternoon, ma'am. Flowers from Dwight. I need to get a signature."

She unfastened the chain and opened the door.

"You might want to put these on the counter first," Andre said.

"Sorry. Sure. Step inside."

Lisa took the flowers and turned around to walk the few steps to her kitchen counter. Andre reached behind and slowly closed the door. He noticed she was wearing a white sweatshirt, blue jeans, and was barefoot. She wasn't carrying anything. When Lisa turned around, beaming, she saw a black automatic aimed at her heart.

"Who are you?" she asked in a quiet voice. "What do you want?"

Andre had thought this through. He didn't want this agent to think he was planning to rape her or kill her. He didn't want her screaming or making a run for her gun, which he knew was probably close by.

"I came for some papers Dwight has. They're important to my people."

"I don't know what the hell you're talking about. Dwight doesn't have any papers here. You must have the wrong person."

"No, he's the right person. It's something he couldn't tell you about until you both were in Los Angeles. I know he's there now."

Andre could see the look of bewilderment in Lisa's eyes. He was enjoying this, playing with her mind. "I know you're both FBI agents," he said. "As soon as I find what I'm looking for, I'll leave. I'm not going to hurt you, but I have to tie you up. Cooperate with me and there won't be any problems. I'm not going to gag you. But don't even think about screaming or I won't hesitate to shoot. Turn around and put your hands on your head."

Lisa did as he ordered.

"Get down on your knees," Andre said forcefully.

He waited until she complied. "Now, cross your legs in back. I'm going to handcuff you, so just follow my commands."

While Lisa was on her knees, staring into the rungs of a kitchen chair, Andre reached into a side pocket of his backpack where he had three hypodermic needles. Quietly holstering his gun, he carefully removed one syringe and moved quickly to Lisa's side. With his left hand, he pressed down on top of her interlaced hands. With his right he stabbed the needle into her neck.

A loud, slow moan was the only sound Lisa made as she fell face-forward. Her head thudded into the living room carpet.

The room was quiet.

Andre pulled on his thin leather driving gloves, walked back to the front door and turned the deadbolt, relocking the door. Looking at his watch, he figured he had about fifteen minutes before the visitor arrived. He grabbed the unconscious body of Lisa Jessup by her feet and dragged her into one of the bedrooms in back and closed the door. She wasn't going anywhere. Walking back into the living room, he glanced at the kitchen table and saw a lot of paperwork and a calculator. It looked like Agent Jessup was paying bills before traveling to Los Angeles. Andre put his backpack to the side of the front door and eased himself into a comfortable chair facing the door.

—◦/◦/◦—

Robin didn't like being early, and she hated being late. She liked to arrive right on time for appointments. At 4:25 p.m. she pulled in front of Lisa Jessup's town home. She glanced up and saw the numbers on the door. With the Jeep still running, she turned the visor down and flipped up the lighted mirror. She touched up her lipstick before getting out of the car.

A minute later she rang the bell and was surprised when a man answered the door.

"Hi, I'm Dwight Jessup," he said. "Are you the young lady who's interested in renting our house?"

"That's right. I'm Robin Mikkonen." Robin held out her hand and the man shook it. He was wearing gloves. "I thought you were in L.A."

"I was just getting ready to leave. Lisa's in back changing. She'll be right out." He pointed to a chair. "Do you know what you're going to be working once you get to the Washington office?"

Before Robin could answer, the phone in the kitchen rang. After three rings and no movement from her host, Robin asked, "Do you want to get that?"

"No. Let it ring. We've been getting some nuisance calls lately."

"Lisa, this is Special Agent Ty Bannister." Robin heard the familiar voice come over the answering machine. "When you get this message, please call the Operations Center right away. Have them patch you through either to me or Doug Gordon. It's important."

Robin didn't even have time to think about why Ty would be calling Lisa Jessup when her cell phone started ringing.

"Excuse me for a second. I need to get that," she said reaching into her purse.

"Let it ring."

She looked up to see a gun pointed at her.

After four rings, the phone stopped.

"What's going on?" Robin asked. "Where's Lisa?"

Bannister thought Kuznetsov was their guy. He was the killer. Everything fit. He matched the profile. He had been there in Vienna with Cal and Lillian Wells. He'd had a relationship with Wells. He was a tennis player, a professional intelligence officer, and a man with a cover that gave him freedom of movement. He had met Sparky Gillespie. Now Sparky was dead, too. Kuznetsov had a storage locker. He could have killed them there. Something had triggered Kuznetsov's violence. His brother was killed by an American missile. If Lillian Wells had given him HIV, it meant an American had issued him a death sentence, too. Maybe that had caused him to snap. Somehow he'd gotten a hold of a specific list of American intelligence operatives and was using that as a death list.

Bannister backed off the accelerator, realizing he was doing fifty in a thirty-five mile zone. He was growing increasingly agitated. Lisa Jessup's name was on the list, same as Cal's. And Robin would be meeting with Jessup right about now. And Kuznetsov had given his tail the slip—no telling where he was, or what he was doing.

Bannister didn't like the situation at all.

He re-checked the address for Jessup's residence. Her unit was on the far end. He saw Robin's Jeep parked in front as he backed into the row on the other side. He called her cell phone as he walked toward the steps. It was irritating to him, hearing her voicemail again. She probably didn't want to be interrupted during her tour.

Just as he was about to ring the doorbell, Bannister heard Robin's voice inside, strong, demanding: "Where's Lisa?"

Something was wrong.

He drew his gun and stepped to the side of the landing away from the peephole. He rang the doorbell and waited. No response. He rang the bell again. He had to get whoever was in there to open the door.

"Lisa, it's me, Adam. Come on, open up. It's cold out here. I've got your package." He didn't want to identify himself, and he counted on Robin recognizing his voice and realizing he knew she was in danger.

"We're going to the door." Robin felt the heat of his breath in her ear. "Tell whoever it is that Lisa's sick. You're a friend from the office and might have to take her to the emergency room." He had Robin's left arm pinned in a hammerlock behind her and the gun pressed into her back. As Robin turned the deadbolt, she noticed the security chain was unfastened.

"Hi," said Bannister. "Where's Lisa?"

"I'm sorry, she's sick. I'm Robin. I work with her."

"That's too bad. She called me earlier and asked if I'd stop by the management office and pick up a package for her." Robin's eyes quickly darted to her left. Bannister shoved the door open with his left shoulder and spun to the right, rushing into the middle of the room. The force threw Robin and Kuznetsov back into the wall. Bannister's gun was in his right hand alongside his leg. Kuznetsov recovered in a second. He switched his left arm around Robin's neck and was standing behind her with his gun aimed at her right temple.

"Don't be stupid," he said to Bannister.

"Where's Lisa?" Bannister asked, knowing he had a couple of seconds. He didn't think Kuznetsov knew he was holding a gun behind his right thigh.

"She's resting," Andre said with a smirk on his face. Robin didn't take her eyes off Bannister.

"I have a word for you," Bannister said.

"What's that?"

"*Bahldung!*"

Kuznetsov frowned, trying to decipher what it meant, but Bannister saw that Robin instantly recognized the TaeKwonDo word for "instep." She stomped her heel into the top of Kuznetsov's foot and dropped to the floor.

Bannister raised his gun and pulled the trigger.

The room was rocked by three blasts. Pain seared Bannister's chest, spinning him sideways. The Russian must have gotten off a shot. As Bannister lost his balance and slammed into the floor, he knew he'd squeezed off a second shot. He gasped and pushed back the pain that was engulfing his consciousness. He looked through the cloud of smoke that hung in the air and saw the body slumped against the wall. He could see that one of his rounds had struck Kuznetsov through the right eye. A second had smashed into his neck.

Robin jumped to her feet, screaming, "Oh, God, Ty, you've been shot."

Bannister asked, "Are you all right?"

Robin rushed over to him as he sat up in the middle of the floor, bleeding from a wound below his left armpit.

"I've got to call 9-1-1," Robin yelled.

"No! Wait a minute. Listen to me." He spoke slowly and firmly. "I'll make the call. Let's find Lisa. Can you help me up?"

With Robin's assistance, Bannister got to his feet and saw the closed bedroom door. With gun still in hand, he kicked it open. Lisa Jessup was lying on her stomach on the floor. He knelt down and detected a weak and rapid pulse.

"She's alive. He must have drugged her."

"Ty, why did Dwight Jessup want to kill us?"

"That's not Jessup. That's Andre Kuznetsov. He's our serial killer."

He could tell nothing was registering with Robin. Their ears were still ringing because of the gunshots. The smell of gunpowder and blood clogged the warm air. His left side was starting to hurt like hell. He wanted to get Robin focused. He wasn't worried about himself, but he didn't want her going into some kind of shock. "Whatever you do, don't touch your face with your hands," he said to her. "You have blood splatter from Andre in your hair and all over your back. He may have AIDS. Do you understand what I'm saying?"

"Yes."

"I need to make some calls," he said

"We've got to stop the bleeding, Ty. I'm going to go find a towel."

He laid his gun down and groaned with pain as he shed his leather coat. He saw the hole near his left armpit. "I believe it's a through-and-through shot," he murmured, as Robin ran back in the room with a towel. She wrapped it tightly under his arm and over his shoulder.

He called 9-1-1.

"This is Special Agent Tyler Bannister with the FBI. There's been a law enforcement officer shooting at 111 Keystone Mill Commons, Arlington. An intruder has been shot. He's dead." Bannister took a second to catch his breath. "I have a bullet wound to my upper chest. Another agent is unconscious. I believe the intruder injected her with a drug overdose, probably Percocet or Seconal."

"I copied that. Your call registers to a cell phone. Is there a landline at that location?"

"Yes." Bannister pulled the card out of his coat pocket and read the Jessup's home number to the operator. She told him an ambulance and police were responding.

In the knapsack beneath Andre's crumpled legs, Bannister found three syringes. One was empty. The autopsy reports of the victims had been burned into his memory. He walked over and collapsed in one of the kitchen chairs. "Robin, would you press the towel on both sides? We have about five minutes to wait."

Bannister called Doug Gordon. "Where are you?"

"At home in my den. Why?"

"Have you got something to write on?"

"Yeah, what's going on?"

"I'm at the residence of one of your agents—Lisa Jessup—it's complicated. I'll explain later. Kuznetsov's dead. I had to shoot him."

"Jesus, Ty! What are you talking about? Are you all right?"

"He got off a round and hit me once. I'm bleeding but I should be okay. The police and ambulance will be here in a couple of minutes."

"Am I missing something here?" Gordon's tone was sending a clear message. Robin folded the towel over and again pressed the ends against his wound. The bleeding was slowing. Bannister winced but didn't say anything.

"I was going to call after talking with Lisa Jessup. Before I could do that all hell broke loose. You've got to trust me a little longer on this. Here's what has to be done. Just listen and write."

Bannister felt bad dictating orders to Doug, but knew this situation could turn chaotic within the hour.

"Kuznetsov stalked Lisa Jessup and came to her townhouse. She was his next victim. I think he injected her with the same drugs he used on the others."

"Is she alive?"

"She's got a pulse, but I don't know how much time she has. That's up to God and her doctors. Call Kaminsky and fill her in. Roger Bell's at the Operations Center waiting for a call from me. Give him a heads up. Call Otis Huggins and see if he can use his connections to get Detective Alvin Weber of the Arlington PD assigned as the primary for this thing. Weber handled the Lillian Wells disappearance." Bannister stopped to catch his breath again and glanced up at Robin. "Talk to me, Doug. You still there?"

"Yeah, I'm still here. My hand's cramping up. For a guy who's been shot, you're spitting out details faster than a copy machine."

"The adrenaline's still working. A couple of other things. The surveillance team's still sitting on the subject's car at the shopping center. The search warrant for the car is still good so we ought to get it towed to Quantico for processing." Bannister looked up at Robin again. Just seeing her face gave him strength. Some of the color was returning to her cheeks.

"Good idea," Doug said.

"Send a forensic team right away to Kuznetsov's apartment. Give it the 'full Monty.' He won't be using it again. You have the search plan with all the players. Just tell everybody the timetable's moved up. One more thing. Better have Kaminsky call Lisa's husband, Dwight Jessup. He's on assignment somewhere in Los Angeles."

"Can we hold off saying anything about Kuznetsov's identity?" Doug asked.

"I'm the only one who can ID him right now." Bannister paused, drawing in a shaky breath. "I believe it's best to level with the locals, but I'll ask them to hold off with the identity of the intruder . . . hopefully, it'll be long enough for Kaminsky to coordinate with headquarters and State Department . . . I'm sure the Russians will go ape shit over this when they find out . . . and go into damage control." Bannister was getting winded and forced himself to take slow deep breaths. "Questions?"

"You don't sound too good right now. Are you sure you're all right?"

"Yeah, I think so."

"You owe me an explanation. I don't know how both you and Kuznetsov ended up at the Jessup's, but we can sort that out later," Doug said. "I hear sirens in the background. I'm going to make a call and see if I can get them to take you and Lisa to George Washington University Hospital. Their ER is a Level One shock trauma center.

They're used to handling the District's drug overdoses and gunshot victims. Good work, Ty. I'm glad you're not hurt bad."

"Ah . . . me, too." The sirens stopped. Bannister hung up as a team of emergency medical technicians and two uniformed officers mounted the steps. Robin ran to let them in.

CHAPTER 34

T he last time Bannister hurt like this was on a hill in Grenada when he'd taken two rounds. Maybe ten seconds after the bullets slammed through his body, hot bolts of pain had seared his back and legs. Back then, the physical exertion and adrenaline surge had forced him to concentrate on the Marine Corps' mission. He saw what needed to be done. The colors of the jungle became brilliantly defined hues, as if he were looking through a giant, slow-turning kaleidoscope, his targets clear images silhouetted on a lime-green hillside. Time clipped forward in gradual movements. He did what he had to do, and then it was over. Enemies were dead and Marines were safe.

Bannister's mind snapped back to the present when an Arlington EMT hooked him up to a plasma IV for the ride to the ER. The EMT's partner, a bald-headed short guy, snugged up the Velcro straps on the yellow backboard on which Bannister was stretched out. He turned his head to the left and saw the motionless Lisa Jessup lying there with an oxygen mask over her face. Bannister was thinking, *it's winter . . . why isn't she wearing any socks or shoes?*

The EMT driver slammed the rear door shut. Bannister overheard him tell the short guy the ride to George Washington University Hospital should take four minutes—enough time for him to enjoy the Whopper he'd picked up at the Burger King drive-through.

——◦//◦——

"Well, how you feeling?"

Bannister opened his eyes after recognizing Doug Gordon's voice, but it still took a few seconds before his vision adjusted to the light. He saw the lost look on his colleague's face.

"You're in recovery," Gordon said.

Bannister looked at the white band on his left wrist. "They took my watch. What time is it?"

"Nine o'clock."

"How's Lisa?" Bannister asked. His throat was raw and his mouth was dry.

"She's fine. Damn lucky you got there when you did. They had to give her a blood transfusion to get the drugs out of her system. The doctors don't expect her to wake up until tomorrow. When she comes around she'll definitely be well-rested. Sort of like Snow White after a long sleep."

"Where's Robin?"

"At our office. Quattrone's bringing her here. She insists on seeing you. She seems to think you two have a thing going."

"We do," Bannister said. He didn't care who knew it.

"A uniformed officer and Detective Weber interviewed her and the PD's tech guy took photos. After that I had one of the female agents take Robin to the office so she could shower. We gave her a sweatshirt and raid jacket to wear back to Quantico. I'll handle getting her stuff cleaned."

"Thanks. What have I missed?"

"Jessup's husband is on a red-eye flight from L.A. The doctors gave you a tetanus shot, a pint of blood, and forty stitches on your front and back to repair the entry and exit holes. You also got a few stitches on the back of your right leg."

"My leg?" Bannister looked bewildered.

"I told you George Washington's ER room was great. They did a complete scan of you to make sure some bullet fragments didn't get scattered around. They found a bone chip next to your femoral nerve and removed it. The doctor was curious to know if you've had any recent leg pain."

"Yeah, matter of fact I have."

"The doctor believes it might have been left over from one of your prior wounds," Gordon said.

"You know, I was worried about my leg. I definitely owe him a drink."

"It's a her," Gordon said. "You can thank her yourself when she checks in on you later."

"What about Kuznetsov?" Bannister asked.

"The investigation at the townhouse is wrapped up. Since it was an end unit, the Arlington PD was able to keep the press and 'looky Lous' on the other side of the tape. Detective Weber has the ticket on the case and everything's going smoothly. Your lady friend and a florist are the only people interviewed so far."

"Did you search Kuznetsov or have a chance to toss his apartment?"

"Yes to both. His backpack had a couple of filled syringes, which we're analyzing now. We found a hat, extra clothing, and a stun gun in the pack. He was carrying ID in the name of Andre Neff. We lifted prints off the wallet and cards and are doing a trace on his gun."

"My throat's scratchy. Could you get me some water?"

Gordon filled a glass with ice water from a small plastic pitcher on a tray. He handed it to Bannister along with a straw.

"His apartment had a couple items of interest. We found a cell phone intercept device. Our techs are going through it tonight to see if it was programmed to record the victims' calls. And Kuznetsov kept some trophies."

"Like what?"

"Quattrone handled the search. He was thorough. He found a photo of Kuznetsov's brother. You know, the one who was shot down. Steve took the photo out of the frame and hit pay dirt. Our guy had hidden drivers' licenses for Wells, Williamson, and Gillespie behind the backing. He also had a newspaper clipping of DiMatteo's obituary."

"That sonofabitch."

"Trooper Bell and Otis Huggins went to the storage locker. The Russian painting is now in our valuable evidence vault. We might be able to use it as a trump card if the Russians start playing nasty."

"What about the press?"

"Kaminsky is meeting them at noon tomorrow. First though, she and the Director are going to the State Department at 9:00 a.m. to meet with the Russian ambassador. I wasn't invited." Gordon grinned.

"It'll be interesting to see how they backstroke on this," Bannister said.

After Gordon left, Bannister took calls from two bosses—Ellen Kaminsky at WFO and Leon Brennan in Atlanta. Both expressed their concern for him and assured him everything was under control.

The pain medication they'd given Bannister was working. He felt mellow. He didn't have anything to read and wasn't interested in watching the television, which was on but muted.

Robin walked into the room. For a moment, they just smiled at each other. She walked around the side of his bed, careful not to trip over any of the cords, leaned over, and kissed him softly on the lips.

"Doug told me you're in great shape and should be released in the morning."

"That's what they told me, too." Bannister observed her standing there, looking like a trainee. Damp hair pulled back severely into a ponytail, gray sweatshirt covered by a blue nylon windbreaker.

"I know," she said. "I look like hell."

"You always look beautiful to me."

Robin's lips started quivering. She began to cry and shake.

"Come here," Bannister said. He pulled some Kleenex for her from a box on the table attached to the side of the bed.

"I'm sorry. You could have been killed. I could have been killed. And I didn't even know what he'd done to Lisa Jessup." Robin's voice was rising as she blew her nose a couple of times.

"I know. But it's over now. You going to be all right?"

"I guess."

"Give me your hand." Bannister extended his right hand, and Robin pressed it between both of hers. He looked into her eyes.

"We don't make a bad team, do we?" he asked.

Her smile returned. "No, we don't."

—⚬⚬⚬—

Bannister spent another week in DC. A headquarters inspector assigned to the shooting inquiry questioned him at the field office for two hours Monday morning. He finished in time for Bannister to join the task force guys and watch the press conference.

Kaminsky appeared on a local DC news station. She looked professional in a dark blue suit accented by a multi-colored silk scarf as she stepped behind a lectern arrayed with microphones from the major wire services. Instead of holding a press conference, however, she read a prepared statement.

"The task force investigating four serial murders has identified the killer. On Saturday afternoon in Arlington, Virginia, Andre Kuznetsov was shot and killed by a member of our task force. Kuznetsov, a reporter for the Russian news agency TASS, was intercepted at the residence of an FBI agent by another FBI agent investigating the murders. Kuznetsov had already gained access to the home and had drugged the first agent when he was surprised by the task force agent. Kuznetsov shot and wounded the FBI agent who returned fire, killing Kuznetsov instantly. Overwhelming evidence links Kuznetsov to all four murders. He was a suspect and was under investigation at the time. His actions had nothing to do with his journalistic duties and were not connected to the Russian Government. The Russian Ambassador deplores this unfortunate incident and expresses his government's condolences to the families of the victims. The Russian Embassy is assisting the FBI in this investigation.

"Preliminary indications are that Kuznetsov had an incurable illness and that self-administered doses of dangerous medications caused him to be delusional. He was obsessed with the idea the United

States was responsible for his brother's death in Afghanistan and that our Government was trying to kill him.

"We are still analyzing evidence and the investigation is ongoing. We will issue a more detailed statement in the future."

Reporters shouted questions at Kaminsky, who ignored them as she turned on her heel and left the podium.

—⁂—

Bannister spent the next couple of days writing up statements and his report. He referred a couple dozen phone calls from reporters to the media coordinator at the Washington Field Office. His last call Thursday was to Robin, who invited him to her graduation from the Academy. That was something he definitely wouldn't miss. On Friday, Kaminsky addressed the task force at its final meeting.

"The Director of the FBI informed the Russian ambassador the United States suspected Kuznetsov of being with Russian intelligence. But he emphasized the murders, as well as Kuznetsov's own death, appeared to have nothing to do with any intelligence operation. The Director requested the ambassador give Russian intelligence a report of our murder investigation outlining the evidence against Kuznetsov."

Doug Gordon raised his hand.

"I'm anticipating your question, Doug. The report will be sanitized, and leave out our surveillance and other sensitive items."

Gordon nodded, and Kaminsky continued. "As a good faith gesture from the US Government, the icon from Kuznetsov's storage locker was turned over to the ambassador. We didn't attach any conditions. Our government's not going to say anything about this artwork's recovery. The Russians can say anything they want or nothing at all."

Kaminsky answered questions before thanking all the task force members for their efforts.

As he checked out of the Watergate, Bannister arranged through the concierge to have two boxes of Godiva chocolates delivered to the emergency room staff of the George Washington Hospital.

He had two more things to do before leaving DC.

He drove to Dulles Airport, not to catch a flight, but to watch one take off. A Russian Aeroflot Illushin lifted off the runway right on time. On board was the body of Andre Kuznetsov, returning to the Motherland for burial. Bannister watched the plane until it disappeared into the folds of the slate gray sky.

As he was walking back to the terminal, he saw Doug Gordon.

"The office said you were coming out here. I'm glad I caught you before you left. I have a copy of a letter Kaminsky opened after getting back from the TV station. She's already notified your boss in Atlanta," Gordon said, handing him an envelope. "The original was sent via DHL courier service from London."

Bannister opened the letter and read it.

Dear SAC,

I'm sending this to you because I know you will make sure the message is delivered to Agent Bannister. I heard about the shooting in Virginia. Too bad the Russian was such a bad shot. Bannister and the FBI have wrecked my life. Tell Bannister that when it's my chance, I won't miss!

It was unsigned. It didn't need to be. Bannister knew who'd sent it.

"It's been great working with you, Ty," Gordon said as they shook hands. "Be careful, okay?"

Bannister had one more stop before driving back to Atlanta. At the National Memorial Park cemetery, he parked along one of the narrow pathways bisecting the graveyard. He had to walk past two rows of headstones before finding the black granite marker for Cal Williamson. It wasn't much to commemorate a man's life. It didn't have an epitaph. Just his name chiseled in stone along with the date he was born and the date of his death. There was no one else in the cemetery. Bannister would have spoken out loud but didn't want to hear his own voice cracking. So in his mind he told Cal they all missed him, that he missed him.

Though it hadn't brought his friend back, it was good his death had been avenged.

With his head bowed, Bannister thanked Cal for their friendship, turned, and walked away.

IF YOU ENJOYED...

The Mile Marker Murders, **don't miss**
Prime Impact

Book 2 in the Tyler Bannister FBI series

Fugitive Terry Hines, suspected of involvement with terrorists, has been on FBI Agent Tyler Bannister's radar for some time when Federal prosecutor Kendall Briggs is murdered, a microbiologist at the CDC is stabbed to death, and a biotoxin is missing. Bannister suspects the crimes are all related.

The investigation takes a personal turn when Bannister's daughter is kidnapped and he is in a race against time to save his daughter and neutralize a biological attack.

ABOUT THE AUTHOR

C.W. Saari is a graduate of Whittier College, Willamette University Law School, and the National War College. He served his country in the US Marine Corps, then spent twenty-seven years as an FBI Special Agent where he supervised undercover operations and espionage investigations. C.W. is currently a private investigator in Lexington, South Carolina, where he resides with his wife, Carol.